USA TODAY BESTSELLING AUTHOR
Dale Mayer

ROGAN 02
SHADOW RECON

ROGAN: SHADOW RECON, BOOK 2
Beverly Dale Mayer
Valley Publishing Ltd.

Copyright © 2023

All rights reserved. Except for use in any review, the reproduction or utilization of this work in whole or in part by any electronic, mechanical or other means, now known or hereafter invented, including xerography, photocopying and recording, or in any information storage or retrieval system, is forbidden without the written permission of the publisher.

This is a work of fiction. Names, characters, places, brands, media, and incidents are either the product of the author's imagination or are used fictitiously. Any resemblance to actual events, locales, or persons, living or dead, is entirely coincidental.

ISBN-13: 978-1-773367-25-5
Print Edition

Books in This Series

Magnus, Book 1
Rogan, Book 2
Egan, Book 3

About This Book

Rogan arrives at the arctic training camp in the midst of chaos and suspicion. Missing men, fires in the kitchen, Magnus still recovering… and Mountain tearing across the tundra searching for his brother…

Lisa was brought in to assist Dr. Sydney in the medical clinic and is only just now catching up on the horrific events that's plagued the camp. She's trying to ignore the distrustful gazes as the only newcomer allowed in, even as everyone is trying to leave.

And yet through it all, the team investigating find some answers and yet a dozen more questions arise. Adding to the confusion, the science center is having unexplained issues with their generator. But with several scientists gone missing their problems are just starting. And those problems spill over to the training center upping the ante for both groups…

Sign up to be notified of all Dale's releases here!
https://geni.us/DaleNews

PROLOGUE

ROGAN WALKED INTO the medical clinic to introduce himself and found Magnus there in one of the hospital beds, sitting up, a cup of coffee in his hand, talking to the doctor. Rogan stepped up and shook hands with Magnus, who looked at him, his gaze intent. Rogan just let him look. Then he turned to face Sydney and smiled.

"Hi, Sydney. I'm Rogan."

She beamed, reached out, and shook his hand. "Am I glad you are on board."

He chuckled. "Yeah, I've heard a bit about the hellish nightmare going on here right now."

"You're not kidding. And I'm getting a new nurse today as well, but I have yet to see her."

"I already heard. She's been here during training, so she's been tapped to come in and to help you with your short-staffing issue."

At that came a knock on the door. A woman entered, smiling as she stepped forward and looked at Sydney intently. "Hey, apparently I've been reassigned as your nurse. I'm Lisa."

Sydney studied her. "That's interesting. I didn't even realize you were here. I thought I was getting someone else."

"I came in a couple days ago on one of the flights where patients were airlifted out," she said. "I've done some sledding myself, quite a bit, but I wanted an opportunity to do it within the military's parameters, only now I have been reassigned here." She turned and looked around. "Apparently this is the most dangerous place on the whole damn base."

Sydney winced. "You could be right. But it's a pretty large base, with multiple outbuildings in this little military village, so I wouldn't count on it. Anyway, this is Rogan, and this is Magnus."

Lisa looked at Magnus, smiled, shook his hand, then turned to Rogan. "I already know Rogan." She acknowledged him with another laugh.

"Yeah, last time I went out with you on a dog sled, you dumped me, the dogs took off, and I was left stranded in that lovely blizzard."

She smirked. "That was your own fault."

"If you say so." He shook his head. "I'm glad to hear that you're getting some training. Maybe by the time you're done here, you'll know how to mush a team."

She rolled her eyes. "Don't be such a baby. If you hadn't screamed like a little kid, the dogs wouldn't have been afraid in the first place."

He snorted. "Screamed like a little kid? You jumped a crevasse."

She shrugged. "Stopping wasn't really an option, and, hey, at least you got dumped on the far side."

Magnus and Sydney watched this exchange in fascination, as Rogan and Lisa volleyed barbs back and forth. Sydney reached out a hand to Magnus, who stood up and wrapped an arm around her shoulders.

Rogan turned his attention to them. "Don't worry. Lisa and I know each other from way back, so all is good."

Sydney smiled and chuckled. "I'm glad to hear that. It

sounds as if you do have a thing going on."

He looked at her. "Oh no, that we do not. She was married to my best friend. That's all there is to it." Then he nodded goodbye and walked out.

Lisa looked after him, and then turned to the two of them and smiled. "He's right. I was married to his best friend, but that was a long time ago. And the marriage itself? It didn't last more than ten months," she shared, with a sad smile. "Teenage pregnancy, teenage marriage, lost the baby, lost the husband, and, hey, life is not what you think it's going to be anymore," she murmured.

"And Rogan?" Sydney asked.

"I think in a way he blames me for the baby and for his friend. I was just as heartbroken. We were both so damn young." She shrugged. "Anyway, Rogan and I have stayed in touch over the years, mostly because of the work we do. And surprise, surprise. Here we are. Let the world bring what it may, I'm up for it."

And, with that, she smiled and asked, "Where's my desk?"

Sydney pointed.

Then Lisa nodded, headed over, and declared, "Okay, let's get to work."

DAY 1, MORNING

Successfully arrived at camp. Assimilation won't be the easiest. Anger among the teams that anyone new is coming in when they all want out. No progress as yet. Stay tuned.

Rogan Matlock stepped into the kitchen area, then headed to the ever-present coffeepot and realized it was empty. Frowning, he turned with the pot toward the kitchen and held it up. One of the cooks in the front rolled his eyes, took it from his hand, and grimaced. "Seems to happen a lot lately."

"As long as it refills throughout the day, I don't care," he replied cheerfully.

The cook looked at him, frowned, and noted, "I don't think I've seen you around lately."

"I was here early on," he shared. "Now I'm back."

At that, the other guy snorted. "Why the hell would you want to come back? I've been trying to get out of here for ages, or so it seems." Rogan considered him, and the line cook shrugged. "Shit's going on here, man. I don't need that."

"Maybe you don't need it," Rogan stated, his gaze searching the place, "but, according to my information, the only people who can come and go from here are any essential services or people involved with the training center since this term began."

"Right, you need your head examined," he muttered, then turned toward the stoves. He returned with another carafe of coffee. "It's a fresh pot after this."

"And what's this?" Rogan asked, staring at the carafe.

"Old coffee. You get that before you get anything else."

He winced at that and looked over at Chef, who was smoking off to the side. His puffs of smoke disappeared out the slightly cracked open door, while Chef openly stared at Rogan.

Rogan asked, "Is this how you guys run coffee all the time?"

"It is. You happen to come back at a time when supplies are low."

"Why are supplies low?" he asked curiously, noting he ought to sound friendlier. "I came in with a load."

"Sure, you came in with supplies, but we were shorted, as always. So, if you don't want that coffee, put it back, and somebody else will grab it. You can wait for the next pot," he stated, his tone tart.

Surprised at the attitude and the comment, Rogan didn't say anything more but put the full carafe on the burner, and, sure enough, several other people jumped up to fill their cups. In a blink, the pot was empty again.

Rogan took the empty pot back to the kitchen. With that, the line cook nodded, disappeared, then reappeared with two fresh pots. "You seem surprised," he told Rogan.

"I am," Rogan confirmed. "Things were a little different when I was here before."

"Yeah, they sure were," he snapped. "People weren't dying. People weren't going missing right under our noses."

Rogan looked over at Chef, the nickname that suited

this man's occupation, who frowned at his line cook, and Rogan nodded. "I get it. Tempers are running hot."

"Hot, cold, and everything in between," Chef declared, walking closer. He eyed Rogan carefully. "I'm surprised they let anybody in. Or, in your case, back in. You were here for a few days, when we were setting up."

"Several people have returned. Maybe they thought we could be a stabilizing influence," he shared, with a shrug.

"I don't know why the hell anybody would think that," the line cook replied, glaring at Rogan. "I want the hell out of here." At that, Chef looked down at him and frowned again. The line cook threw up his hands. "Look. I want to get out of here alive. I no longer sleep at night. I'm looking over my shoulder all the time."

"Hang on a minute," Rogan interrupted, trying for an innocently shocked tone. "I understood the one guy and the nurse were involved with stealing drugs, and they are both gone. Right?"

"Even if you heard that much, you're doing better than most," the line cook noted, with a half laugh. "Yet I've got to tell you that that's only part of the story."

Rogan waited for more feedback to come, but Chef shushed his line cook with a stern stare and sent him back to work. At that, Rogan raised an eyebrow. Chef shook his head. "We can't have that talk, not in here," he explained in a low voice. "I'm not sure why the hell you're here because I remember you, and I remember you from other places too," he declared, barely in a whisper. "Watch your back."

"Any reason in particular?" Rogan asked.

"Yeah, because anybody involved with the investigations into this base is a suspect. So, whether or not you are another investigator," Chef added cryptically, "the fact that you're even here means your presence is suspicious."

"And why is that?"

"Because we were told that nobody else was being allowed in."

"And yet we had a new nurse, and we had a couple other new guys. That was bound to happen sooner rather than later, what with people on waiting lists for these survival training sessions."

"Right, and yet"—Chef studied Rogan closely—"the brass won't let just anybody in at this point. They'll be majorly vetted."

At that, Rogan gave him a lazy smile. "Good point."

"Keep your head down, before somebody sees your presence as a challenge." And, with that, Chef turned and walked away, leaving a very surprised Rogan.

A challenge? What did Chef mean by that? Rogan had never considered his presence here in that light. He pondered that, as he walked over to the dining room tables and sat down among the others.

Instant silence swept around him. He waited to see what the general reaction would be to him; then several people started speaking almost at once.

"What the hell are you even doing here?"

"We heard that nobody was allowed to come in or out."

"How did they allow you back?"

"Are you on the investigation team?"

He looked around at the table at a lot of confused, angry, and perplexed faces.

"Some of us had to come in or go out for various reasons. I brought supplies with me, so I presume you want me here."

"Not really," replied one of the guys, almost joking. "I

wish we were on that supply plane, leaving with or without you."

"So I've heard before," Rogan replied. "I'm not sure what's going on around here."

"Yeah, nobody does," murmured one of the other men. "None of us really knows what's going on, and nobody's talking, and the fact that nobody's talking makes all of us even more suspicious. I've already put in several complaints with my superior, and I've asked for a chance to get the hell out."

"What response did you get?" Rogan asked, eyeing him curiously.

The guy looked down at the table and shrugged. "Not a terribly positive one," he noted, with a frustrated sigh. "Something about making a big deal out of nothing, with a tone that suggested they may as well have told me, 'Suck it up, son. You're a soldier. That's why you're here.'"

Another man rolled his eyes at that. "It's one thing if you're up against an enemy," he explained, with a shrug, "at least an enemy from another country. But to find out you're up against enemies within your own training mission?" He waved his hand around, as if warding off some form of evil. "That's a whole different story."

"Do you know for sure that's what it is?" Rogan asked, looking at him closely. "Do you have any information that nobody else has?"

"No, of course not." He glared, looking around the table at the others seated nearby. "However, believe me. This place is rife with rumors." And he stood up, slammed down his cup. "And you best grab a hold of whatever it is that brought you here and turn around and get the hell back out again." And, with that, he stormed off.

Watching him leave, Rogan turned to look at the others, but they all suddenly appeared to be busy. "You're all of the same opinion?" he asked, amazed when a couple men shrugged. This place was itching to blow, and that was never a good situation.

One of them stated, "Don't know what the hell is going on, so everyone is on the edge. ... I'm Ryan, by the way." Then he reached out a hand and shook Rogan's.

"Rogan," he replied, smiling. "I've never been in a situation quite like this."

"None of us have," Ryan noted. "I think that's the problem. People don't know how to handle new and different." He got up then and added in a controlled, yet bitter tone, "As a friendly warning—because we don't know what the hell is going on—keep an eye out, will you?" And, with that, he turned and left as well.

Rogan looked at the last two guys remaining at their table, both staring at him sideways. Rogan shrugged. "Can't say I ever expected to feel as unwelcome as I do right about now," he stated in a conversational tone.

One of the guys snorted. "That's all right. You'll get used to it soon enough." And, with that, he was gone too.

The other guy winced. "Hey, I remember you from the beginning. Not sure why you left or why you're back, but, considering what's going on here, you've got to see that things have changed. I'm Reed."

"Hi, Reed. And I do see that they have changed." Rogan tilted his head toward the door, where the others had walked out. "I hadn't expected a welcome, but I didn't expect to be treated like a leper either."

"It's not so much that you're a leper as much as the circumstances make everyone feel wary of newcomers and jealous of those who get shipped out. On the whole, most would prefer to leave. Most of us have asked for transfers," he shared. "We all committed to a certain amount of time here, and we generally honor our commitments, but we didn't realize it would be such a damn nightmare."

"No, and I wasn't really filled in on it either, but, whatever is going on, it's palpable."

Reed added, "You may want to turn around and leave. Most of us are confused and don't know what's going on, but we do know that several people have gone missing—two still are. Plus several guards were attacked by one or two who were stealing drugs here. Not to mention we've also had some men get hurt in very strange ways. Two died in training exercises, and recently a man who tried to rape our doc was murdered."

"Maybe a little bit of suspicion is healthy then," Rogan noted cautiously, "but too much of it, and things can go south very quickly."

"I think we're already at the too-much part, and things are definitely going south," Reed replied. "So just a friendly warning to watch your back." Then he smiled and asked, "Do you have a room to yourself?"

Rogan shook his head. "I'm bunked where one of the other guys used to be. It's also a bit hard to digest that the morale at this base has dropped so drastically. If the brass could find answers, it would help," he suggested casually, as he stretched out his legs.

"Sure, it would, but, so far, no luck in that department. I guess I'll be seeing you around." Picking up his cup, he stood to leave, then turned back to Rogan. "I'm heading out to do a check around base. I'm on watch, if you want to come."

"Absolutely." Rogan rose. "I also need to acclimate to

the Arctic temperatures again."

"Yeah, is there an easy way to do that? I sure as hell haven't found it," Reed muttered, as they walked to the exit, where they quickly bundled up in multiple layers of heavy outdoor gear.

"I always liked it up here," Rogan replied, with a chuckle. "I know it's not for everybody, but something's very peaceful about this frozen world. I respect it but also enjoy it."

"Something peaceful, yes, usually. However, right now, something is so wrong."

"I heard that one of the missing men was found in a snow cave." He slid a sideways glance at his companion.

"Yep. Terrance. And he's in a bad way. The doc here was kidnapped by the villagers, specifically to help Terrance. Followed by a shooting during a search-and-rescue event. I admit, people were wondering whether she was telling the truth or not."

At that, Rogan turned and looked at Reed. "People suspected the doc or her nurse?"

"The nurse, Joy, now she ended up being something else, what with stealing drugs from the clinic. Not sure anyone saw her coming. Not so much about the doc, and maybe *suspected* isn't the right word. *Jealous* maybe, *on the outs* definitely. But then the doc has gotten quite close to one of the other guys now, so err on the side of caution because any speculation about Doc Sydney will get your ass kicked."

"With good reason I would think. From what I heard, the doc has already been treated pretty roughly, and I can't say any of the rumors I've heard so far about this base have included her."

Reed laughed heartily. "Most likely because Magnus has

been pretty strict about what people say." He stared at Rogan and added, "But she is hardworking, and she didn't even know most of the people here, so you've got to admire that she's even stayed through this mess."

Rogan definitely admired that, particularly when he saw so many people looking to get out of here as soon as they could. It was never good for morale when people wanted to get the hell away. Yet, if they were all targeted, as much as they all believed they may be, Rogan couldn't blame them. It was one thing to die for your country, but another thing completely to die for the bullshit such as was happening here.

LISA WALKER WORKED away at the clinic's computer, trying to get caught up with the information and the reports that had been filtering in on the rest of the staff. She looked over a couple times to see Sydney working with a patient who had just arrived—one of the kitchen staff, with a small burn. She frowned when he finally left and told Sydney, "Seems to be an awful lot of burn accidents happening here."

Sydney turned toward her, frowning. "That's the only one since you've been here," she noted cautiously.

"Sure, since I've been here, but I've also heard about multiple others, plus I've inputted a few in the computer."

"That's true," Sydney acknowledged. "We're not too sure whether that's a problem yet or not."

"I would think it is, if only a diversion from the bigger events here," Lisa muttered. "But, hey, don't mind me. What do I know?"

Sydney laughed. "Apparently you know a fair bit."

"Not really, and not anywhere near as much as I want to. Of course I didn't really plan on being a nurse on this mission," she admitted, with a shrug, "but I'm happy to help out."

"I'm happy to have you, and, if I don't need you at times, … believe me. I will be more than happy to have you go off and do your training. So, if we get a chance for you to ever do that, please feel free."

Lisa twisted around in her seat to fully face her boss, raising one brow.

"Yes, I mean it," Sydney stated, with a smile. "I don't need staff all the time, and you would think that, in this place, we shouldn't need more than a doctor on call, but, so far, it hasn't worked out that way."

"No, I can see that, especially under these strange circumstances," Lisa muttered. "Yet I'll keep that in mind, and thank you. I really want to get out on the sleds at some point. What about you?" she asked, studying the doc cautiously. "Have you done any sledding?"

"No, at least not by choice," she replied, with a wince.

At that, Lisa frowned, her expression curious.

Sydney shrugged. "You'll probably hear about it anyway, so I might as well tell you now. At least that way you'll get the real story. In all this mess, I was kidnapped and taken to a village nearby—the Inuit settlement, as it's called by the locals."

Lisa looked terrified for a moment, then tried to mask her features.

"I was kidnapped to help one of our own people in the village," she explained.

"Really?"

"Yeah, if they would have asked me, I would have gone

in a moment. But I gather the man in charge thought I would refuse and avoided any discussion with me."

"So, they kidnapped you?" Lisa couldn't imagine.

"Wouldn't be so bad but they knocked me out and asked questions later, and that took a little bit longer to recover from."

"Ouch," Lisa replied. "That would give you a very different feel about it all."

"Exactly, but they figured the man found in the snow cave needed help, and he had told them that nobody here could be trusted."

At that, Lisa turned and looked at her in shock. "He said that?"

"Apparently, which was a pretty strange thing to say, especially since the cumulation of questionable events happening here came *after* Terrance went missing," Sydney answered, with a curt nod. "When I reached him, he was nonverbal, so we don't know his story, and, as far as I understand, he still hasn't woken up stateside either. So we may never get answers from him."

"Shit," Lisa replied.

"Yeah, you and I both are not terribly impressed with any of this."

Lisa pondered that. "I hadn't really considered that this would be that kind of dangerous up here. At least no more than any other training session here in the Arctic."

"And I don't think you will be in danger," Sydney shared. "However, as always, in a case such as this, you need to look after yourself. Stay safe, and take all the necessary precautions."

"Got it." Lisa quickly returned to the work at hand.

Frowning, she finished up the paperwork, looked down

at her watch, and announced, "I've finished this section, so are you okay if I knock off for the day?"

"Yes, of course," Sydney agreed, walking over. "If you wanted to get outside for a bit, the weather is nice right now."

"Wouldn't that be fun," Lisa stated, looking around the room. "Being hunkered down inside, you forget what the outside even looks like."

"Go, go on," Sydney encouraged her. "If you want to be outside, get going." Her words were drowned out when a knock came at the door, and Magnus stepped in. At that, Sydney laughed. "Lisa, you're definitely off duty now that he's here."

And, with that, Lisa hopped up. "Perfect." She beamed a big smile at them, walked out, and headed back to her room. As soon as she got there, she sat down and tried to give herself a few minutes to assimilate some of the information she had read and heard, figuring out what she was supposed to do with it.

What she read had not been public knowledge; it was all within private medical files, and, while some of it could be important, much of it might not be. She really had no way to know. When a knock came at her door, she opened it up to see Ted.

He stepped in, closed the door, and looked at her intently. "And?"

She shrugged. "I'm not sure there's anything to say. I spent most of the day working on the medical files, trying to get things caught up." She looked at him curiously. "What is it exactly you're asking me to look for?"

"Nothing ... and everything," he replied.

"So, in a way, you're looking for information on Sydney?"

"She's been cleared, at least as far as everybody else is concerned."

"But you're not so sure?" she asked, staring at him.

"It's not that I'm not sure, but I would feel better if a little more time goes on, and she's not involved."

Lisa nodded at that slowly. "Fine, but I don't particularly enjoy spying on my coworkers."

"Maybe if people didn't continuously get hurt and go missing around this place, that wouldn't be such an issue," Ted explained, looking around at the room, and back at her. "Yet it is an issue, so I need you to keep your eyes open." And, with that cryptic comment, he was gone.

Lisa was still unsure exactly what her involvement in this would mean, and she really did hate to spy on anybody she was associated with, but hopefully this was harmless and was more of a security check than anything.

As she walked toward the cafeteria, she heard laughter. It was muted, but people appeared to be relaxing somewhat. Then again, if it was a good day outside, the chance to get fresh air and natural light would change the attitudes around this place for the better.

She walked in just in time to see several people packing meals. She stared at them with envy. "Are you guys heading out on training?"

They laughed and nodded.

One guy said, "You're the one who got suckered into first aid. That's one of the reasons I didn't do any medical training. If you ever need to be called up, that's what they do. Then you lose out on all the fun stuff. And it's the fun stuff that keeps us here." He rolled his eyes. "Particularly now."

She thought his name was Wilson but wasn't too sure. It would take her a little bit to get their names pegged. She nodded and smiled. "The doc did say that, as long as it was pretty calm at the clinic, I could go out and enjoy as well."

Wilson stopped and added, "That's a surprise, but, hey, look at you, all free and clear. Why don't you see if you can join us?"

"Maybe," she muttered, as she looked around. "Not sure what's going on though. What training are you heading out for?"

"In this place there are always multiple training opportunities, so maybe you could figure out which one still has room and join up." And, with that, Wilson gave her a mock salute and was gone.

When she turned her gaze, she caught Chef studying her intently. She winced. "What? Do I have something on my nose or something?"

He shrugged. "Or something." He looked back at the guy she had been watching. "He's all right to a certain extent, but if you're not the outdoor person …"

She snorted. "Really doesn't matter when you're here, does it?"

"No, it sure doesn't." Chef grinned. "You decide, and I can set you up something to take out for lunch today or tomorrow, if they have room for you."

She really wanted to partake in the training events but was afraid that, since she'd been loaned out to the doc, it was probably way too early to be asking for sledding time. "But I've gotten into this clinic position, where I've been asked to help out, so it feels as if I'm one sour grape if I don't give the doc a hand."

"And yet how much of a hand does she need?" Chef

asked. "Honestly, if you want to go out and get some training, then go out and get some training. You won't get this opportunity again."

And that, in fact, was quite true. She hesitated, as if trying to think, and then Magnus entered the room. He saw her and walked over, with a grin. "How was your first day so far?"

She shrugged. "It's been fine, and I wouldn't begrudge the shift in my duties," she admitted, with a rueful smile, "until I found out that the weather is improving, and everybody's heading out to train."

"Go if you want," Magnus suggested. "I'll be on base, so I can stay."

She hesitated, then lowered her voice and asked, "So, is this a babysitting position or is it really a needed position?"

"It's necessary, and it's a babysitting position," he replied, with a smile.

She groaned at that. "That doesn't help much."

"Maybe not," he agreed, "but go. I'll be around tomorrow too, so feel free."

And, with that, Chef smiled, and, as soon as Magnus was gone, Chef added, "He means it. He's always keeping an eye on the doc, so, if he says go, don't worry about it."

Then another voice spoke behind her, and this time it was Rogan. She groaned. "And I suppose you'll tell me to go too?"

"What? Go to hell, go somewhere else? Where to?" he teased, with a note of interest. "Where are we going?" She glared at him, and he snickered. "Am I not invited?" Then he spied the to-go containers offered to her and whistled. "Ah, you're trying to figure out if you can go on the exercise trip tomorrow? Or even one today?"

She nodded. "But I've been assigned to the medical clinic, so …"

"What did Magnus say?"

"That he would be around, so I could go out this afternoon and even tomorrow afternoon."

He stared at her for a moment. "And that's bothering you?"

She lowered her voice and added, "I thought I was here to help out at the center, not to be a bodyguard."

"I think in this case, the position is both in a way," he suggested.

"It'd be nice if people had told me that ahead of time," she noted in exasperation. "In which case, I'm not going sledding tomorrow for sure."

"And yet didn't Magnus say that he would be around all day? And if you don't go out tomorrow, make sure you grab some sun and fresh air today."

"Sure, but where does my clinic duty start and stop?" she cried out in frustration.

He grinned. "Considering you're on duty regardless, I wouldn't worry about it."

"Maybe, but, if somebody tells me I can go on a dogsled run, and then I get in trouble for it," she pointed out, glaring at him, "then what?"

"Good point," he agreed, with a nod. "Either contact the colonel and ask for clarification or go with what Magnus told you."

"Why would I rely on Magnus's word and not the colonel's?" she asked curiously, and then she stopped, looked around, and whispered, "Unless you know something I don't."

"I know lots that you don't know," Rogan replied, with

a snicker. "And, if Magnus says that you can go, believe me. You're cleared to go."

As she grabbed her cup of coffee and headed to check the training schedule roster to see where the numbers were, she felt a hard gaze behind her. She turned, looking around, and caught sight of a mountain of a man in the far corner. He openly studied her.

She frowned at that too. Something was very unnerving about him, not only his size but that look. Not so much a predatory look as much as that he knew what she was thinking or doing, even from a distance. Though she wasn't doing anything wrong, at least not according to everybody else, it still felt that way, as she read the assignment board.

The colonel was here, speaking to the staff sergeant responsible for making schedules and assignments. The colonel gave her a searching gaze. "I hear you want to go out," he barked.

She winced. "It's not so much that I want to go out, sir," she noted. "However, I came here for training, and, despite my reassignment to the clinic, I still want to get any training that I can." His gaze was hard, and she held up her hand immediately. "And I understand that's all shifted since I'm assigned to the medical clinic to help out, and I'm perfectly happy to do so."

He didn't say anything. Then he turned on his heel and walked out.

"And with that, I guess I'm not going anywhere." She headed back to her room.

DAY 1, MIDMORNING

A LITTLE LATER, Lisa walked to the cafeteria for breakfast, but she was on the late side, so headed straight back to the clinic. As she got there, she opened the door to find Magnus visiting with Sydney. Lisa smiled at the two of them. "I guess this is a regular thing then, isn't it?"

"It is, and will be for the rest of our time here," Magnus replied.

"And after that too?" she teased.

Magnus nodded. "I sure hope so." He grinned at Sydney. "I've got to go." He stood, walked over to the door, and sent a look back.

Sydney groaned. "I already know what you'll say. I promise I will be careful."

"Good, then maybe you won't get into trouble." And, with that, he was gone.

Lisa chuckled as she faced the doc, who shook her head.

Sydney muttered, "He can't see that we're out of danger now."

"Are you though?" Lisa asked. "I'm still getting caught up on all that happened, particularly as I'm now privy to more info, being here in the clinic with you." She shook her head. "When you're out there in the general population, you don't hear all this."

"No, you sure don't," Sydney agreed. "And, if you

weren't part of this group, you wouldn't hear it either."

"Yet, with so many people talking about things—mostly rumors, it seems—the general public is getting a lot of the information wrong."

"I know," Sydney noted, "and I'm all for people being informed, but I can't go against the rules."

"The rules suck," Lisa stated begrudgingly.

"They do. So, I thought you were going out training today. What happened?"

"Yeah, well, the colonel didn't seem to like the idea."

Sydney frowned. "I'm sorry to hear that."

"Whatever. I understand that I'm here to do a job, so it's fine. Maybe I'll get another opportunity." And, with that, Lisa pushed down her disappointment a little further.

However, Sydney seemed to be fairly bothered about it, and, by the time it rolled around closer to lunchtime, she got up with a burst of energy and announced, "I'll be right back."

She quickly walked out of the clinic, leaving Lisa to stare after her. When Lisa got a summons to the colonel's office a little later, she walked in to see him frowning at her.

"Take a seat." She sat down, and he continued. "Now look. Apparently the doctor wants you to go out and get as much training as possible. So, if you still want to go, you can go."

She winced. "I wasn't complaining to her," she replied earnestly. "I understand I have a job to do in the clinic, and that's the priority."

"No, that's all right," he corrected her in a very formal tone. "It's not a problem. I understand from Sydney's point of view how valuable that training is, particularly with the circumstances happening around here. Thus any winter training that you complete is of benefit, particularly in case we must go after injured personnel. I just need to ensure that our medical clinic is covered. She made it very clear that she is perfectly capable of handling it on her own." He gave a partial eye roll. "She was very insistent, in fact." He gave a half laugh.

Lisa was completely surprised at his lighthearted reaction, expecting him to be much more negative about Sydney getting involved in this. Yet Lisa didn't dare say anything about that.

"So, as of tomorrow, we'll put you on training for half of your days," he declared, "and we'll find somebody else to give Sydney a hand, if needed."

"I'm fine to stay," she protested, not wanting him to get somebody else in to do the job that she was fully capable of doing. "Although, in all honesty, she doesn't need help most of the time."

"She only needs help when she needs help," he noted.

"And in that case, I'm fully on call," she declared.

He nodded. "Maybe, we'll leave it with that."

"I don't know what training Magnus has, but if he has any medic field training, you might want to consider him too." The colonel shot her a look at that comment. She shrugged. "He does spend a lot of time there."

"As long as it's his free time, I don't care," he snapped.

She winced. "I didn't mean to imply anything other than that." She hoped the colonel wouldn't take her suggestion the wrong way. "I was just thinking that, since he's already there some of the time, maybe he could do some of the relief work too."

He studied her, still frowning. "We'll see. You're dismissed."

She immediately turned and left, being summarily dismissed. As she walked into the clinic, she glanced at Sydney. "I might have gotten you and Magnus in trouble," she apologized. "I'm not sure what I'm supposed to do about it though."

"What happened?"

When she explained, Sydney laughed. "Don't worry about it. He already knows about Magnus and me, so that's not an issue."

"And yet I don't think he liked it."

"He's just being himself, worried about his responsibilities, and that's how it should be. Plus you're right. Magnus does have some medic training. I don't know that it's enough to step into this position on an on-call basis, but, if there was an emergency, that's a whole different story."

"Right," Lisa murmured. "Anyway, I'm released to do some training, since apparently you thought it would help me in my work."

"It absolutely would, so you need to participate whenever you can while the chance is there. We only have so many weeks, and then hopefully ..." She stopped and winced. "I shouldn't even say, *Hopefully it will be over* because, when things are going great, this is a really unique experience, and it will come to an end sooner rather than later anyway."

"I get it," Lisa noted. "I didn't want to get the two of you in trouble and wanted to warn you if I did."

"Not a problem, and thanks for the heads-up."

"Do you think the colonel will call you about it?"

"He might, but I'm not worried," she replied. "Even if I get sent back home, it's all good."

But it was a worry Lisa lived with, so she was very excited when shortly thereafter she was assigned for some training. She called the staff sergeant who did the scheduling to double-check. He laughed and confirmed. "Yes, you can join in this afternoon's outings. This is dog training, sled running, and the first day on the run, so everybody will take part in this, including you."

IT WAS A nice bright afternoon. Cold but crisp and clean outside. Rogan was checking on the dogs, not surprised to see Magnus talking to Joe, the dog handler. Lisa was cuddling one of the dogs in the pack. *Smart dog, has good taste.* He thought the dog was Benji—Rogan's personal favorite too—yet hard to tell, as several other dogs kept butting in, looking for attention. They were a rambunctious bunch and a lot of fun. These dogs helped ground all the personnel eager to hug and love these furry friends, especially when they were so happy to have the attention.

Rogan joined Magnus and Joe. "You have a couple injured ones, I hear."

"I do," Joe confirmed. "They won't be going out."

"Wouldn't the run help them?" Rogan asked.

"Maybe, but pulling won't." Joe's tone was sharp.

Rogan nodded. "No offense intended. I was just curious."

Joe frowned at him. "My dogs, my decision." And, with that, he returned to the sleds, where he'd been waxing some of the skis.

Rogan looked at Magnus, who shrugged. "He's still a little sensitive that his dogs were shot," Magnus shared.

"I would be too," Rogan agreed in a low voice. "That's complete bullshit. And we still have no idea who it was, right?"

"No, we sure don't." Magnus hesitated, then asked, "You going out today?"

"Absolutely. We've been waiting for some sunshine and the chance to get out. I got the roster earlier this morning and checked it over and realized that both you and Lisa are on it. I'm surprised she's coming, but I know she'll be happy too. She loves dogsledding."

"Exactly."

And with that, they headed to where everybody was gearing up, while Joe was strapping in the dogs. What followed was training on how to deal with the dogs, working in detailed patterns, strapping in the dog harnesses, basic care of the sleds, and what to look out for in case of problems. Then, with Joe on one sled and leading a group on another sled, they slowly set out on their first training trip in a while.

For Rogan, this beginner info was frustrating because he did have some experience sledding, but it couldn't have been half as frustrating as it was for Lisa, who was bundled up and sitting on one of the sleds, as her musher ended up making a complete mess of it.

By the time they were to set off again, she'd shot Rogan enough horrified looks that he was surprised she had remained seated on the sled for so long, letting this guy bumble his way through it. Lisa was a spitfire—which could be off-putting to someone who didn't know her or someone with a fragile ego to defend. However, Rogan knew Lisa to be good people, although it had taken him a long time to not automatically think of her as the wife of his good friend Barry.

Rogan shook that thought from his head and focused again on Lisa, holding back his grin as she made her newbie musher stop. Then she quickly got out and organized the leads better, giving the newbie musher a few quick pointers. Joe stopped his team, waited for the other team to slowly catch up. When they were side by side, he muttered to Lisa, "He still has to learn."

"He does, but he lost track of a few things," she snapped back in a low undertone.

Joe smirked, but he kept an eye on their team the whole time.

They would be out for a good three to four hours, with the teams to return long before sunset. They stopped at one point in time to go over emergency procedures for crevices, ice melts, and broken equipment. This was an intro course for some of the new guys, with a smattering of more advanced information, depending on which sled you were paired with.

As they turned around, Joe changed routes, making a more circuitous ride back to base. Rogan approached him when they stopped for a break and asked him curiously, "Any reason for this route?"

He nodded. "Yeah, it's that damn snow cave. Since Terrance was found there, and then Magnus used it to save himself… and my dogs, I check it out every time. It's a habit."

"I want to see it myself," Rogan added.

"Stay in a straight line, and you'll hit it," Joe replied. "It's coming up."

And, sure enough, there it was. Approaching it cautiously, they got up to the edge and stopped, while Joe explained the history behind it. "You can see it's partially caved in. Nobody's been here recently, but, as far as outdoor survival on a temporary basis, this wasn't a bad idea. It still won't save you if you're badly injured or without food for too long."

Everybody took a few moments to examine the snow cave and to go over how it was built and how long it would take to create one from scratch. Then they all started back home again.

By the time they pulled into the base, the wind had picked up, and the chill factor bit into their faces, as Rogan helped to undo the harnesses. Glancing at Joe, Rogan asked, "Have you ever seen anybody around that snow cave?"

"Not recently."

"But you saw the tracks?"

Joe looked at him sharply and nodded. "I did."

"What do you think?" he asked, glancing around to confirm they were alone. They were in the outside pen with the dogs, who raced around, rolling in the snow in joy. They couldn't care less about the biting cold or the encroaching darkness. Benji came over to Rogan, shoving his nose in hands, looking for neck scratches. Rogan scratched him, as Joe appeared to weigh his answer.

"I suspect it'll be someone from the village," Joe finally replied. "The locals found Terrance in that cave. I'm sure they check it out constantly, as I do." He sighed heavily.

"Could be. That makes sense. However, you never really know until all this shit breaks loose, and we understand more of what went on."

Joe walked away, looking back at Rogan. "Could be somebody is keeping an eye on us."

"Why would somebody do that?" Rogan asked.

Joe stared at him, "You tell me." And he turned and walked away.

DAY 1, DINNERTIME

COMING IN FOR dinner, making her way to the dining room, Lisa felt just how much the cold had zapped her energy. She rubbed her arms and shoulders as she walked in. Chef took one look and frowned. She nodded. "I know. I know. I've been outside all afternoon and picked up a bit of a chill."

"And you know better than to get a chill." He quickly served her a hot bowl of soup.

"I do. I wasn't expecting that today"—she accepted the bowl—"but I'll be better prepared for tomorrow."

He snorted at that. "You might not get another chance, particularly if they can see how cold you are now," he noted, with a shrug. "Get down some of this hot soup and maybe a hot coffee too." He motioned toward the pot. "And do it fast."

Although she already knew how to deal with the chill, it was still nice to be fussed over. She gave him a gentle smile and thanked him and found a seat. She looked up while drinking her soup to see Magnus frowning at her.

He walked to her side and stared at her. "Are you that cold?"

"First time out in quite a while. It was absolutely beautiful out there, but I seem to have picked up a little bit more of a chill than I expected."

"Looks like it." He studied her carefully. "Make sure you keep an eye on it."

"I will," she noted. "Everybody seems to be so concerned."

"Exactly, and with good reason," he stated simply. "When we're here in this Arctic tundra, it's on all of us to watch out for each other because it really is all of us or it's none of us."

He sounded almost cryptic and had Lisa immediately frowning.

Magnus continued. "We don't need any more people hurt, particularly you as a medic here."

She winced. "Meaning that everybody would think I should know better."

He chuckled. "I don't know that you'll be charged with *you should know better*, but that you got too cold, and maybe, as our only nurse, you shouldn't have been out there in the first place."

"*Right*," she grumbled, "as if I need that either. Colonel didn't want me out there to begin with, not until Sydney spoke to him."

Magnus laughed. "As I mentioned, much better to get warm … and fast." He tossed her a few pocket heat packs for her hands. "You can always put a couple of these on your hands."

She shook them to activate the heating and pulled her sleeves down over her hands.

As she worked on her soup, Magnus added, "Then I suggest a good night's sleep."

"I plan on it," she muttered, wishing he would let it go.

At that, he gave her a hard look. "You might just be cold, but it's not a case of *just cold* up here. We can't fool around with it here, not with our limited resources." And, with that, he turned and left.

She let out a sigh, but wished she hadn't the minute Rogan spoke up from behind her.

"He's right, you know?"

"I know he's right," she snapped. *Why did Rogan rub me the wrong way?* "I'm here getting some soup to warm up, and, as you can clearly see, I am fine now."

He snorted. "Don't give me that BS. You're still shivering, even with the hot packs I saw Magnus pass to you. And I know you too well. If you weren't fine, you wouldn't tell us, would you?"

"I would. I'm not an idiot," she replied crossly. "I did everything right today, but I hadn't yet had any exposure to this cold for this long, and so here I am, freezing. Now can we leave it alone?"

"Sure." He chuckled, giving her a knowing look. "Besides, you aren't the only one. A couple other people are suffering from today's trip." When she stared at him in surprise, he nodded. "You didn't think it was just you, did you?" He gave her a smirk, and she rolled her eyes.

"Does anybody need help?" she asked, frowning into her soup. "I'm capable of coming and getting myself some soup, but what about the others?"

"I believe a couple of them are on their way in, and one of them is already in the clinic."

"Ah, crap," she muttered, as she immediately put down her soup bowl and stood to head for the door, but Rogan grabbed her before she got far.

"No, Sydney's got it. You need to finish your soup."

"Right, of course she can handle one or two patients." Lisa brushed the hair off her face. "Still, I don't want to think that she needs help, and I'm not there."

"If she needed more help, she would call you," he stated immediately. "Now dinner is being served, so go grab yourself some more food, and let's make sure you're okay."

"I'm fine," she cried out, angry at herself now for even letting anyone see that she was so cold.

He looked at her, snorted. "You don't look it. And don't get upset when people show concern. Or is this just the reaction you give me?" He didn't wait for her answer to that question. "It's in everyone's best interests to look after each other. However, since you are the only nurse in this place, it's best that you look after you, so you are in a position to truly help the others."

"I'm not upset," she snapped but couldn't say it without her tone turning snippy. She groaned, then closed her eyes to get a grip. "Look. I don't want a big deal made out of it. I know, in some situations, it is a big deal, but that's not the case right now with me."

"Good thing. So, eat up, and then you can go check up on Sydney."

"You mean, Magnus isn't?"

"Oh, Magnus is," Rogan confirmed, with a smirk. "He already took food to her because she isn't leaving any patient right now. Hypothermia, *as we all know*, is nothing to fool around with."

"No, it isn't," she agreed calmly. She stepped into line and looked back at Rogan. "Are you eating?"

He nodded. "Yes, then I'll go out on security watch."

At that, she froze and turned to look at him, one eyebrow raised.

He shrugged. "I shouldn't have mentioned that. Seems you are worried about me." He waggled his eyebrows at her.

She waved her hand at him, downright serious now. "Yeah, you shouldn't have," she replied, studying him intently. "Anything you want to tell me about?"

"Nope, not at all."

When he gave her a bland smile, all it did was piss her off.

She quickly loaded a tray with her food and, rather than eating it here, she raced to the clinic to see how Sydney was doing.

ROGAN BUNDLED UP in multiple layers, before stepping out into the frozen night. He had a big thermos with him and a rifle over his shoulder, standing outside the kitchen's back door, waiting for his body to acclimate, then stepped out briskly into the snow drifts. First stop was the generator shed, right next to the kitchen area. As he stepped in to make sure all was well, he surprised Chef, who looked at him in alarm. "Everything okay?" Rogan asked him.

"Yeah, it's fine," Chef said. "I always come out and check the generator. Being so low on supplies, I can't have anything spoil."

"Sure, but wouldn't everything just be more frozen than usual?" He studied Chef curiously.

"True," Chef agreed, "but, in the past, we've also had a few unwelcome local predators, helping themselves to our supplies."

"Can't blame them for that. They're trying to eat to live too."

"I know, and sometimes I really feel sorry for the poor buggers." Chef smiled. "Yet I can't have it, not at the risk of our needs." Chef quickly headed back inside.

He wasn't even dressed for the cold, but, if it was as he had told Rogan—Chef was on a quick trip—then that made sense. Although not many men would be so acclimated to this frozen tundra. With a frown, Rogan looked toward the kitchen area, seeing a well-worn path to underline Chef's comments.

As Rogan stepped into the generator room, he checked it over carefully to ensure all was well. It appeared to be fine. A lot of fuel tanks were off to the side, and, as long as their supplies kept coming in on a regular basis, they would be fine. If something went wrong, that was when everything fell apart. Rogan checked for anything suspicious, but everything appeared normal.

He stepped back out again and headed to the sled dogs' area. As he walked in, Joe sat there, talking to one of his dogs.

Joe looked up. "Problems?"

"Just doing rounds."

"Good." Joe nodded.

"Is everything okay out here?"

Hearing Rogan's voice, Benji woofed and raced over to greet Rogan, leaning against his legs and looking up adoringly.

Rogan chuckled and bent to give him a good scratching behind the ears. "He seems to be doing much better. I see Magnus is always over here, visiting with Toby. Better watch it. He might steal him from you."

Joe snorted at that. "He's mentioned it a time or two."

"Still, the dogs must be a good warning system. Outside of us dog lovers."

"They are, and things are fine. I haven't had any unwanted visitors, so I'll take that as a good thing," Joe muttered.

"But then again, you prefer four-legged critters to two-legged ones when it comes to company, don't you?" he asked with a smile.

Joe stared at him. "Yeah, I sure do."

"How are the dogs doing?"

At that, Joe reached down and brushed Benji's coat, even as the dog woofed and squirmed at Rogan's feet. "This is one of the two that were shot. He's still healing. He always seems to have a chill now, although you'd never know he's not 100 percent to see him now." Joe frowned. "I might end up sending him home, instead of keeping him here."

"Where is home?"

Joe looked over at him. "Alaska."

"Ah, so not somewhere warm?"

"Benji enjoys the cold," Joe stated, followed by a headshake, "but that doesn't mean he'll be okay out here for the long term. So I need to make sure he's healthy enough to do the job."

"Of course," Rogan agreed. "I wouldn't expect anything else."

Joe didn't say more, not before staring at Rogan for a moment. "I don't remember seeing any sentries before," he noted, abruptly looking around.

"No, you probably haven't, but that doesn't mean there shouldn't have been, though."

At that, Joe's eyebrows shot up, and he nodded. "That's a good point."

"So let me know if you see anything out here that hits you the wrong way."

"Will do," Joe replied.

With that, Rogan gave one last cuddle to Benji, wishing, not for the first time, that he had a less nomadic lifestyle and could keep a dog, and headed back out again. He did a full circle around the base, checking for tracks. In the distance, he turned to look in the direction of the scientists' camp.

Out of sight farther up, Rogan got a weird nudge inside him that warned him something wasn't quite right. He backtracked and found Joe again.

Joe stared at him and frowned. "Did you find something?"

He shook his head. "No, but …"

Joe immediately straightened. "But?"

"Do we have very much to do with the scientists' camp?"

"The scientists?" He shrugged. "I haven't seen them myself, but I know we have lots of interactions back and forth because they've had generator problems. You should probably talk to Magnus about that, as he's helped out several times."

Rogan nodded. "Okay. I can do that." He frowned as he turned, not liking what he still felt.

"If you've got anything to say," Joe added, "I really want to hear it first."

"It's not so much that I've got anything to say," Rogan corrected him, "except something doesn't feel right."

"Then contact Magnus," he stated sharply, "and let's head off a problem before we get there."

At that, Rogan pulled out his phone and contacted Magnus. There was no answer, so he quickly sent him a text.

When Magnus phoned him a few minutes later, he said, "Good instincts. They're having generator troubles again. Worst-case scenario, we'll bring them down here, until they can get their own systems all back up and running again."

"That would suck," Rogan replied. "We're already in tight quarters as it is."

"We are, but I'm hoping this generator issue isn't that bad tonight."

At that, Rogan looked up to see Magnus walking toward him, yet still talking on the phone. Rogan told him, "Pretty shitty night for a trip up there."

"No such thing as a good night for that trip," Magnus replied, with a burly laugh.

"Do you need somebody to come with you?"

Magnus looked at him and shrugged. "I won't say no to the company. No one should be doing these trips alone as it is."

"Ya think?" Rogan muttered. "I'll come."

"You any good with generators?"

"Nope," he answered cheerfully, "but I'm great at navigating, even in the dark—or whiteout conditions."

"That's good," Magnus noted, "because usually up here we're navigating in the blind. Clear it with the colonel, and we'll get going."

Twenty minutes later they were in the snowcat, slowly traveling toward the scientists' camp. "What exactly are they doing up here?" Rogan asked Magnus.

Magnus raised his free hand, palm up. "Good luck asking them. They act as if it's top secret. It isn't though. It's scientific research stuff."

"And we know for sure it's strictly scientific research stuff, and nothing weird is going on?"

"I have no reason to think it's anything other than what we've been told. I wouldn't be at all surprised if they had more than a few difficulties that they haven't shared." When Rogan looked at him sharply, Magnus nodded. "They're not even considering sabotage or any other problems."

"Why would they though?" Rogan asked. "Most of us don't make that immediate assumption."

"True, but up here you need to look at everything, and I tend to think they're on the naïve side, now slowly waking up to a new reality."

"Shit, you really think somebody is sabotaging their camp?"

"I don't know," Magnus admitted.

"Does make you wonder if the sabotage of their camp is in any way related to the mess at our base, right?"

Magnus gave a one-arm shrug. "Too soon to tell. However, I did mention that sabotage premise to them last time, and they got pretty upset at the idea."

"*Pretty upset* is one thing, but ignoring it completely is a whole different story. Have they had that many issues?"

"You'll get a chance to ask them yourself," Magnus noted, "because we're about there." As they came around the corner, several shadowed structures appeared. "Yeah, the lights are out."

"Don't they do that for their own rationing though? Or maybe they shut it down when they have fuel issues?"

"Sure, but they're also having generator issues." And, with that, they pulled into the camp. The door opened almost immediately, letting them in. As they stepped inside, six people stood there, staring at them.

"Hey, Magnus," greeted one of the men, with a forced smile. "I honest to God don't know what we'd do without you."

"Freezing," quipped another scientist off to his left. "It's been a shit show since the beginning."

"No, that's not true," corrected a woman, her voice calm

in the darkness. "Everything was working fine, up until a little while ago."

"When you say a little bit ago, what does that mean, time-wise?" Rogan asked her, curious.

"A few weeks back. I've been up here for a couple months now," she stated. "The work we're doing is coming to an end, at least for our shift. We wanted to finish, so we didn't have to send anybody else up anytime soon."

"I'm all for that," declared one of the men, "but not without heat."

"No, we cannot do without heat up here," the first woman agreed. "Any suggestions, Magnus?"

"For starters, you need two decent generators, so you have one as a backup, and more fuel of course. I don't really understand why this generator keeps conking out on you," he admitted. "The only other option I have is to move you all down to our military base, until you can set up something better here for your group. That option must be discussed with our commander first."

"If you've got heat and food," she replied, her voice full of laughter, "I'm pretty sure everybody here would be jumping all over that idea."

"Only if we can't get your generator running again tonight," Magnus noted in a casual tone. "In that case, we do whatever we need to in order to keep everybody safe."

"And we appreciate that, young man," replied a white-haired woman, stepping into the little bit of light that there was, giving Rogan a better look at her face. She looked to be the senior scientist on board, and, as she spoke, everybody fell silent, giving more credence to the respect that she naturally received. "And I would be okay with that too." She nodded at the two military men. "We just need a few more days, a week at the most."

"I don't even know what you do up here," Rogan admitted to her. "Seems to be a lot of expense and hard work. I hope it's worth it."

"We're scientists, so, for us, it's all about the data. … Information-gathering is pretty much everything," she stated, with a half smile. "I get that, for you guys, keeping track of temperatures, wind-chill factors, polar Arctic species, and local vegetation doesn't really matter"—she gave him a stern gaze—"but it does to us."

"I didn't mean it as a criticism," Rogan added immediately.

"And I didn't take it as such," she replied equally quickly. "Still, like you're playing war games up here, we're doing what's important to us here as well."

He winced at that. "I guess to you guys it does seem like war games."

"It does," she agreed, "and from what we understand, there have been some issues down in your corner too."

One of the other scientists noted in disgust, "Yeah, if anything, that would stop us from moving to your place. I don't want to get murdered in my bed."

DAY 2, MORNING

THE NEXT MORNING, Lisa woke up, shivering in her bed. She waited until her shakiness calmed down, realizing she had to get up in order to get some hot food and hot drinks. She also grabbed a couple more of the small hand warmers that Magnus had given her earlier. Dressing in heavy long johns under her normal clothes, she headed to the kitchen to grab coffee. Moving to an empty table, she huddled around her steaming cup.

When Rogan found her a little while later, she looked up. "Hey," he said, studying her intently.

"I'm fine," she reassured him. "I'm fine."

He nodded. "We may end up with company soon." He sat down opposite her. "I traveled to the scientists' camp with Magnus last night, and they're definitely having some ongoing generator issues. They'll probably need to join us here, until they can get airlifted out."

She nodded. "Did they come in by air, or did they come in by dogsled?"

"Both," he replied, with a laugh. "Seems some people were doing other work relatively nearby and had been here for a little bit longer. Then, when the camp opened up, those scientists ended up joining the rest of them. They do work here in the summer and the winter."

"Summer here I could understand maybe," Lisa shared,

"but, man, wintertime? ... It's something else."

"It is, indeed. ... Are you really doing okay?"

Clearly he wasn't convinced about her condition. "I'm doing fine," she repeated, bolstering her smile. "I slept like a log, and, since I obviously woke up, it's all good."

He burst out laughing. "Glad to hear that. Have you checked in on the clinic?"

"Not yet this morning." She frowned. "Is there any reason to?"

He looked at her, shrugged. "None that I know of."

"Good," she said. "In which case, I'll finish my coffee, and then I'll refill it and go check on Sydney."

"As far as checking on Sydney goes, I'm pretty sure Magnus has got that one down."

She leaned forward and asked, "Are they sharing accommodations?"

Rogan nodded. "He was assigned as her bodyguard, and, once they became an item, no need to shift things again."

"No." Lisa smirked. "But, man, I can see a lot of benefits to having a warm body at night," she let slip out. She flushed, as she added hastily, "I was pretty-damn cold last night."

"Yet you wouldn't admit that to anybody, would you?"

She glared at him. "I'm fine."

"Of course you're fine," he repeated, with an eye roll. "And if there was ever a statement guaranteed to make people think you're *not*, it's that one."

She groaned and waved her hand at him. "I really am okay."

"That sounded a little better," he admitted, "so don't go getting snappy and upset when people are just checking on you. It means we care."

And, with that, he got up and headed out, leaving her sitting in the dining room, staring after him. She had to admit that, of everything she had found out about over the past couple days, knowing that Magnus and Sydney were sharing quarters and noting how cold Lisa herself had been the night before, both made a huge difference to her outlook on the world.

To have a partner to share this stressful scenario with would make it all very different, and keeping her warm in the night was only part of it.

She hadn't had a full-time partner in a very long time. Relationships were something she didn't really do easily, not with the work she did. She was forever off on missions, always volunteering, always wanting to be out and about. However, she also knew that part of the reason why she always wanted to be busy was because she didn't have anybody at home. She had no reason to go home, nothing to keep her there either. So she might as well go out and explore while she had the chance. At least that's what she told herself.

With coffee in hand, she headed to the clinic. As she opened the door, Sydney stood there, talking to somebody who obviously had spent the night. Lisa hurried in. "How is everything?"

Sydney looked over, smiled. "He's doing better, but he'll need some hot coffee and some hot food."

"I've got a hot coffee here in my hand," she stated, looking over at him. "I'm happy to make another trip." And, with that, she quickly gave him her cup and returned to the dining room. As she walked in again, Chef looked at her and frowned, his question evident in his expression. She smiled. "I'm here to collect coffee for the patient."

"Good, I was hoping he made it through the night okay."

"Do you know him?" she asked.

"I try to get to know everyone here." Chef smiled. "I know that kid is from down south, has no meat on his bones, and isn't in any way geared for this cold."

She snorted. "Hey, I used to spend a lot of time in the south, so we can adapt."

"Do you now?" he asked, with a smirk. "I don't know how you feel right now, but you looked pretty cold yourself last night."

She winced. "Yeah, okay, I'll give you that one," she muttered.

She quickly filled three cups of coffee, doctored one with sugar and powdered creamer, and then headed back to the clinic with the tray. She handed Sydney hers and then walked over to the patient. Seeing he had downed the first cup already, she placed the patient's second one on the small table nearby. "I know you had some already, but I put sugar and cream in this cup to help with the cold."

"Thanks," he replied, with a bright smile. "I didn't think I'd sleep much last night, but then half the time I was afraid I wouldn't wake up again. The doc kept telling me that I'd be okay, but I wasn't sure I believed her."

Lisa chuckled. "Are you part of the British team?"

"Nope, the US team. Sydney is part of the British team though." He nodded at the doc.

"As long as you didn't come here just to visit with her," Lisa teased.

"Nope, I can do that anytime." He chuckled. "Besides, she's got Magnus, so no point in coming to visit her now." He gave an exaggerated sigh.

At that, Sydney rolled her eyes. "You've been in a couple times to see me anyway, Willy," she noted, "so it's all good."

"Yeah, but if I'd known you were in the market for a boyfriend ..." Willy smirked.

"I wasn't," she declared, turning to give him a look. "But, when it's right, I guess, ... you don't even think about it."

"Aye, I hear you there," he agreed, with a sage nod. "Glad the two of you hooked up. He's a good guy."

She smiled at Willy. "He is, isn't he?"

"Yeah, everybody respects him. And there is something to be said for that," He reached over and picked up the coffee, but his shivers had his hand shaking way too much.

Lisa gave an exclamation, then snapped the cup from his hand. "Let's not have you wearing that," she murmured. "It's one thing to be cold, but let's not have you burn yourself."

Willy nodded. "I can't stop shivering."

Lisa pulled out one of the pocket warmers she'd been given, shook it to heat it up for him, and tucked it up against his chest. "Here. Hug that for a little bit."

He gave a sigh of joy as the heat washed through him.

She turned and looked over at Sydney, who shook her head at his antics. Lisa walked closer to Sydney to get some distance from their patient to speak privately. "Do you think he'll be okay?"

"Yes, he's fine." The doc looked up and smiled at Lisa. "He's cold, but that's okay. I also caught him trying to get dressed, and he wasn't wearing the right amount of clothing for this Arctic weather either—even inside—so now he's caught a chill again. He needs to sit back, relax, and enjoy being here. At least until his temperature normalizes."

"Yeah, I don't think any of the men enjoy being here in

the clinic," Lisa noted, with a knowing smile.

"No, but, unless he warms up, I'm not letting him go."

Lisa sat down across from the doc and in a low voice asked, "Did you hear that we might end up with company?"

"Yeah, I heard." She snorted. "It'll cramp us a bit but not too badly."

"And they might need your services."

"I hadn't heard that," she admitted, looking over at her nurse. "Did you hear something I didn't?"

"No, maybe not. I was thinking that, if they're all cold enough that they move down here …"

"Oh, it's one thing to be cold and not have a reliable way to keep the heat on, making it prudent to move here until they can get out," she stated, with a shrug. "It's an entirely different thing if they're injured or possibly frostbit."

"I don't think I'm expecting them to be injured as much as I'm worried about so many people moving in, making things here more difficult. We already have mysterious goings-on. Bringing in strangers is dangerous."

"I think less than a dozen scientists are in that camp now, and we're not up to full capacity here anyway," Sydney noted. "So finding the rooms won't make that much difference. Plus I think Chef is rationing our food, preparing for the worst. Therefore, it seems he's got a stockpile, even if our supplies are delayed, due to the weather here."

Lisa didn't say anything to that, but it was a relief to hear Sydney's positive reaction to it all. That was the one thing about Sydney. She didn't get ruffled over much. That was a unique experience for Lisa because so many people—mostly women, though she hated to say it—got overly dramatic regarding changes, especially when it came to accommodations. But, if Sydney was okay with it, then they would work it out.

By the time noon rolled around, Lisa and Sydney had revised their attitude toward their patient. Willy was getting belligerent, and that wasn't normal.

Sydney shook her head. "I was really hoping this wouldn't happen," she muttered, and then swore under her breath as she checked his vitals. "He's not warming up on us. He was, but now he's not."

"Damn," Lisa whispered. "What will you do?" she asked, as Sydney stayed close, hovering around him.

"We'll do our best to keep him warm," Sydney replied. "Take these blankets to Chef and see if he can get them warmed up somehow."

"Dryers?"

"No, but he's got a little warming oven down there. Uses way less energy than a dryer, yet takes a bit longer. See if he can toss those in for us." With that, Lisa quickly took off.

As she reached Chef in the back corner of his kitchen, he took one look, nodded, and rose to get the blankets from her. He was obviously familiar with the practice.

"Is he struggling?" he asked Lisa.

"Apparently, but it's all of a sudden."

"Yeah, it can happen that way up here," he noted, with exasperation. "Unfortunately we go from everything being calm and normal, then suddenly it's not so calm and not so normal. I hope he picks up quickly."

"Yeah, you and me both," Lisa agreed. "I hadn't seen it go south like this before."

"When you stay here long enough, you'll see that the body can cope, right up until it can't anymore." Within a few minutes, he pulled the blankets from the warmer, quickly wrapped them in an insulated bag, then handed them to Lisa. "Get these back to her quickly."

And, with that, Lisa took off running. When she returned to the clinic, Sydney was taking Willy's temperature again. She grabbed the blankets and quickly pulled the sheet off the guy. Willy cried out in shock from the cold, but she wrapped him up immediately with the heated blankets, and, with Lisa's help, quickly bundled him up in both warm blankets, as he moaned against the heat.

He sagged back on the hospital bed and asked, "You won't let me die, right, Doc?"

"I won't let you die," she stated immediately.

"Yeah, it wouldn't do for you to lose a fellow member of these teams," he noted, with a crack at a joke.

"It wouldn't do to lose anybody," she declared. "However, I need you to eat and to get some liquids down."

"Be happy to," he snorted and turned with agitation, "but I don't think I can swallow anything. My teeth are chattering too much."

And, even now, it was hard to understand what he had to say, but Lisa was off and running to get a hot drink for him and a straw.

By the time she got back, he had calmed slightly. As soon as he was out of danger, Lisa looked over at Sydney. "Does this happen often?"

She nodded. "It can happen more often than not, once you catch that chill," she explained. "It's pretty-damn easy to think you're fine, but then that chill races back, and suddenly you're not."

"Yeah, ... I've never seen it return so fast like that," she admitted in concern.

"It can happen so fast that it's really a problem," she murmured. "So if you ever caught a chill yourself"—Sydney turned to assess her nurse—"then please be very careful and don't go outside on those days."

"No, I won't," she murmured. "But it does make me wonder how we can continue to do all these winter training programs if this is what's in store for some of us."

"Also, in Willy's case, he wasn't dressed properly, but he didn't want to let everybody know he'd caught a chill, so now it has to go in my report. That means he'll get sidelined, probably for the rest of this training session. And likely shipped home."

"*Great*. That won't make him feel very good, will it?"

"No, it sure won't, but making him feel good isn't my job. It's all about keeping him alive," Sydney declared, with half a smile. "Sometimes they make my job damn difficult." Sydney added, "I've got meetings to go to right now, so will you be okay here on your own for a few hours or so?" With Lisa's nod, Sydney left the clinic.

Keeping a close eye on Willy, as his temperature fluctuated up and down, kept Lisa busy throughout the day, and she was glad for it because, the more he shivered and fought the chills, the more it made her aware of her own issues.

Finally Willy noticed and snapped at her. "You're cold too, aren't you?"

She nodded. "Yeah, it's not just you," she admitted cheerfully.

"That makes me feel better," Willy shared. Then he gave her a cheeky grin. "Unless you want to curl up in here, we could use our combined body heat to warm ourselves up."

She burst out laughing. "Nice try."

He shrugged. "Hey, if you can't, you can't ..." Then he started to shiver more. Moaning, he now shook visibly again. When he finally calmed down, he noted, with a forced smile,

"That was a bad one."

"I don't think it was as bad as what you've had earlier, so I do think you're making progress. As long as you stay warm and don't over exert yourself, you will continue to gradually improve."

He nodded. "Can't say I expected this."

"No, I don't think anybody ever expects it," she stated, with a smile.

"Including you? You've done a lot of this training, haven't you?"

"I have," she confirmed, "and that's why I was pretty surprised when I got so cold too, … but I also got a little bit wet out there, and once that happens …"

He winced. "Yeah, sucks when that happens, doesn't it? But, hey, hopefully I'm well enough to get out."

"Get out as in leave the clinic or leave the base or get back out as in outside in the winter weather?"

"I'm totally okay to not go out in that blizzard-ridden mountain of snow anymore," he shared. "Yet I get it. We're all supposed to do a certain amount of survival training, and I have done most of my weeks, so thank God for that."

"And, if we're ever in a war, will we do this stuff?"

"That would be a different story," he noted, with a groan. "In that situation, we'd be in total survival mode. However, in this case, it's just a different lifestyle."

"Absolutely."

She checked up on him a few more times, and Sydney finally returned from her series of meetings. Lisa looked up at the doc's face, then immediately asked in a low voice, "Problems?"

Sydney shrugged. "We might end up with the scientists a little earlier than we thought."

"Oh." Lisa frowned at that. "Will that make a whole lot of difference?"

"They are working on room assignments right now," she shared, with a nod.

"Do we have supplies for them?"

She nodded. "The scientists will bring whatever supplies they have, but that's not the worry right now. It's more a case of making sure we have room and that everybody is aware of what's going on here at our base."

"The people on base shouldn't care though, right?" Lisa asked curiously.

"Ordinarily I wouldn't think so," Sydney replied, "but, with our current situation, it'll add stress to an already tense scenario."

"Right, I hadn't thought about that. I guess not everybody is happy to have company, are they?" Although Sydney had been blasé about this all before, she looked concerned now. That change was more concerning to Lisa.

Sidney grimaced. "Not only are some people here not happy to have company but, from the ugly talk I've already heard, the scientists are deemed close enough to have been a part of whatever has been going on here. Therefore, some people will probably want to question the scientists."

"That's hardly fair." Lisa snorted. "They were off in their own world."

"They were, but now they might not be, and that is part of the reason why the brass has held off inviting them here, hoping we would solve whatever the hell was going on with this mess, so the scientists wouldn't get dragged into it too."

"I understand their point," Lisa admitted, with a nod. "Who the hell would want to play any part in this mess? From the scientists' perspective, they're only doing this because they're forced to, due to those power issues at their own camp, which could have severe consequences. They were hoping to make it another week, but it doesn't seem to be possible, at least not unless they can make arrangements here."

"Which, in a way, might be quite doable and could even result in an opportunity for cross-training. It could be a great thing for everybody. The scientists are presumably going off to various sites during the day, right?"

"Exactly," Lisa confirmed. "They go out to their sites, collecting data, and all that good stuff that goes along with being a scientist."

Sydney frowned. "I don't exactly know what they're working on, though I'm not sure that it's top secret or anything that's got to be kept confidential. However, I know the colonel is still fussing about the whole thing."

Lisa didn't say anything about that because, when the orders came down, as they always did, they would all buckle down and deal with them.

Sydney added, "In the meantime, they're up there still trying to stick to themselves and to not worry about it."

"Will the move be today?" Lisa asked.

"I don't think so. They're still trying to get the generator up and running, but, if it comes to a move, we'll probably see them tonight or tomorrow, something like that." Sydney shrugged. "I can only tell you that Magnus is heavily involved in trying to keep their generator operational. Yet, at some point in time, he'll need parts and pieces that they don't have, and it won't work out any other way."

"Right." Lisa nodded and went back to work on Willy. This would be an interesting mess to sort out.

Lots of movement outside, whether on foot, skis, dogsled, snowmobiles or the new snowcat that replaced the Arctic Cat prototype—regardless of the weather. No sign of Teegan. Lots of snow. Lots of maintenance to keep airfield open.

Rogan grimaced. Mountain continued to send daily texts regarding Teegan to Mason, with copies to Rogan and Magnus. Mountain resolutely held out hope of finding his brother alive, but, with each passing day, it had to be eroding his hope.

Rogan and Magnus headed to the colonel's office. When they stepped inside, the colonel glared at them.

"Why the hell can't that generator be fixed?"

"I'm not sure," Magnus replied, then hesitated. "Colonel, I'm not so sure it isn't being sabotaged."

The colonel's eyebrows shot up. "Oh, hell." He put down his pen. "Do you have any proof of that?"

"No, I sure don't," Magnus admitted, "but I keep looking for it. I don't have any cameras to check, nothing that would work in these cold temperatures anyway. We can't set up any video equipment, which is a nuisance, so we have nothing on that angle."

"No, the ice and the snow keep covering any cams. I get that. But why would anybody want to sabotage the scientists' camp?" asked the colonel.

"I can think of a couple reasons," Magnus replied, "and none of them are good."

"Speak up," the colonel barked.

Magnus was still for a moment, then shrugged. "It could be anything, whether the threats to the scientists are coming from within their own camp or could be coming from our base. Regardless, my theories are that the scientists want their group brought here for whatever reason, besides just the issue of heat, as in their food supply is threatened too," he suggested a bit hesitantly. Then he sighed. "If the threat is within the scientists' camp, then the perpetrator has more potential victims here, while living among us in our base," he noted, with caution. "Or it could be somebody within their own camp is against their staying out here any longer. I guess this research was supposed to end a while ago, and this could be one way of making sure that the scientists head back home sooner rather than later."

"True," the colonel agreed, "but they're all scientists, and they've all signed up for this. As I see it, they would wait all year for this."

"And that would be a good reason for getting some more information on them," Magnus suggested, "particularly if you aren't certain about bringing them in to live temporarily at our base."

"I don't want to bring anybody else into the scenario we've currently got going on here. While the scientists are certainly aware of some of my reasons for my hesitancy, they aren't aware of all of them, and I don't want them to be," he snapped. "It's bad enough that we have this mess on my base, without everybody else hearing about it."

Rogan stood silently at Magnus's side. Suddenly the colonel pinned him to the spot. "Do you have anything to offer?"

Rogan shook his head. "No. However, of the ones I've met from that group, they seem to be dedicated scientists. A couple of them want to go home, I think. Whether that's a timing thing or if they're thinking it's a bad deal and going home is a better solution for all, I don't know. I can't see any of them sabotaging their own equipment, and I'm not sure any of them would even know how."

"And yet it's possible?" the colonel asked.

"It is possible," Rogan confirmed. "Plus we saw tracks all over the damn place that don't make a lot of sense."

At that, the colonel shot his gaze back over to Magnus, who nodded and replied, "I would agree with that. The scientists told me that they haven't been out walking around the camp"—he shrugged—"but I don't know that they're telling the truth. Somebody made those tracks."

"*Great*," the colonel muttered, "so it could be that we're bringing in another headache by allowing them to join us."

"It's possible," Magnus murmured. "We don't have any way to know."

"Go back up there and see if you can get that damn thing running again."

"The generator was running when we left, and I promised them that I would return tonight and check on them."

"Have they sent out an SOS?"

"No, not yet," Magnus replied, "but somehow I figure it'll come at any time. I'm doing what I can, but I can't fix what I need parts for. Still, I'm not even sure, in this case, that parts will help."

"Why is that?"

"Because one of the shafts was broken clean off," he shared. "I don't know whether that was a failure due to the cold or to vandalism."

The colonel pondered that. "I've got my own headaches right now. I really don't want to bring any more potential victims into this mess," he explained. "Keep it running as long as you can, and, ... well, obviously we'll help them out if it comes to that because that is what we do. However, I want everybody to know that's an absolute last resort. We don't want to get them here and ..." Then he fell silent.

Rogan nodded. "Agreed." He looked over at Magnus. "I'll come with you."

"You're welcome to, but, if you don't have any experience with generators," he began apologetically, "you might be better off here."

"I'd certainly be more comfortable here, but, while I may not have the same experience you have with generators, I come from a long line of can-do outdoor people, so I've certainly seen my fair share of them."

"Good enough," Magnus acknowledged. "In that case I suggest we go gear up now." He turned and looked at the colonel, one eyebrow raised.

The colonel nodded. "Yeah, you do that." Then he stopped and turned to Rogan. "What about that nurse of yours?"

Rogan frowned at him. "Nurse of mine?"

"Yeah, the one who's filling in at the clinic," the colonel confirmed. "I hear you guys are an item."

"I don't know where you heard that," he replied. "Lisa was married to a good friend of mine a long time ago, but I haven't seen her until recently."

"That's not what the gossip says, and, if you were planning on keeping a relationship quiet, forget it. News spreads pretty quickly around this place."

"That may be the rumor, but they've got it wrong. We aren't in any relationship."

The colonel pounced on that. "At this point in time."

"Yes," Rogan agreed flatly, rolling his eyes. "At this point in time, nothing is going on. We've known each other for lots of years, but no romantic relationship exists between us."

The colonel nodded. "Remember. If that changes, everybody here will know in a heartbeat," he announced, more as a warning than a statement. "Isn't that right, Magnus?"

As Rogan eyed his partner, Magnus returned the look, his lips twitching. "Absolutely, sir." Then he burst out laughing.

"It's a good thing you're totally okay with it," the colonel muttered. "I never could stand to be the laughingstock of a group myself."

"I really don't give a crap what the others think," Magnus stated, with a snort. "Besides, it lets me keep an eye on her."

"Yeah, I hear you," the colonel replied. "Let's make sure no more trouble is going on around here. In the meantime, go solve this generator thing up there so the scientists' problems don't become ours."

Both men were dismissed and now walked along the hallway, back to the clinic. "He means so our problems don't become theirs, doesn't he?" Rogan muttered to Magnus, as they reached a safe distance down the hallway.

"That goes both ways." Magnus picked up the pace. "Enough shit is going down here right now that we don't need more people to look after."

"Yet nothing new has happened, right?"

"Nothing new?" Magnus turned to face Rogan. "Not in the sense that you mean. We've got Willy in the clinic under observation. Lisa has moved into the clinic job, replacing the traitorous nurse. We shipped out the injured guards. One's back on duty, and the other has returned stateside. Before that, Terrance was rescued and sent stateside for advanced care. So, other than that, no, nothing new. But we still have missing men, dead men, plus the murdered Russian guy named Helsky."

Rogan grimaced. "Right. So, although nothing is new, not everything has been solved either."

"Exactly," Magnus murmured. "That means we haven't gotten any answers yet. We don't know where the missing men are. We found Terrance at the Inuit settlement, or Sydney found him, after the villagers had kidnapped her. Those two original deaths are bizarre as hell, becoming more suspicious as this other shit happens too. Not to mention that Sydney had to shoot Joy right in the clinic."

Rogan looked over at his buddy. "That would be the nurse that Lisa replaced, right?"

Magnus nodded. "Has Ted the investigator talked to you yet?"

"No, should he have?"

Magnus didn't say anything but had increased his speed, forcing Rogan to pick up the pace to keep up.

"Should he have?" Rogan asked again in a pointed tone.

"I would think so, if for no other reason than to check that you're aware of what's going on, plus to see if you're involved."

"I don't have any involvement," Rogan claimed. "I'm back, and you know why."

"Sure, I know why, but remember. Nobody else gets to know why." On that odd note, Magnus checked his watch and looked back at Rogan. "I'm leaving in about forty-five minutes. So go grab some food, some coffee, and get geared up. I'll meet you outside at the snowcat in forty-five." And, with that, he was gone.

Rogan meant to ask Magnus about using fuel on the snowcat versus taking the dogs or snowmobiles, but, considering what had happened the last time Magnus took out the dogs, maybe it was for the best. Saving the dogs for the training was good, but the base needed the fuel too. Maybe that's just another reason why the colonel wasn't happy about these trips to the scientists' camp.

Mulling all of that and more, Rogan headed toward the kitchen, where Chef called out to him.

"Hey, I heard rumors that we're getting extra bodies." His facial expression revealed such misery that it looked almost comical. "I don't have supplies to support that."

Rogan nodded at Chef because that much Rogan had gathered already. "Okay, I'll let you know if and when that changes. However, my understanding is that we're trying everything we can to keep them where they are, and a move here would be a last resort and only for their safety."

"That would be good," Chef stated, clearly exasperated. "Otherwise, somebody needs to get me more food and supplies in here and do it damn fast."

"The scientists may bring some fresh and canned goods with them. So maybe you need to put things on tighter rations here," Rogan suggested. "Between you and me, I'm guessing they'll be here within the next day or so."

Chef winced, then groaned. "*Great.* Time to go reassess the kitchen." And, with that, he turned and was gone.

DAY 3, MORNING

WAKING THE NEXT morning, Lisa lay in bed, sensing a change, but that same unnatural feeling permeated the new morning of a new day. Lisa got up and around to discover that the scientists were still at their own camp. Yet it felt as if something were brewing under the surface.

She smiled at Chef as she grabbed a coffee. "A reprieve for another day, *huh*?"

He rolled his eyes. "I really don't mind if they come, and we're here to assist anybody who needs help of course. It would just be nice to know which way we were going with more than a minute-by-minute notice."

She chuckled. "I think the scientists probably want to know that too."

He grinned. "You could be right, but I've still got to be prepared, just in case."

"It's not that many extra people though. So it won't be that big of a deal, right?" she asked, with a curious tone, trying not to upset the applecart. If Chef was determined to be upset, he would be. However, if he was fairly laid-back and calm, then this was just another twist in his day.

He chuckled. "If I start rationing the coffee," he pointed out, "what would your reaction be?"

She stared at him in horror and immediately topped up her cup.

He burst out into guffaws. "As I said, that's when the rationing would start."

"You are kidding me, right?"

"Depends how often we can get supplies, if they can get these people out fairly quickly, or if they need to stay here long enough to finish whatever they're doing," he explained, with a shrug. "And then there's the weather factor. If we get caught up in a days long snowstorm, no one is leaving, and no supplies are coming in."

"Would the scientists stay here until they finish this research?"

"Why not? We're an international military base right now as it is." Chef smiled. "So, if we're bringing in more military personnel, trainees, or scientists who need to complete a job, what difference does it make?"

Lisa pondered that as she headed back to the clinic. There she found Sydney, but only Sydney. "So you released Willy, *huh*? You must be relieved at that."

"Definitely I am. He's gone, and he's doing fine." Sydney grinned. "So that means you can head off to the next training op and get back into the swing of things. If I need anybody, I can call you." Lisa hesitated, but Sydney immediately shook her head. "Go. You're fine. Most of the time I don't need anybody anyway, and, unless something major happens, then I can call you." Sydney gave a wave of her hand.

"What about the colonel though?" Lisa asked, with a wince. "If I've been reassigned, I've been reassigned, right?"

"Yeah, and I already had a talk with him about that. You've been reassigned back to your training team, and you'll be on call for the clinic on an as-needed basis. That's the arrangement I have cleared with him." Lisa stared at her boss in delight, and Sydney laughed. "Did you think I didn't know that's where you wanted to be?"

"I come up here for the training," she agreed, "and it did take a fair bit of effort to get called up for it."

"Understood," Sydney noted. "So go on."

And, with that, Lisa called out her thanks and raced to where her team was already laying out plans.

Peter, her team lead, looked up, smiled, and acknowledged her. "Guess who's back with us?" he stated, with a nod in her direction, and everyone focused on her.

She grinned. "Unless something blows up in the medical clinic, I'm back."

"Understood," Peter stated. "And, in reality, depending on the size of the blow, there could be more than just you called in."

Then she considered how many here had varying levels of medical experience associated with their service. "Got it," she stated, as she headed off to pack up and to get ready for another day out on the trail. She gave herself a talking to about the cold and to do a better job of layering up. What she couldn't afford to do was to get sweaty and hot, overheat, and then chill down—something they were working on today.

She had her own team of four, and they were to take turns walking the dogs. And, with Joe out with them, giving strict instructions on the dogs, Lisa realized they were still operating short of one dog team. She winced as she talked to him. "How are the two injured dogs?"

"They're fine," Joe snapped, with a retort more sour than necessary, "but they won't be back out for this season. And Magnus and Rogan are spoiling them rotten."

She nodded. "I guess that makes sense."

"It does for them," Joe stated, casting her a glance. "One of the worst things you can do is overexert them, particularly when there's no need for it. I know a lot of people are training here, but nobody has to run the dogs hard. It's always about keeping the dogs safe."

"Which goes without saying, I would presume." She cast a glance around at the other dogs. "I'm sure everybody's being very careful with them."

"They better, or they'll answer to me," Joe vowed, his voice harsh. "I've got two injured, and the most I ever had out before is two." Determination glared through his tone. "I will not tolerate a third."

"How are the recovering dogs handling being left behind?"

He shrugged. "I'll be bringing Benji, not that he'll be doing any of the training today, but he needs to be exercised to get some of that leg movement back. When he tires, I'll put him on a sled." Joe finally grinned.

Realizing that the dogs really were in the best hands possible, Lisa quickly headed to her assigned sled. By noon they were sitting out in the middle of nowhere, at least it appeared to be nowhere, and a calm surrounded them. White was in every direction, blue sky beaming down, the sun hot, the snow freezing cold, and yet it was a glorious day. She smiled, grateful that she was back out here, when one of her teammates walked over and asked her how she was doing. She smiled. "Grateful that I made it out here today."

"I'm not at all surprised," he said. "That's what we came for, isn't it?"

"You're Salmo aren't you?"

He nodded.

"Got it. That's the thing about being at this Arctic base,"

she explained. "We're all here to get out in this frozen tundra and learn how to survive these elements. All of us want to experience what we can, though being short a couple dogs isn't helping."

At that, he winced, looked over, and nodded. "And even though the injured dogs are running, they're not in shape to pull, according to Joe."

His neutral tone had her staring at him. "You don't agree with that?"

He raised an eyebrow, shrugged, and pointed to Joe. "He's the boss, so that's not my problem." And yet his words had a disgruntled note in them.

"Sorry if it means you didn't get as much training as you wanted," she added. "Me? I'm just glad to be back out again."

"Of course you got called into the medical center, didn't you?"

She laughed and nodded. "That's what happens when you're a nurse," she noted. "They tend to pick you up as relief."

"Which is probably also how you were brought into the program," Salmo pointed out. "I know dozens who weren't accepted."

"I hadn't considered that, but, yeah, you're probably right."

And, with that, Salmo walked off with a huff.

The more she thought about it, the more she realized that was exactly why she'd probably been given a slot for this training session. Even though a two-person medical team had been onsite, that didn't mean they didn't always need backup, as had been proven already.

Still, Salmo seemed upset that she had been chosen over

others.

Maybe those guys should have gotten their own medical training that ensured they would be chosen on ops where they could fulfill two positions.

Sighing, yet determined to not let Salmo's sour grapes affect her, the day passed without any issues. When she finally got back, chores done, she was wiped out, more than tired. While still hot under several layers, she felt the chill starting to set in.

She shook her head. Something about donning or shedding that outerwear made maintaining an even temperature damn-near impossible. She walked into the medical center not long afterward and checked on Sydney, who sat at her desk, doing paperwork.

Sydney looked up, smiled, and asked, "How are you doing?" Her gaze was watchful, as if she already knew all about her.

"I did pretty well," Lisa replied. "Only in the last bit, coming in, did I get that chill again."

Sydney nodded. "Go curl up in bed for a few minutes and see if it gets any better." She pointed to the warming packs left behind on the hospital bed by Willy. "You know better than to let it get worse."

"I was thinking I would pick up some dinner and take it back to my room, if that's possible."

"It's absolutely possible, but, mentioning that chill again, I'll be coming in to check on you," she declared firmly.

She tossed her boss a glance and reiterated, "I'm really okay."

"Good, glad to hear that." But the doc's gaze was watchful, as she studied her nurse's features.

"I guess that's really a problem here, isn't it?"

"It is, and you can't argue about it. In here everybody is strong, everybody is capable, everybody knows what they're doing, yet not everybody is as self-aware as they need to be," Sydney explained. "And when you're working in these temperatures, we can't take a chance."

"I'm feeling fine, but I would do a lot for a hot cup of something."

Sydney laughed. "I can bring in a heated blanket, if you need it, but, other than that, training for hours in this tundra is a bit rougher as each day accumulates, which can turn a trainee into a patient. That's one of the things you must watch out for up here," she offered, with a smile.

"I am fine," Lisa repeated, "but you're right, I'm a little on the chilled side. So, I'll go grab my dinner and then curl up in bed, and, if you had access to a heated blanket, I wouldn't turn it down."

SYDNEY NODDED. "GET moving. I'll be coming to your room behind you." With that, she got up, grabbed a couple blankets, and headed to the kitchen. When Chef saw her and the blankets, he rolled his eyes. She smiled. "I know. I'm coddling them." She chuckled. "But I'd rather coddle them than have them miss any signs and have a bigger issue on our hands."

"No, I hear you," he noted, as he quickly led her to the back. There she sat, while the blankets warmed, and then bundling both up in an insulated bag, she quickly walked to Lisa's room. When she got there, Lisa wasn't. Frowning, Sydney headed back to the kitchen because the last thing she wanted was for the heat of the blanket to dissipate before Lisa had a chance to enjoy it. As Sydney headed for the cafeteria, she caught Lisa heading to her room.

"I'm here. I'm here," Lisa called out in a hushed tone, but her skin was already starting to turn pale. "Honest, I've been trying to get through the line." She carried a tray with her food, but her hands shook a little bit.

Sydney quickly removed the tray from her hands and handed her the warmed blankets. "Get your ass into bed."

"You don't have to tell me twice," Lisa muttered, as she took off one layer, then hopped into bed, her long johns still on, and there she sat, wrapped up with the blankets, while propped up in a corner.

Sydney ordered, "Now I don't want you moving until I get that temperature of yours raised. And you might want to rethink going back out tomorrow."

Lisa stared at the doc and groaned. "That's not how I wanted to spend my time up here—out one day and sick for several. This is madness."

"Maybe not your cup of tea," Sydney noted, "but, if the brass finds out this is what's happening, you'll be benched anyway."

Lisa winced at that and nodded. "Isn't that the truth," she muttered.

DAY 3, EVENING

Happily, Lisa stabilized relatively quickly, and, by bedtime, she was nice and cozy, feeling fine. When Sydney came to check on her later, Lisa smiled. "I'm fine, Doc."

"Glad to hear that," Sydney replied, "but, if you don't mind, I still want to keep an eye on you."

"Please do. Nothing quite like falling asleep while knowing there's a good chance you won't wake up anytime soon."

Sydney grimaced. "Not a bad way to die. ... I'd just prefer it not be on my watch."

"Anybody else sick?" Lisa asked, forcing her eyelids to stay open, even though she longed to sleep.

Sydney shook her head at that. "Nope, and you're not sick either, but you're still recovering from a hypothermia episode, and that can be brutal."

"And yet I thought I was doing fine."

"You were, right up until you weren't. Besides, you went back out and thoroughly enjoyed yourself, I gathered?"

Lisa nodded at that, with a smile. "I really did, and it was absolutely stunning out there today."

"Good, so, if you don't get back out again, you'll know what you're missing."

Her eyelids opened, and she looked over at her boss. "You'll bench me?"

"Not this time, depending on what you're like in the morning," Sydney replied, with a lazy wave of her hand. "But if this happens a third time, we'll consider it pretty seriously."

"Great," Lisa muttered in frustration. As Sydney closed the door, Lisa curled up on her side, all but ready to fall asleep, when a hard knock came on her door. She groaned and called out, "Who is it?"

Instead of answering, Rogan stepped inside and glared at her. "You shouldn't have gone out today. You know that, right?"

"It was a great day, and everybody thought it'd be okay," she answered cautiously, not sure why Rogan was so mad. "I wanted to give it a try, and I didn't think I did too badly, until now."

"Yes, but that's only because you were ignoring the signs again," he snapped in exasperation.

She didn't say anything, but stared at him, feeling disgruntled.

Rogan continued. "We've dogsledded a lot. You're basically a pro—but not in these conditions."

"So, did you have a reason for stopping by, other than to give me shit?" she asked, her voice harsher than she intended. Or maybe not. Maybe it was a good thing to keep him out of her world. "Did you get the generator going? I'm assuming you went along, since you seem to be aligned with Magnus now, and that's where he was at."

"We did get the generator going at the scientists' camp, and they did get more supplies. They will try and make it through another week or two up there. Some of them want to stay, and some of them want to leave. So, as soon as there's an opportunity, we may be helping a few of them get out."

"And they didn't come prepared for all that?"

He nodded. "They were, but, at some point, another group of researchers joined them. Therefore, although they have supplies, … they don't necessarily have the means to get out all at once. So they'll leave in stages. In fact, that other group has already left."

"Which makes sense."

He nodded. "Often it makes more sense, but it's such a chaotic time, not to mention that they must put the camp to bed when they go."

"Right, and that can take some time too."

"It sure can," he agreed.

Even as he spoke, his gaze was intent on her face. She waved her hand. "I really am okay."

"Glad to hear it. I'm confirming for myself."

She eyed him inquiringly. "Why?" Maybe it was the bluntness of her tone. Maybe it was the surprise of her question. Yet the question did seem to throw him.

"Why not?" he asked. "I don't hate you. You do realize that, right?"

"You don't have any reason to hate me," she declared, feeling suddenly awkward. They'd been good friends once. "And you really don't have a reason to check up on me all the time either."

She yawned just then, and he smiled. "I'll chalk up your crankiness to your condition."

"Am I cranky?" she asked, opening her eyelids. Then considering it, she nodded. "I guess I am at that."

"Yeah," he agreed, with a mild chastising tone, "you definitely are. No, I don't hate you and never could." Hesitating, he added, "I know that you and Barry weren't happy, and I wish to God you'd never gotten married, but, hey, that was a very long time ago."

Her gaze stayed glued on him, and she nodded slowly. "That's the thing to remember. It was a very long time ago."

"You never did tell me why you guys broke up," he added, after a moment.

"No, but you never asked either."

"I'm asking now."

She shifted in the bed, frowning at him, then the fatigue and the cold hit her all over again. She asked in a resigned tone, "Do we have to do this now?"

He shrugged. "Maybe not, but I want to know the truth."

"*The truth.*" Something about the way he sounded caught her attention. "Meaning?"

"Meaning that I heard something from Barry that I wasn't sure of. I hoped that he was wrong. I guess I want to think that he either made it up or just maybe he used it as an excuse."

"You mean, Barry told you that I had an affair, which I never did?"

He nodded slowly, his gaze studying her. "Yes. Exactly that."

"I didn't have an affair," she declared. "We were only married for ten months, and he became incredibly paranoid. Every time I went out for anything, he was sure I was out with somebody. I think in the beginning maybe, it was his way of showing me that he loved me, but I'd become more of an obsession to him by the end of our marriage. Eventually it was so bad that I felt completely smothered and had to go," she explained. Lisa watched him, as colors of uncharted emotions lightened up his face. "I don't really care if you believe me or not," she added in a mild tone, "but that's the truth."

"Thank you for that," he said, as he stared off in the distance for a long moment. "It's hard to reconcile the man I knew with what you're saying, but thank you for your honesty."

"If you consider for a moment that I didn't have an affair and that there was absolutely no reason for Barry to even suspect such a thing, you must also look at where he was getting these ideas from and why he kept perpetrating the same accusations over and over again. He became very controlling and very difficult, especially in the privacy of our own home," she noted. "Every time I went on a mission, he was certain I was cheating on him while I was gone. Then, while he was away, he just knew I was involved with somebody else at home." As she spoke, fatigue and irritation made her tone unpleasant. "Believe me. Even though it was a long time ago, when you bring it up, it doesn't seem that long at all."

"Did he ever hit you?"

She stared at him for a moment, and then slowly shook her head. "No, he didn't."

Rogan tilted his head and frowned at that. "You don't sound very positive."

"No, he didn't hit me, but I believe that was where things were headed. By the end he was always angry, constantly yelling, not happy about life in general. It got to the point where I couldn't stay," she said. "I know that the relationship was over long before I left, and my mistake was letting it go on for far too long."

"I'm sorry," Rogan added. "I didn't realize he'd gotten that bad."

"You didn't realize it because you weren't around, and you probably weren't around because Barry didn't want you to be. If you'd been around, you would have seen what was going on, and he didn't want that. Barry didn't want anybody around," she stated.

Rogan shook his head. "And again, that seems so far-fetched from the man I knew."

"Which is why I don't talk about it," she declared. "The marriage broke up, and that should be enough for anyone out there. We divorced amicably. I went on my way, and so did he. Well, I assume so. I don't know, since I haven't had any contact with him in all this time. I presume that you, as his best friend, still do, but …" Then she shrugged. "I don't care, since that has nothing to do with me."

When he looked at her oddly, she stiffened, glaring at him.

"What?" she asked him. "Am I still supposed to care about something that happened so long ago? It was a bad deal that was only getting worse, and I needed to get out and to move on with my life. Hopefully it made things better for him too. Barry was terribly unhappy."

"Lisa, Barry is dead," Rogan muttered.

She sat back against the bed pillows and looked at him in shock. "What? Really? I hadn't—" She took a deep breath, before she sunk down on the bed. "I hadn't heard."

He nodded. "Probably not the circumstances you would have expected either."

"I don't know what the hell that means. What are you talking about?"

"He was murdered."

ROGAN STUDIED LISA'S face, as she realized the truth of his words, and he knew that she'd had no clue. Unfortunately every answer she'd given him made a weird kind of sense. He hadn't really expected her to tell him the truth, if that was the truth—and yet he had no reason to doubt her, particularly after hearing everything else that had happened to end his friend's life.

"What do you mean?" she asked, dumbfounded. "To think that he was murdered is just—"

"He was murdered in jail," Rogan added. "He did get married again, and he beat the crap out of her, as in seriously beat the crap out of her, and put her in the hospital. He ended up with domestic violence convictions, went to jail, and was killed there. So, believe me. When I asked you if he'd ever hit you, it was a serious question." She stared at him, stunned, and he nodded. "It isn't that I don't believe you. I do. It's just, as his friend, it was hard to understand, when I hadn't seen it happening."

"You hadn't seen it," she repeated absentmindedly, as she pulled the blankets closer, "because he didn't want you to see it. You weren't invited to our home, once we got married, and neither was anyone else. You were intentionally kept out of it so he could work on that whole control thing," she explained, "but I didn't handle it well. I'm the one who left and asked for the divorce, but I left first and asked for the divorce from a distance. Maybe he learned from that. I don't know. I'm sorry if whatever happened between us made him so angry that he hurt his second wife because that violence was definitely something within him, and I was doing my best to avoid it."

Rogan sucked in his breath. "I'm starting to realize that I may not have known him at all."

"He changed. He wasn't always paranoid and possessive." She shrugged. "I don't even know what to say. Obviously I'm sorry he's dead, but I'm not sorry if that prevented his wife from being hurt further. I'm sure she would be worrying about him ever getting out of jail."

"It's possible," he agreed, with a sigh. "Still sucks though."

"That it does," she muttered.

"Do you need anything?" he asked, as he stepped toward the door.

She shook her head and winced. "No, and you've certainly given me lots to think about."

"I'm sorry. I had no idea you didn't know."

"When I told you that I walked away, I meant it, but maybe the truth of the matter is I, more or less, ran away," she corrected, looking away. "Nothing about things at the end of our marriage were healthy, even though he tried for the longest time to get me back. I just couldn't."

"No, and it's a good thing you didn't," Rogan agreed.

"And his second wife, is she okay?"

"Yeah, as far as I know," Rogan replied. "I kept in touch with her for a while, but we drifted apart after the court case. Once Barry died, I sent my condolences, and she responded in kind, but that was the end of it."

She smiled. "I'm sure you were always wondering what happened between me and Barry, once you heard more about his second marriage."

"Yeah, for sure." Rogan shrugged. "How could I not? I went to high school with Barry, continued to see him out in the field all the time with our military enlistments. So we worked together, were on missions together—and then to find out this stuff?" He shook his head. "It was a shock."

"And yet, you also know that a lot of guys come home, and they can't handle life there after being on active duty."

"Sure, and he was married to you, and you're also military."

"That was always my thought too. That we should do well together because we both understood our world in the military, but apparently I was being naïve."

"No, you were young. Hopefully you loved him while you were together, until things changed," Rogan said. "No other explanation needed."

As he walked toward the door, she called out behind him. "Did you ever get married, Rogan?"

He turned to face her and shook his head. "No, I never did find anybody willing to take that walk with me."

"Or one that you were willing to take the walk with," she pointed out.

He snorted. "That could be it too." And, with that, he walked out, leaving her curled up in the blankets behind him.

Unsettled, he headed to the kitchen, searching for coffee, and found instead hot water and a bunch of herb teas. He frowned at them, not being much of a tea drinker.

Chef came up and saw Rogan studying the tea selection intently. "You might want to get used to a few of these, in case we run out of coffee." Rogan stared at him in horror. Chef chuckled. "Hey, it could happen."

"Don't even joke about that." Rogan shuddered. "I can't imagine everybody here with caffeine withdrawals."

At that, Chef burst out laughing. "Good point, but we would make certain that the colonel had coffee."

"Maybe I should go try to make friends with him then," Rogan quipped, with a smile.

"Good luck with that," Chef replied in a low voice.

The colonel wasn't by any means the most favored person here, but, as long as he did his job and kept everybody safe, people were prepared to ignore any deficiencies in his leadership. Yet everybody hadn't been kept safe, and, once things had gone south, Rogan imagined that everyone's attitudes could change pretty quickly.

DAY 4, WEE EARLY MORNING HOURS

LISA AWOKE IN the early hours of the morning, shivering. She quickly bundled up tighter into her bedding, wondering what had woken her in the first place. There was an eerie silence in the place. She frowned, as she tried to sort it out. Then it hit her hard; the generator wasn't running, as she shifted upright, testing the air, and realized that the base had definitely dropped in temperature.

She winced, grabbed her phone, and sent a text to Rogan. **Did the generator stop?** She didn't get a response, but whether that was because he was asleep or he was already outside working on it, she didn't know.

Knowing that she wouldn't fall back asleep again without knowing for sure, she quickly dressed in multiple layers, grabbed an extra hoodie, and crept toward the kitchen, the room closest to the generator shed. Everything was quiet, calm, and felt almost empty in the base.

As she got to the dining room area though, it was a different story. Several people were meeting in the back of the kitchen. She looked over the group, hoping to recognize somebody but didn't. They all appeared to be either new people or people who she didn't have a whole lot of dealings with. She recognized some faces but didn't know their names.

As she walked toward the coffeepot, Chef stepped out

and shook his head at her.

"Sorry, no coffee."

She stared at him, nonplussed, then again looked around at the others, who were all huddling over something. "What are they drinking?" she asked in a low voice.

"Tea, hot water."

With a raised eyebrow, she quickly made herself a cup of tea, before it was rationed as well. "Why no coffee?"

"It doesn't work well on the wood stove," he shared. "I'm getting campfire coffee going now, but it will be a bit yet."

She nodded, and then in the same low tone she asked, "The generator's out, isn't it?"

"It is, but they're working on it," he replied. "I trust them to get it back up and running."

She nodded. The alternative was not something she even wanted to think about. Adding this issue to those they already had was too much to contemplate. She didn't even want to go there. She took a step closer to the kitchen and finally saw Rogan.

He peeled himself from the group, walking toward her. "How are you doing?"

She shrugged. "I'm okay." She tried her best to stop a shiver. "I woke up and realized it was way too quiet. So I came out to see if it was the generator had stopped."

"It had, and we're working on it."

She stared at him. "But you're the one who does the generator repairs, so why are you here?"

He grinned. "I'm not the only one. Or the main guy—that's Magnus."

"Sure," she agreed, "but, if you're the one who went out to the scientists' camp, why aren't you looking at this one?"

He tilted his head toward the meeting. "That's why."

She stared at the people behind him, shrugged, and added in an undertone, "Still seems as if people are focusing on the wrong thing."

"People are looking after the generators, which is a big deal," he told her calmly, "but it's really early, about five," he noted, looking down at his watch. "Why don't you head back to bed?"

"Sure, now that I'm totally secure in the knowledge that everything here is fine." She winced at her unintentional sarcasm. She was sure everyone was working hard to fix the situation.

"It will be," Rogan declared.

Hearing that confidence in his voice, she felt better. "Good, okay then." And, with that, she headed back to her quarters. As she walked past the clinic, the door opened, and Sydney stepped out, all bundled up. Lisa stopped and explained the situation.

"Okay, good," the doc replied. "I wondered what the hell was happening."

"The generators. They've got wood stoves burning and kerosene lamps going, but, if I don't need to be at the clinic, then I should be in bed."

"Right." Sydney nodded. "I'm fine to stay here. You could too, if you want. Just curl up in one of the hospital beds." Sydney eyed the cup in her nurse's hand with greed. "Is there coffee?" she asked hopefully.

"No, hot water and an herbal tea assortment. They're getting campfire coffee going."

"Yeah, I'm surprised it isn't already done."

"I don't think Chef has been up all that long." Lisa chucked, as she remembered his grumpy face. "He looked as if he had just tumbled out of bed."

"Considering it's barely even five yet, I wouldn't be at all surprised." Sydney smirked. "On the other hand, as long as they're on it, I'll curl back up in bed. Hopefully, the next time I wake up, this will be over with." And, with that, Sydney walked back into the clinic and closed the door, forgetting the offer that she made for Lisa to stay.

Lisa wondered if Sydney was sleeping in there, or if she had somebody in there who she needed to keep an eye on. But it wasn't Lisa's place to interfere, unless asked. Yet, considering the clinic was a smaller room and potentially warmer, maybe it was a better place to be after all. She hesitated and then knocked on the door.

When she heard a call to come in, she opened it gingerly. "Did you want me to go back to the kitchen and get you something?" Then she realized that Sydney was sitting at her desk. "I thought you were going back to bed."

"Yeah, and then I realized that I needed to check on stuff here and sat down, which is always a mistake," the doc noted, "but I should go back to bed."

Lisa yawned just then. "Go back to bed if you can. Otherwise I'm more than happy to go grab you a cup of hot water for some herb tea."

"I'll wait a little bit and see if they've got coffee," Sydney said, with a smile. "But thanks." She waved Lisa along. "Go get back to bed and stay warm."

And, with that order in mind, Lisa returned to her room, where she quickly curled back up into bed, sitting against the wall so she could curl up, holding her hot tea. To have all the heat go out was a major survival issue here. They had water, if they needed it. They had wood, if they needed it. They had oil, if they needed it. They had all kinds of emergency heaters, so definitely no need to panic yet. It was one of those inconveniences that happened on this base, given the extreme weather. Also, one of some other very strange scenarios, but, hey, this one could be fixed, so she was fine with it.

Only as she almost drifted off did she hear footsteps in the hallway—but not normal footsteps. These footsteps tiptoed gently down the hallway, as if someone were sneaking around. It struck fear in her heart, yet she had absolutely no idea why. Other rooms were up and down this entire hallway, with no insulation between rooms, so people easily heard things going on in other rooms. If people wanted to sneak around, they certainly could and would do it. She had certainly seen several couples doing exactly that, but this? The solo footsteps skulking in the hallway? … This sounded different. It sounded off.

Quickly rising to a sitting position, she waited as the footsteps stopped outside her room. It wasn't the first time, but it was the first time it hit her as wrong. She winced, wondering if she should call out, but her instincts kept her from saying anything. She closed her mouth and waited. Then after a heart-stopping moment, the footsteps continued, until they disappeared into the distance. She sagged back onto her bed, holding her breath still, as she contemplated what the hell that could have meant.

ROGAN WALKED INTO the kitchen to see the meeting still on. No sign of Mountain, no sign of Magnus. Rogan frowned at that, then quickly checked to see if there was coffee, and it wasn't there, so he turned and walked back out again, ignoring a jibe from Chef. Under the circumstances, it would be a tough time for everybody if they couldn't get the base's generator under control.

Fully geared up now, Rogan stepped outside and headed toward the generator shed, wanting to ensure everything was okay. When he got there, he heard voices. He looked inside to find Magnus standing there, parts and pieces of the generator machinery in his hands, and others scattered about.

Magnus looked up and nodded at Rogan. "We're getting there," Magnus noted, with half a smile.

"Glad to hear that," Rogan replied. "I came to ensure everything was okay out here and to see if I could do anything to be helpful."

"Not at the moment," Magnus stated, "but, if you can calm everybody inside, that would be good. It would also be a miracle …"

At that, one of the other men at Magnus's side snorted and added, "Isn't that the truth? Everybody is already pretty freaked out. Some of the guys have been doing this trip for years, without a fraction of the problems they've had this time."

Another guy looked up from his work and groaned. "Plus we're already getting slammed from every country involved in the training here for the shoddy equipment, the pissy management, the whole works," he confirmed, with a clipped nod. "The colonel is getting the wheels slammed down on him."

Rogan nodded, not knowing what he was supposed to say to that. "That won't make anybody happy," he muttered. At that, he headed back toward the kitchen but first detoured to check on the dogs and Joe, since he refused to bunk inside. Instead Joe chose to always room with his dogs. Rogan would love to keep Benji—one of the two injured dogs, as he'd quickly become Rogan's favorite. It appeared mutual. Rogan wasn't sure Joe appreciated that.

As he walked in, Joe lifted his head and groaned. "Tell me coffee's over there."

"As of five minutes ago, there was not," Rogan informed him. "Although I have it on good authority that the problem is soon to be fixed, and, either way, coffee is being made over a wood fire, as we speak."

At that, Joe snorted. "I don't know, but this whole session seems to be pretty badly hexed."

"Somebody else was saying that too." Rogan chuckled. "Apparently people have been coming up here for years doing this training, and they've never had headaches like this."

"I would agree with that," Joe added grumpily. "I've been coming up here myself for years, and we never had these problems," he muttered. "Once we had the generators go down, but they flew in new generators, within twenty-four hours."

"In this case it could definitely take a week," Rogan noted. "They are working on it, but, last I saw, the generator was in a million pieces."

"That is not encouraging." Joe snorted. "I get that we're supposed to have a lot of mechanics and engineers here," he said, with a shake of his head, "but, if they don't have hands-on experience, they're no good up here." Joe glared at Rogan.

"What about the dogs? Is everything okay here?" He looked around for Benji. The small dog door exploded open, as Benji raced inside to say hi. Rogan dropped to one knee to keep the dog from jumping with his injured back leg.

Joe's face broke into a smile. "The dogs don't give a crap about human stuff. They've got their food here that doesn't require heat. They've got me, which is their comfort, and we have a way out of here if need be, … at least some of us." Then Joe gave Rogan a knowing grin.

"Right, because we don't have enough dogs and sleds to get everybody off base, do we?" Rogan suddenly realized the truth of his own words.

"No, we sure don't," Joe stated, "especially not with two dogs down. I wanted to bring more dogs, so we'd have some backup, but I was shut down. I have another eight at home, and I wanted to bring six of them." Joe shook his head. "But, no, the brass complained how it's too expensive, too much airtime, no budget, all of the above, *blah, blah, blah*," he complained. "We would at least be covered for getting everybody out, if that were the case."

"We still have skis, snowmobiles, the snowcat, etcetera," Rogan replied. "If worse comes to worse, we can make it to the local village."

"Sure, we could." Joe spat on the ground. "But, at this rate, with the number of people dead or missing," he explained cryptically, "we won't even worry about it."

More than a little disturbed at that comment, Rogan waved and headed to the kitchen. As he walked in again, Chef looked up and nodded.

"Yeah, so the first pot is done and gone. Second pot's on and will be ready in a minute." Chef pointed to the pot. "I'm trying to get ahead of the curve to get the pots filled outside. We still have no working generator, but the wood stove is doing the job."

"Wood always will." Rogan smiled. "It'll take a little longer to get there."

"Yeah, it sure does and requires constant feeding, which is why we have the generator and every other heating technology you can imagine," Chef muttered.

"And you're still okay for food?"

"I'm okay for food." Hesitating, he looked over at Rogan. "Any idea what caused the generator problem?"

He shook his head. "No idea. However, I haven't talked to anybody about it yet."

"Why? You should be interested in knowing," he noted.

"Why is that?"

"With all the other shit going on, you've got to wonder if maybe it wasn't some foul play, right?"

"You think so?" The thought had crossed his mind, and, if it had also crossed Chef's, then it would be on everyone else's minds too. "It would be bad news if that attitude got out though," Rogan noted. "We don't need people thinking sabotage will be the new normal."

At that, Chef gave a crack of laughter. "And yet it is, at least on this trip. I almost didn't come." Chef was looking around his kitchen, his arms crossed. "I've done my time, so I was heading for the South Seas to get a little bit of rest and relaxation for a while and to figure out what to do with the rest of my life. But the colonel called. And where he goes, I go, at least for now."

At his phraseology, Rogan looked closer at Chef and realized that he was older and rougher than Rogan was. "You've done your twenty years?" he asked.

Chef nodded. "And a hell of a lot more. Right about now the Caribbean looks mighty fine."

Rogan smiled. "I wonder how long before you'll be bored to tears."

"Hard to say." Chef grinned. "I'm looking forward to

giving it a try and seeing how it works out though."

"Send me a postcard, man. Let me know how you like it."

"What about you?" Chef asked, staring at him.

Rogan shook his head. Nobody understood why he was here or what the deal was, but he'd been following along with the shenanigans going on here this whole session. "I was here earlier on, and they needed more men, but nobody else new was allowed to come in, at least not for a little while." Rogan gave an eye roll. "I thought when the nurse and her drug-addicted boyfriend were killed and their bodies shipped off, then everything was fixed, but apparently not."

"*Nah*, shit was starting to hit the fan, that's all." Chef snorted. "But I don't get who's got the time or inclination for all this crap."

"A lot of people apparently," Rogan suggested, his tone serious. "When you think about it, an awful lot of people out here would much rather drift away on their spare time than doing something good with their life."

Chef grimaced. "Anyway, maybe take a cup of coffee down to the doc, will you? She hasn't been in yet."

"Will do," Rogan confirmed, picking up a cup. "She probably thinks there isn't any."

"Which is why you'll take her some coffee to let her know that some things at least are back up and running. Breakfast will be delayed about twenty minutes, and it won't be anywhere near as elaborate as it could be, but you'll get fed."

"Sounds good to me." Rogan poured a second cup of coffee and walked toward the clinic.

As he entered, both Lisa and Sydney sat huddled together. Instantly the conversation died when he walked in. He raised an eyebrow, walked over, and handed the coffee to the doc. "I didn't know you were awake," he stated, looking over at Lisa.

She shrugged, then sniffed the coffee, and her eyes widened.

He nodded. "It's up and running."

And, with that, Lisa bolted from the clinic.

He grinned, turned, and looked at Sydney. "Why did the conversation stop when I walked in?"

She looked at him and then in a low voice shared, "Lisa heard footsteps stop outside her room this morning, and it unnerved her."

His heart stilled at that. "What do you mean?"

Sydney explained, repeating what Lisa had told her, and then added, "You need to double-check with her on the details because I heard what she said of course, but it's better if you get it first-hand."

"Did anyone knock on her door or try to get in at all?"

She shook her head. "No, he stood there outside her door, as Lisa heard him breathing. She initially thought it might have been you, hesitating to see if she was awake. However, when you didn't call out or say anything, her instincts told her to stay quiet."

He stared off in the distance, thinking about what she would have gone through and then nodded. "That was really good thinking on her part, and I will talk to her. Thanks." And, with that, he turned and raced back to the kitchen. He soon found her heading to the clinic again, walking carefully with a full cup of coffee.

She looked up and frowned. He frowned right back, checking if the hallway was empty, and, in a lowered voice, he asked her about the visitor. She shrugged. "I don't even know what to say, really. It was so weird, and, if they hadn't been standing there for so long, it wouldn't have felt so off, but this person stood there at my door. And I don't mean for a few seconds but several minutes," she declared, staring up at him. "And I did think maybe it was you at first, wondering if I was awake. However, when you didn't say anything, I quickly realized that chances were good it wasn't you. So, I didn't want to know who it was."

"And yet you do want to know who it was," he stated immediately.

"Sure, but I didn't want to find out the wrong way," she corrected, lifting her chin. "Believe me. Nobody here has forgotten the fact that we still have missing people and some dead people. We still have a murderer on the loose."

"I know," he agreed, as he glanced around, leaned closer, and whispered in her ear, "There are some suspicions that the generator was sabotaged."

She stiffened, instinctively moving closer to him, then pulled back enough so that she could look into his eyes. Letting out the breath she'd been holding, she muttered, "That doesn't make me feel any better."

"So, if anybody comes to your door at nighttime," he declared, with a headshake, "don't let them in."

"No, I won't." She winced. "Now I wish I was in one of those doubled-up rooms, where I had a roommate."

"I can get you reassigned, if you want," he added. "I don't want you scared."

"Too late," she said. "I'm already scared."

DAY 4, LATER THAT MORNING

AFTER TELLING ROGAN how she felt, Lisa realized it really was the truth. She was scared, and something was terribly wrong in this place. She realized that, for all of the efforts everybody made to stay positive and jovial, everybody else seemed to sense the underlying evil too. When she walked back to the clinic, after Rogan had headed somewhere else, she sat down across from Sydney.

"You told Rogan?" the doc asked her.

"Absolutely. The last thing we need to do is tiptoe around and make a mistake that'll cost another life." Lisa winced at that. "I did tell him that I was halfway wishing I was in one of those doubled-up rooms, so I had somebody there with me."

Sydney burst out laughing. "I'm sure he offered immediately. Not very subtle, Lisa."

"He did." Lisa frowned. "Was that foolish of me?"

"Not at all, you two obviously have a relationship."

At that, Lisa stared at Sydney in shock, then shook her head immediately. "We don't. We never have. Not like that."

A smile played around the corner of Sydney's lips. "Not one you've acknowledged," she clarified, "but you have a history there."

"Yes, a history is there, all right." Lisa then explained

about Barry.

"Oh my." Sydney dropped her head in embarrassment. "That's not what I expected."

"No, of course not." Lisa gave her boss a rueful look. "It's not something I talk about, but, when I found out from Rogan what happened after my divorce, I was pretty rattled. I had seen that violence in Barry but hadn't experienced that side of him. Yet I had been with him long enough to realize how dangerous he could get." She shook her head. "I'm really sorry to hear about his second wife and then Barry's own death in prison, but I don't know what I could have done about it."

"There wasn't anything you could have done about it," Sydney stated, looking at her nurse. "Even if you had accused him of being violent, how would that have gone? It's not as if he would have admitted, *Oh, gosh, you're right. Let me go get some help.* That's not how abusers work."

"No, I got away, then told him I wanted a divorce, and filed. Shortly thereafter I jumped into the navy and buried myself in work because ... I was eighteen, nineteen? Who the hell wants to be a divorcee at that age? Talk about feeling like a failure," she muttered. "Of course my parents didn't do anything to help that. They really liked Barry, and my mom was very vocal about what she thought about me walking away and 'giving up' so quickly," she relayed, with air quotes. "She called me a quitter."

"Interesting," Sydney replied. "Wonder what she would think now."

"I don't know. I haven't had a whole lot to do with her since then. Nothing like realizing you're a complete disappointment to your family to stop you from keeping in touch, right?"

"Exactly." Sydney nodded in agreement. "And what about Rogan, did he ever marry?"

She looked at the doc and shook her head. "No, and I did ask him about it. He told me that he never met the right person." She looked over at Sydney to see that same damn smile tugging at the corner of her lips, and Lisa shrugged. "I'm not sure what that smile's all about, but, if you think he's been holding a torch for me, you're wrong."

At that, Sydney burst out laughing. "Rogan might not have been holding a torch for you, but I think he needed to hear the truth from you to understand something about your relationship with your husband. And I suspect maybe that has been holding him back."

"I've not seen him for years," Lisa said in exasperation.

"And maybe that was deliberate, who knows? Maybe he needed to avoid seeing you all this time because—"

"Now you're being fanciful." A grin tugged at Lisa's lips. "Sounds as if you're a romantic."

"Maybe," Sydney admitted, "but, on the other hand, I know there's electricity in the air when you two are in the same room, whether you want to acknowledge it or not."

Lisa glared at her, but inside she had to wonder.

As the day went on, she buried herself at the clinic, helping the doc go over supplies and ordering more. Lisa finally asked, "Do you really think so?"

Sydney made no effort to pretend she didn't understand exactly what Lisa was asking about and nodded immediately. "Yes, I do. Rogan more than likes you."

"Interesting," Lisa murmured. "I really liked him back then. He was great, the life *of the party* guy but not in an obnoxious way. He and Barry were best friends, … but then suddenly Rogan wasn't invited over. More than that, he wasn't allowed ever again. I didn't know what was going on, but Barry told me at one point in time that he didn't trust Rogan anymore."

"Didn't trust him?" Sydney repeated, looking at her. "In what way?"

"He didn't say, but now I'm wondering if it's because of, as you mentioned, maybe Barry saw something there between Rogan and me and didn't trust me or didn't trust him around me."

"I wouldn't be at all surprised, particularly if your ex-husband was as paranoid as you say. Somebody who's always jealous and accusing you of having affairs would never want a guy like Rogan around. Or any other man for that matter."

"It never even crossed my mind that Barry was trying to keep Rogan away from me," Lisa noted. "All Barry had talked about was what a great guy Rogan was and how they'd been best buds since forever."

"And was Barry jealous?"

"Absolutely he was jealous, even after we got married. He told me how he was jealous because he still wanted the single life, and then would immediately apologize and tell me how much he loved me and how I meant the world to him. Then in the next breath he'd rant and rave about me seeing other guys. I never saw any of that during the courtship, only after we married. Then he started using drugs. I fought him on that, but he argued that he needed it to get over all the things that he'd seen while he was on missions. Having seen some things myself, I understood to a degree, but it wasn't my pathway. I didn't like that it was becoming Barry's pathway." Lisa shook her head. "I know a lot of people put up with that, but I didn't."

"And now you're feeling guilty because he's dead."

Lisa winced. "I guess that's foolish, isn't it? I didn't even know he was dead, and here I am, feeling as if I did something wrong."

"That goes back to that whole gaslighting thing, where you feel you're the one who's done something wrong, and yet really you haven't."

"Haven't I though?" she asked, almost on the verge of tears. "In a way I ran away from him. I couldn't handle what he was doing and what he was like, so I left as soon as I could and got as far away as possible."

"Lisa, that's not wrong. In fact, I'd call it self-preservation. You probably understood the self-destructive and violent tendencies within Barry and were desperately trying to ensure you didn't get caught up in it."

DAY 4, DINNERTIME

LISA THOUGHT A lot about that for the rest of the afternoon. When she got to the kitchen that night to get dinner, she checked out the dinner offerings, then looked at Chef, who was loading rice into one of the big pans. "Does this mean we don't have generator problems anymore?"

He smiled. "Nope, seems they got it fixed." He spread out the rice, his movements efficient and fast.

His voice was calm, quiet, and patient, which she appreciated. "I'm glad to hear that. Some of us were getting a little worried."

He shot her a look. "And that's never a good thing. Paranoia can build to the point that it's not something you see happening, yet, once it starts, it's hard to stop." Again it seemed as if Chef's words were almost prophetic because that was the paranoia her husband, Barry, had been dishing out on her about relationships.

When Lisa sat down to eat her dinner, several other people joined her, and the conversation focused on general topics, until somebody brought up the generator. One of the guys leaned forward and asked, "Any idea if that was sabotage?"

Lisa shook her head. "We don't have any reason for thinking that. All that talk will do is cause problems." When he glared at her, she shrugged. "Listen. Only so many of us are here, so what you're suggesting is that somebody here would have done that. I, for one, don't need to participate in that talk." With that, she got up and walked out.

ROGAN HEARD HER words, as he was standing nearby, in line getting food. He appreciated her immediate attempt to stop that gossip and to not perpetuate what he had warned her could be an issue. He ate his dinner here in the dining room but quickly, being social in an effort to not stand out. By the time he was done, half of the dining room was empty, and most people had left, with some gathering to play cards, as they did to pass the time each evening.

When a huge shadow dropped down beside him, Rogan looked up to see Mountain. Rogan leaned forward. "Where the hell have you been?"

"Not here, that's for sure."

Indeed, Mountain looked tired.

"I went back to the village settlement, trying to do some interviews with the locals on our missing people. I was trying to get the villagers to open up and talk to me, but, of course, they're not terribly impressed with anybody from our base."

"Of course not," Rogan agreed. "They don't want any interference, and, if we can't even take care of ourselves, why should they look after us?"

"How is the scientists' camp doing?" Mountain eyed him over the rim of his coffee cup.

"They're holding for now. Magnus was up there a couple nights ago looking after their generator, and, so far, no other calls for help have come in."

"That's good." Mountain lowered his cup and turned his

gaze to the lineup at the food buffet. "We also need to keep an eye on them a little more often to make sure they *can* call for help."

At that, Rogan stiffened and turned to him. "Do you know something I don't?"

"Not yet, but …" He leaned forward and, in an even lower voice, added, "Did you hear anything about our generator?"

"Only that there was a suspicion of sabotage."

He nodded. "Confirmed."

"*Great.*" Rogan groaned. "But, outside of inconveniencing us, and making more people paranoid, what good would that do?"

"I guess it depends on how long our generator would have been down. As it was, we fixed it. And it's now guarded," Mountain added, with a nod.

"And, yes, you're right. It's an inconvenience, but most of us are weather survivalists, so it's not as if it'll stop anything on a permanent basis, but it might shut down the base for this particular training session," he added, with a look around at everybody else still in the cafeteria.

"Maybe. But because of what was happening, we already reduced some of the training and shut down many parts of the international competitions."

"Ah, and the dogs are doing fine where they are?"

He nodded.

"Apparently Joe wanted to bring more dogs to ensure that he had enough to get people out, if need be, but that was shut down to reduce costs."

"Yeah, of course it was," Mountain noted, with a harsh tone. "As much as we might want to love to hate him, the colonel is getting a lot of flak over what's going on here."

"Yeah, I'll bet," Rogan replied. "The colonel's frustrated and fed up, and, at the same time, worried because these deaths are on him—which they aren't really—but I get it. Leadership comes with a price."

At that, Mountain nodded. "I need to crash, but I have to eat. Did you already have dinner?"

He nodded his head in affirmation. "Where's yours?"

"Chef's bringing it."

Rogan raised an eyebrow, as Chef walked out with a huge platter and set it in front of the big man. Mountain tucked in, and Rogan looked around to see if anybody had noticed. Nobody appeared to be paying any attention. "Now that is one hell of a lot of food."

"It is, and I'm a big guy," Mountain noted. "I also haven't eaten for quite a while."

"They didn't look after you at the village?"

"No, I ended up being escorted out, once some of my questions pissed them off," he shared, with half a smile.

"I presume you felt fully justified in asking those questions?"

"Oh, absolutely," he declared, "but I'll have a hard time bringing anybody to justice if that village is where the problem is coming from. It's a tight-knit group."

"Did they see anybody?"

"They did, apparently somebody female."

"*Great.*"

Loud sounds came from the doorway, as a group of guys came in and took up a large table, where they started playing card games. One of the men got up to grab some drinks and food and then sat back down again.

Rogan waited until Mountain finished eating.

As soon as he downed the last of his meal, Mountain

pushed away his plate and stood. "I'm heading out to check on the dogs."

"I'll come with you." Rogan immediately hopped to his feet, and the two men walked out to check on Joe. Rogan immediately sought out Benji and cuddled him. The dog always, even when not feeling well, had a heartfelt greeting for him, reminding Rogan once again of a different lifestyle, where he could have a dog like Benji in his life on a more permanent basis.

Joe looked up and frowned at them. "I'm fine," he declared in a grumpy voice. "Tired of the BS and ready to make sure I'm the last man standing in this place," he muttered.

"That's not so far-fetched," Mountain replied. "What I don't want is to come out here one day and find out that it's the opposite."

Joe stared at him for a long moment, then nodded reluctantly. "Point taken," he admitted grumpily. "I am isolated, yet I do have weapons. So, if somebody were to sneak up on me, well, you and I both know it wouldn't be good."

Rogan stayed quiet, watching the two men interact. This was Joe's domain, but Mountain? Well, he was hard to ignore or resist. He also appeared decent at not stepping on toes.

"No, it sure as hell wouldn't be good," Mountain agreed.

The affection in his voice revealed to Rogan that Mountain knew Joe from way back.

"Take care of yourself, will you?" Mountain leveled a glare at Joe.

"I will," Joe said. "What about you though? You were gone for quite a while."

"I was. Were you worried about me?" A grin lit up

Mountain's features and almost made him look like an enormous teddy bear.

"I wondered if I should take out a dog team to see if you were stuck somewhere. I did check the ice cave, just in case."

Mountain nodded. "So did I, but I didn't see anything."

"No, but I saw your tracks, so I knew you were out there somewhere."

He chuckled. "Yeah, it's a little hard to hide mine when I'm out and about."

Hearing this conversation between the two old friends, Rogan realized that both of them were still actively investigating that site. It should have surprised him, but ... he focused on scratching Benji's chin, chuckling at the dog's look of rapture.

These were very affectionate animals, showing that Joe cared deeply for them. Still, there were a lot of them and only one Joe, and the dogs were all anxious for a little extra attention. Several others walked over to them, one shaking off a coat of snow onto Rogan. He stepped back, laughing, trying to listen in on the conversation between Joe and Mountain and still not be so distracted by the canine energy. "Do you want to clue me in as to why that ice cave site is so important?" Rogan asked them.

"Because it's a place of shelter, if somebody gets caught out there," Mountain replied, without looking at Rogan but staring at the dogs. "It is still a place to go, if you have the navigational ability to get there."

"Which the dogs would have," Joe acknowledged, "but I'm not missing any dogs. Thank Christ for that."

"Of course, if you were, it'd be a hell of a different scenario, wouldn't it?" Rogan asked.

"Damn right." Joe spat out the chew in his mouth onto

the ground. "I ain't got no truck with anybody hurting no dogs. They're mine, not military equipment that people can abuse and hurt. I'm already mad enough about two of them getting shot as it is," he muttered.

"But they're doing okay, right? They'll survive?" Mountain asked in concern.

"Yeah, they're doing fine," Joe confirmed, "but they won't be doing any pulling up here, and I want to get them shipped back home again. Honest to God, I wouldn't mind if all of us got shipped out."

"How much longer are you supposed to be here?" Rogan asked.

"To the bitter end," Joe stated, a snarl in his voice. "God help me, to the bitter end."

As the two men walked back to the main base, Rogan looked over at Mountain. "Any word on the missing men?"

He shook his head. "No, and, if the villagers have them or know anything about them, they're not talking." Mountain swore out loud. "I was so sure that my brother would have made it that far. It's pissing me off that I can't find any answers. And, in these weather conditions and the heavy snow, … it could be a long time before his body ever surfaces."

"Do you think he's dead?"

"No," Mountain declared, stopping and looking at Rogan. With their faces bundled up, it was hard to read expressions. "I really don't."

"Have you ever been in a scenario like that?"

He nodded. "Yeah, I sure have." He looked off to the side. "Not exactly the same thing, but I've learned to trust my instincts, and right about now they are tingling. Anything happen around here that we don't know about?"

"Not that I'm aware of. Everything was shut down, and it's been pretty well an inside day, while the generator was brought up again. Once that happened, I don't even know what people were doing. It was pretty much a day off, I guess." But with an eye roll, he corrected himself. "There is no such thing here of course, but it would have been cleaning and probably reasserting rules and that sort of thing," he muttered.

"Yeah, they're good on that." As they walked inside the base, Mountain stopped and looked back at the dog area. "Some days I think it might be safer if we slept out there."

"I'll keep that in mind"—Rogan laughed—"if it ever gets that bad."

"I'm not kidding," Mountain stated. "The dogs are a hell of a good warning system, and something is still pretty rotten in this place. Everybody's been interviewed. Everybody's been checked, and, so far, nothing is popping."

"One thing did happen that set my nerves on edge." Then Rogan told Mountain about the footsteps outside of Lisa's door.

"I gather she's new?"

"No, she's not new." Rogan quickly gave her description to Mountain.

Mountain nodded. "I remember her. She's a nurse?"

"That's right, but, when nothing's happening, she's been out getting in some of her training, since that's what she came here for."

"And, as long as she isn't needed by Sydney, I've got no beef with it."

Rogan laughed at that because Mountain spoke as if he were in charge. They would have been in a hell of a different scenario if that had been the case. "Has everybody been questioned? You sure no one was missed?"

Mountain nodded. "Everybody was interviewed multiple times, to the point that people were getting pissed because their word wasn't believed. Of course, in a scenario like this, you can't trust anybody."

"Yet, at the same time, we ended up with two dead Russians—one suspicious death, ruled an accident at first, then the death of Helsky, the Russian who tried to force himself on the doc. Not to mention a missing Russian too."

"Yegorahn," Mountain added.

Rogan nodded.

Mountain continued. "So believe me. The Russian government is all over the US government on this one. Thus the colonel is catching hell, and, so far, his hands are tied. He needs to produce somebody who's guilty."

"Let's hope the colonel only produces the guilty party," Rogan said, his voice sharp. "The last thing we need is to have somebody railroaded over a murder that he didn't commit."

At that, Mountain gave him a ghost of a smile. "I don't want to see that either, but, more than that, I don't want to see anybody else turn up dead or missing."

DAY 5, EARLY MORNING

LISA WOKE THE next morning to a knock on her door, Rogan's voice calling out gently, "Lisa, you awake?" In a muffled voice, she called for him to come in. He opened the door and stepped inside. "How is it you got a room to yourself anyway?" he asked, looking around.

She shifted so that she sat up against the wall, trying to clear her head. "Is that what you came for? You're fishing for sleeping quarters again?" While she was clearly still trying to wake up, she couldn't respond to his instant grin.

"Not exactly," he replied, with a laugh, "but I do understand the appeal of having a space all to yourself. Seriously, why didn't you end up in a double room like almost everyone else? Pretty sweet deal."

"Maybe, although it might also be a little bit warmer with two bodies in one room," she muttered.

"It would," he confirmed, frowning as he looked over at her. "Have you seen Ron at all?"

"Ron?" She repeated the name, trying to put a face to it.

"Yeah, he's on the Swiss team."

"No, I don't think so. Why?"

"Did you see him yesterday?"

The way he asked her so carefully about it—as if to make sure she understood—had her staring at Rogan. "Is that the guy with the red hair, a little slim, but really strong?"

He nodded. "Yeah, that would be him."

She shook her head. "I don't think I did, but I was rattled enough by all that was going on that I basically don't remember."

"There were some trainings yesterday. The scheduled programs were canceled but some groups got together to keep busy. Were you part of that?"

She winced. "Nope, I skipped it and mostly hung out in the clinic." His eyebrows shot up. "I know. I know. ... I shouldn't have, but I wasn't feeling all that great," she admitted honestly.

He frowned at her. "Still cold?"

"A little bit, yeah, and after the generator incident, ... I just can't seem to shake this chill. So I decided to stay inside and to stay warm for the rest of the day."

"That's fine, as long as you report it."

"I did, and I also had Sydney check on me."

"Good, in these cases, the more people checking on you the better."

She shifted and asked curiously, "Why are you looking for Ron?"

"Because nobody's seen him."

Her mouth opened and then closed. "What do you mean, *nobody's* seen him?"

He nodded grimly. "He's not in his room. He didn't show up last night for dinner, and, when a friend went to his room to check on him, he wasn't there. Ron's friend didn't think much of it last night, but, when he returned to his room early this morning, before they headed out for training, he called at his door and couldn't find him. He checked the kitchen and didn't find him there, and then he reported it. The colonel was contacted, and now we're doing a room-to-room check."

"Jesus, how does somebody here just disappear?"

"Ron is very accustomed to this weather," Rogan shared, "so, if anybody will be okay out there, I would suspect it to be him."

She shook her head at that. "No, that's not good enough," she argued, throwing back the covers and immediately grabbing the hoodie beside her. "Because, if he's got a head injury, or if he's stuck in a whiteout, or if he isn't properly clothed and supplied, you know it won't really matter. He can dig himself into the ground and hope for a rescue, but why would anybody go outside alone, especially without telling the rest of the team? That's the number one rule," she muttered, as she struggled into her hoodie.

"I know it, as should all of us here," he noted. "Listen. Have you ever heard anything about some betting going on in the base? Betting on how long people can stay outside, plus how far they can go on their own and still make it back, safe and sound? Or having to call in for help?"

She stared at him, her mouth hanging open. "What in the hell? You mean like those stupid water bucket challenges on the internet?" she asked, her voice incredulous. "No, of course I haven't heard of that here. Please tell me that you haven't either. Nobody should be stupid enough to taunt Mother Nature out there."

"I've heard whispers of it, but it seems to be within a very small group of people."

"Yeah, it would have to be. In a larger group, chances are somebody with some sense would have reported them. Jesus, how could they be so stupid?"

"Apparently this Ron guy was one of the group but didn't want anything to do with it. Now, whether he got egged into doing it or maybe he threatened to report them—"

"And what? Somebody stopped him? Jesus, Rogan." Her eyes went wide, as she stared at him. "That would be horrific."

"Not only that"—he shook his head, as he stared around at her room—"supposedly Ron had a pretty bad argument with Helsky, the Russian who was murdered. Apparently Helsky was egging Ron on, all about not being good enough to do survival training on his own, begging to come to a training base like this, instead of being invited, such as Helsky."

"Jesus, I'm sure the colonel really loved hearing about that."

"We hear that shit all the time but always on the down-low," Rogan shared, "since that talk is never allowed."

"Of course not," she muttered. She looked around, frowning. "I don't even know what time it is."

"It's around six-thirty."

"And you had to wake me up early?" she asked, with an eye roll. Then she immediately remembered why. "Give me five to get dressed, and I'll come join the search."

"No way," he argued in a strict tone. "We don't need you getting hypothermia. Just be on alert at the clinic in case we bring in Ron," Rogan told her. "I'm heading out now with the dogs and Joe, along with a couple other teams on skis."

"So, people really expect Ron to be outside of the complex?" she asked in shock. "Dear God."

"Maybe he went outside and decided to spend the night with the scientists or in the Inuit village," Rogan suggested.

At that, she stiffened and looked at him. "Are there

women in the village?" she asked hesitantly.

"Oh, absolutely. There are women in the village," he confirmed, with a nod and a grim smile. "Some of us had that thought too."

"Well, crap, they are close enough for a night out, I suppose."

"They are. It's just not what we thought would be happening up here."

"And yet, if he's on his own time, he could do what he wanted, right?" she asked pointedly.

"Yes, and believe me. Plenty of people are saying he has every right to date a local woman, as long as he is welcomed."

"And that could be why he hasn't returned," Lisa suggested.

"However," Rogan added, "I know somebody who was there recently, and he didn't get a warm welcome."

"*Great.* The last thing we need is the gift of an unexpected pregnancy being left behind for the locals to raise."

"And whether they would look at it as a gift is a whole different story," Rogan pointed out.

She winced. "God, how the hell did this base run off the rails so fast?"

"It shouldn't have, and that's something the colonel will likely face some scrutiny over."

"Crap, these consensual sexual events are hardly his fault either," she muttered.

"And yet, if he were running a tight ship, this would not be happening," he pointed out.

She wanted to agree with him, yet, at the same time, she also knew that people would be people. Plus she had seen some military men and women pull off some pretty dumb stunts, no matter where they were. And, when they were bored, the stunts they came up with were even dumber. "So, are we thinking Ron got suckered into any of those bets? Because that isn't a bet you'll win."

"No, it isn't," Rogan agreed. "Listen. I'll wait outside, while you get dressed. Then I'll take you to the kitchen."

While she quickly got dressed, she considered his wording. As she opened the door and stepped outside, she was a bit abashed to see him waiting there. "You make it sound as if I'm under guard or something."

"It's not that you're under guard, but we're not exactly sure who and what and why this is all hitting the fan. So, until then? Believe me. Everybody is being paired up."

She nodded. "So presumably that'll be me with Sydney?"

"It's me and you right now. Then I'll sign you over to Sydney, and the two of you are to stay together for the rest of the day, while I'm out hunting."

At the term *hunting*, she stopped and looked at him.

He gave her a grim look. "Yes, that's the term, at least as far as I'm concerned."

She lowered her voice, looked around, and, in a quiet whisper, asked, "You think Ron's dead, don't you?"

He nodded. "Yes, I do."

WHEN ROGAN MET the rest of the search team outside, everybody was quiet, their faces grim. As Rogan looked around, he saw no sign of Mountain in any of the groups, but Magnus was here. Rogan walked closer to Magnus, who looked up and pointed at him.

"You're with me."

Rogan raised an eyebrow. "Where are we going?"

"To the scientists' camp."

"Good enough," Rogan replied. "And what about the locals' village?"

"Somebody else has gone there."

While Magnus didn't say as much, Rogan suspected that *somebody* may have been Mountain. Rogan asked Magnus, "So everybody else is heading out in groups? Do we have trackers?"

Magnus nodded grimly. "It didn't snow overnight, so there's a hard crust, but no fresh tracks that we can see."

Rogan stopped and looked at him. "So, what are you saying?"

"Chances are, Ron disappeared last night."

"Shit." Rogan groaned, as he walked over to the snowcat.

"Joe is leading the dogs. He's got two trackers with him, so, with any luck, they can find Ron," Magnus added, as he tightened his hold on his backpack. "We'll go up to the scientists' camp, double-check that they're fine, and see if they've had any contact with Ron."

With that, they got into the snowcat. In the distance Rogan watched the others as they took off on skis and sleds. "What the hell is going on?" Rogan muttered in the cold interior, as they set off.

"I don't know, but we've got more brass involved, so we might see a change at the top here very soon."

"I'm not surprised," Rogan replied, "though I'm sorry about that because I'm not sure the colonel deserves whatever is coming his way."

"As you well know, that doesn't matter one bit in the military. Failure is not an option."

"Definitely been a hell of a lot of failure here so far," Rogan agreed, with a nod. The rest of the journey was made in eerie silence. Though, if it weren't for the circumstances, Rogan could really enjoy the breathtaking natural beauty. He focused on surveying the area, trying to find any sign of their missing man. "We're absolutely positive that Ron's not back at the base, right?" Rogan asked.

Magnus nodded. "You were part of the room-to-room search. A full search has been done. Every bed's been lifted and checked—still no sign of him."

"But couldn't he have a hiding place we haven't considered or found?"

"Anything is possible," Magnus acknowledged, with a shrug. "He'd be an idiot to be still hiding though."

"Unless he has no choice."

"Believe me. We thought of that too, and even the freezers were checked. I don't know what more to say. When I say that a full check's been done, I meant a full check has been done."

"And presumably that was done under orders from the colonel?"

"He ordered it, but he didn't personally supervise it. Just another reason why there will likely be a change at the top."

"So, they want all hands on deck for this," Rogan muttered.

"Yeah, and, at this point in time, the colonel might be thinking somebody is trying to make him look bad."

"Wow." Rogan faced Magnus. "I hadn't even considered that."

Magnus continued to concentrate on navigating them safely. "Yes, it's a possibility. I can't see anybody giving a shit, … unless they're trying to make him suffer. Maybe trying to make him pay for something. In that case, ... I wouldn't be at all surprised if somehow something goes wrong. And the colonel ends up staying here because then it would mean that he was part of the targeting."

At that, Magnus fell silent again, as Rogan contemplated what it would look like if somebody were trying to get payback on the colonel for something. "I suppose nobody did any checks into the colonel's background, did they?"

Magnus snorted. "Good luck getting that, though things may have changed by now because of Ron. However, it probably depends more on what the outcome of this search is. If we find nothing's wrong, and it turns out that Ron is fine, then the colonel will probably skate on this. Yet, if Ron's isn't fine, I suspect we'll find out that the colonel is being heavily investigated."

"Right, but that still doesn't mean he's guilty."

"Absolutely not, it doesn't mean he's guilty of anything. Somebody could have something against him, and they're determined to make him pay."

"By making it look like this entire charade is his failure?"

"Yeah, by having multiple guys die or go missing under his watch, it goes without saying that the colonel's completely useless as a leader."

Rogan added in a sad tone, "Man, it's a shame to think about deaths due to revenge or just sheer incompetence. Nobody deserves to die over that."

"No, they sure don't," Magnus confirmed, "but, if somebody is prepared to kill—just to make someone else look bad—they sure don't give a crap about the ones they are killing. And they really don't give a crap about what you or I think about it."

"That's great," Rogan muttered. "You could have lied

and told me this would all blow over," he joked.

"Yet you and I both know it won't."

"No, it sure doesn't feel like it."

"Did you find out anything through your questioning?"

"No, nothing besides the *betting against Mother Nature* thing. Even with our guys increasingly bored and forced to stay inside, I can't believe we have any segment of people who are crazy enough to risk their life for some ego trip or pennies or whatever. Plus I'm still trying to figure out who the hell would have been standing outside Lisa's door."

"You may want to change your sleeping arrangements, if it matters to you that much."

"What do you mean, if it matters to me?" he asked, his anger seeping through. "To have any of the women targeted matters to me."

"Sure, but, in this case, we've got men being targeted as well, so—"

"Meaning?"

"*Everybody* needs to be careful, and everybody needs to be working on a buddy system," he spelled out for him.

"Right." Rogan nodded. "I wasn't sure what you were trying to say."

"I was trying to say that you're sweet on her, so don't bother with excuses. If you're worried about her, you may want to change your sleeping arrangements."

Rogan stiffened at that and turned to look at him, but Magnus was totally unaffected by Rogan's glare.

"Don't refute it," Magnus stated, "because I can see the truth every time the two of you are together. You lean in closer. You're always very solicitous, and your eyes follow her every time she gets up and leaves a room."

"Crap," Rogan muttered. "I can't say I even noticed, and

I've put it down to being friends."

"You may have been firmly friend-zoned or you friend-zoned her at some point in the past, but something has shifted, and it feels weird."

"Yeah, it feels weird all right," Rogan said under his breath. "It also feels weird that everybody else seems to have some idea of what the hell is going on between me and Lisa, and yet I don't have a clue."

At that, Magnus burst out laughing. "Get used to it, buddy. In this place, there's nothing to do but analyze everybody else around you, so it happens. And now you know. Get yourself up to speed or move on." He pointed up ahead. "Almost there." As they approached, he swore.

"What's the matter?" Rogan asked.

"I don't hear the damn generator." He parked outside the front entrance, and together they raced inside. As he opened the door and stepped over the threshold, he felt the chill. "Hello! Hello! Where is everyone?" No sign of anyone in the main room. Magnus walked through and sniffed the air. He looked at Rogan, who had the same somber expression on his face. "I don't like that smell," Magnus roared, racing back to the front door, propping it open, and immediately covering his face with his hoodie.

"That's gas," Rogan snapped. "Stay here." He raced through the center to where the sleeping quarters were, opening the doors to find still bodies in the beds. He raced to each person, checking for pulses. He took two on his first trip out.

Magnus raced to meet him by the door, helping to get the first two into the Cat.

"It might be carbon monoxide poisoning," Rogan suggested. "They're in bad shape in there." Both men raced to the bedrooms, carrying two people over their shoulders. "We don't have very much room with this machine," Rogan said, with a groan.

"Doesn't matter. We'll stuff them in here anyway. Thank God the other team was just visiting and left shortly thereafter," Magnus stated. "You can stay behind, if need be."

"That's fine," Rogan agreed, "or I can ride on the damn roof even." They double-checked the scientists' camp for any more people, but only found the six that they'd already loaded up. They sent a message back to the base, putting Sydney and Lisa in the clinic on full alert.

Rogan took one last look around. He left a note on the front door, in case the rest of the scientists were out collecting data. By his count two people were missing. One female doctor and one male geoscientist.

With that, knowing they were literally racing against life and death, they climbed on the snowcat and headed back to base.

DAY 5, MORNING

HEARING THE MEDICAL alert from Sydney, Lisa raced to the clinic, as several people were roped into getting more beds set up, until she had what amounted to cots placed in the medical clinic and even took over the closest bedroom, which happened to be Sydney's.

By the time the men brought in the first of the scientists, two of them had started to wake up. The first man groaned and whispered, "We went to bed, and it was fine. We had somebody on watch all night to ensure the generator was okay. I think it was my turn, and I didn't wake up," he said frantically. "I didn't wake up."

Sydney immediately calmed him down, putting an oxygen mask on him, as Lisa came around and checked his vitals. Sydney told him, "I need you to stay calm. Take deep breaths and don't worry. It's all good." She looked back to Lisa and nodded. "We've got to get oxygen on everybody." She turned to the next man and reassured him. "We're setting one up for you right now."

"Give it to them," he said immediately. "Give it all to them. I'm breathing fine."

"You're breathing," Lisa confirmed gently, "but your saturation levels are extremely low."

He nodded and collapsed back down again. "That goddamn generator."

"Did you have any idea that it could do this?"

"No, but we've had nothing but problems with the damn thing. We kept trying to filter heat back into our camp by rerouting the exhaust system, and we knew that would be dangerous, but we were also freezing. We had separate rooms at first, but then we crowded into the one," he explained. "I have no idea how we ended up like this."

"First off, let's focus on getting you all back on your feet," Lisa suggested. "Then we can figure out the rest of it."

"Will everybody make it?" the lead guy asked, looking at her in horror. He tried to sit up again, but she pressed him back down firmly.

"They're alive," Lisa replied, "and that's what we're going for right now. What's your name?"

He turned his head her way, tears in his eyes. "Myles, Dr. Myles Rand. My God, we should have shut it down instead of trying to last for a little bit longer. The data is important but not worth losing our lives over."

"I gather some people thought so?"

He nodded, and then he added in a whisper, "Oh no," he added. "We've got a team out. They radioed that they were staying overnight, but they don't even know," he said. "They'll walk back into that. They don't know."

She was hard-pressed to keep him calm, while she sent a text message to Rogan. When she got a message back that the men had left a note, she told Myles, seeing the overwhelming relief on his face.

"Thank God." He was almost on the verge of tears again. He lifted his mask. "Dr. Robinson and Dr. Amelia, they went outside. … They're both in great physical shape and are well used to these kinds of conditions." He shrugged. "But I know how it is when you come home, and you want to get in where it's warm and where you're safe, so you can have a hot cup of tea and relax. I don't want them coming back to that scenario."

"If we had been any later," Rogan announced from the doorway, "they would have come back to a completely dead camp."

At that, her patient winced. "Thank you for your timing," Myles replied, his voice heartfelt. "Jesus, ... I can't believe, ... I can't believe we were so stupid."

"It happens, and it's not as if you were trying to commit suicide or murder everybody, right?" he asked, and his tone was light, but the look in his gaze belied it.

Myles immediately shook his head. "No, we were making plans to go back home again." Myles yawned, only to start coughing.

Lisa immediately strapped the oxygen mask back on him, and he gasped and sucked it in, leaning back on the bed. She looked over at Rogan sternly. "Can we do this later?"

He nodded. "I'll be back in a little bit." He headed over to the other patients and talked to Sydney, who was doing the rounds, as she checked on everybody.

"Their oxygen levels are very low," Sydney confirmed, "but it seems you got them out just in time."

Rogan nodded. "And, for that, you can thank Magnus for going up there. We were also looking for Ron of course."

"Yeah, any news on him?"

"No," he replied in a low tone.

She nodded, her face grim. "This really is an op from hell," she muttered. "Certainly not what any of us expected."

"I'll go check if any of the teams searching for Ron are back," Rogan shared. And, with that, he disappeared.

Lisa walked over to Sydney, her voice low as she whispered, "Some of them are barely hanging on."

"Some of them may not wake up," Sydney murmured in response. "We need to get them airlifted out immediately. The colonel is trying to make that happen. An ugly weather pattern moving in complicates matters."

"Of course," Lisa said bitterly, "but it still needs to happen."

"We can't seem to catch a break."

BUT THE MEDICAL team did pull it off, although the airlift wouldn't be here for several hours. When the opportunity came, they loaded up the worst four to be evacuated to a proper hospital and left the two who were doing a little bit better to await the next evac trip. Myles, the man Lisa had spoken to earlier, sighed with relief when the others were loaded up and on their way out. Myles and the other scientist, Anna Millwork, stayed behind. Anna was in the best shape of all of them but was still in shock.

"Jesus." Myles let out a long sigh. "I'm happy to stay behind and to get this fixed. I'm sorry Anna had to remain here too. She wanted to go home as it was."

"And when you say *fixed* ..." Rogan began, with Sydney and Lisa by his side, all frowning.

"We still must shut down the camp for the winter," Myles explained and coughed hard. "We can't have all our work be for naught because we didn't preserve and share the data we almost died trying to get. I've got to collect the laptops for example, deal with the food, and generally winterize the place."

"Right. I can take you up there later and give you a hand," Rogan offered. "I want to have another look at what happened anyway. Plus, with supplies here at our base on the low side, any foodstuffs you've got left that would help out here, we'd gratefully accept."

At that, Myles nodded. "Okay then, I'd appreciate the help. Of course anything we have, you are more than welcome to." He hesitated. "I presume I'm supposed to return there," he added, his voice almost defeated.

"Not sure about that," Rogan admitted. "Regardless we need to confirm that your camp is safe, particularly as others of your team are still outside."

He nodded. "I do need to get word back to the other two team members."

"I left a note on the door," Rogan stated.

"Yeah, so that means they could be there, working on the generator, trying to fix it, or are still not back—which would be concerning—or they're on their way here."

"Regardless, you need to relax," Rogan stated. "We got your friends out of here faster than we thought possible, but it's been several hours, and you still haven't recovered enough to be on your own."

"*Great.*" Myles rubbed his face. "I do feel kind of rough."

"Get some rest," Lisa said. "Stretch out and sleep. You're here for the duration, so relax."

With that, she turned and motioned Rogan out of the room, leaving their two patients under the watchful eye of Sydney. Out in the hallway, Lisa asked, "How did you guys get that rescue together so fast?"

"A navy ship was close enough to help," Rogan explained. "Whether it will be enough to save those people remains to be seen, but thankfully that's on them now."

"They are far better equipped," Lisa noted. "This is definitely not the place for that."

"No, and maybe somebody knew that too."

She turned and looked at him in shock. "You don't think it was deliberate, do you?"

"I don't know. I'll go back up and check." Rogan stared at Myles through the open doorway. "We will find out."

DAY 6, MORNING

EARLY THE NEXT morning Rogan stared at the generator at the scientists' camp. Magnus and two other men from the compound were with him. One of them was supposed to run a full report. Another was to stay in contact with the colonel and provide an ongoing description of what the hell was going on here during their inspection. Rogan was here with Magnus to try and figure out what had happened and how it had happened and whether any of it was deliberate or not. Rogan could only hope it was accidental. Myles was doing okay, but he was still on oxygen, and everybody was grateful that the rest of the team had managed to get out, except for Myles and Anna.

The navy transport wasn't coming back for the two of them, as far as Rogan understood. They also had yet to find Dr. Amelia and Dr. Robinson, but it was too early to make anything of that. At Sydney's request, oxygen and other critical supplies were dropped off when the transport came in, for which she was thankful, since she had been running low.

They were hoping for another food supply drop as well and also were assessing what was available at the scientists' camp to take back to the base.

Rogan wandered through the scientists' camp, studying their setup. Magnus had brought their own military equipment to provide data on the oxygen carbon monoxide levels, but, with the generator off and the doors open, everything had reverted back to normal, so they were fine. Rogan looked back at Magnus. "Are you getting any insights into this?"

He looked over at him and nodded. "The exhaust was deliberately set up this way, that much is quite clear. The question is why, and did the person know what they were doing would basically kill everybody, or was it a case of being so cold they didn't care anymore? On that, I have no idea."

Rogan winced. "Is that even possible? We are talking about scientists here."

"Absolutely it's possible. And honestly I'm going with stupidity because these pipes were rigged up and secured to run into the main building with the fresh oxygen coming in as well, but the strapping they used to hold them up was just this duct tape." Magnus shook his head. "It has fallen from the weight, and, even though these piping ducts were lightweight, the structure they put them on wasn't secure enough to hold it. So the piping dropped, filling the room from the bottom with the exhaust gases. The fresh air intake was up high and wasn't enough to combat the exhaust. So, in an effort to stay warm, they almost died, which we have seen before."

"Why didn't they contact you about the generator, instead of rigging something themselves?" Rogan asked Magnus, turning to look at him with a frown. "They have all along when their generator breaks down, so why not this time?"

"That's a question I'll ask Myles and Anna," Magnus noted, "because they should have. And I've never refused to come, so it can't be that. Now, I did say that we might move them over to our base, but that didn't seem to be that big of a deal to them. Obviously it's not what they wanted, but they were here to get a job done and were all here willingly, so I didn't see that as being the issue."

"And was the generator working? Because, if it was working, I don't understand why they needed to reroute the exhaust in the first place."

"Because the generator wasn't up to full function, and they couldn't get it to crank up any higher. And that's part of the problem they were having before," he muttered.

As two men walked toward them with large boxes and crates between them, Rogan smiled at them. "I gather you found some supplies?"

One guy nodded. "Yeah, Chef wanted anything perishable, but not an awful lot is here though."

"That's fine. It will stretch our resources." Rogan went back with them for another load, and they quickly packed up the bulk of the remaining food supplies in the scientists' kitchen, leaving some pantry goods behind—in case the other team came in, looking for groceries themselves.

"I feel bad doing this," Rogan noted, as he looked around, "because they could use a lot of this themselves."

"Then they can come to our base," Magnus declared, as he wrote another note on a few large parchments and left them hanging at multiple locations, explaining what had happened and where everybody was. "We'll put that note back up on the door." He pointed to another banner-size canvas.

"Myles didn't seem to be too bothered that they aren't back yet," Rogan shared. "Is that normal?"

Magnus sighed and looked over at him. "I was wondering about that myself. Plus I'm not sure how much we can trust Myles."

"Exactly, and I hate feeling that way. The guy has been through a lot," Rogan acknowledged. "I don't know what's going on, but it seems to be one more anomaly in this training session."

Magnus laughed. "Yeah, this seems to be the training session from hell for our military base, but also for the scientists. Most of them are very experienced, and they've been up here several times, so I can't say that anybody is trying to sabotage or cause trouble at that level. They must have noticed something. I mean, what's the point of coming up here to get rid of your coworkers?" he asked, with a shrug. "Unless there were some internal issues."

"Maybe," Rogan agreed, "but, even then, it doesn't seem right."

With the rest of the gear loaded, they headed back to the military base. After unloading the supplies, Rogan went in, shed several layers of clothing, and walked into the kitchen to grab some coffee. When Chef popped his head out, Rogan asked, "Were the supplies of any value?"

He shrugged. "Most of the supplies are dry goods, so we can use them in a pinch, but they didn't have much of anything in the way of fresh, unless you guys didn't raid their cooler."

"We didn't find an operating cooler. The one we did find had been shut off, probably to preserve electricity because of the generator."

"Got it. Good that if we have their food, we also have two of the scientists here now, with two more coming, from what I am hearing. Is that right?"

"Two more possible, yes, but only if they can find their way here. We're waiting for the two people from their team who were out on a mission and missed out on the carbon monoxide poisoning," Rogan explained. "I do feel bad that we stripped most of the remaining food supplies from their camp, when they're due to come back."

Chef frowned at him. "That's not good."

"I know, and we did leave them notes and left enough pantry goods to get them by until they can move over here. However, considering we only have two of their people here now, I'll admit it felt weird to take the bulk of their provisions."

At that, Chef glared at him. "That was the colonel's orders, I understand."

That comment earned him an eye roll from Rogan. "Yes."

"The cost of that rescue is huge, if the scientists care," Chef added, "but I sure hope they show up here looking for meals. I'll feel like a piece of shit if they don't."

"And yet you needed everything that was available."

"Yeah, but I didn't think anybody was going back there, at least not permanently."

"I have to take Myles back up there again pretty soon to try and get their equipment out. We did get a bunch of it today, but it needs stable temperatures, and I'm sure we missed even more of that."

"Will the computers handle that kind of temperature?"

"I don't know. I guess we'll find out," Rogan said, with a wry look at Chef. "I'll talk to Myles and see if I need to go back up again right away." With that, he grabbed a coffee and headed to the medical clinic to talk to Myles, except he had been assigned a single room on his own.

As Rogan knocked on the door, he heard a voice call to come in. When Rogan stepped inside, he smiled as he saw a much better color evident on the older man's face. "Hey, how was your night? You pulled through in fine form, I see."

"You can bet I was damn grateful every time I had an opportunity to wake up and to breathe again," he replied, with half a smile. He shifted a bit in bed and looked around the room. "What time is it anyway?"

"Almost noon."

Myles looked at him in horror. "What?"

Rogan nodded. "We've just come back from your camp. We brought in some of the supplies to help stock up ours, and we checked out your generator."

"What about the other equipment?" Myles asked anxiously, as he threw back the covers. "That's one of the reasons I'm still here, … I need to go back up with you and pull in all our electronics."

"Absolutely," Rogan agreed, "that's not a problem."

"Give me a minute, and I'll get dressed," he said frantically. "They've been in the cold too long as it is."

"I'll give you a little more than a minute," Rogan told him. "I'll be in the kitchen, and we'll head straight up there."

"Thank you." Myles quickly started to get dressed.

Rogan stepped out and went down to the kitchen. He found the colonel sitting there in the dining room, having coffee, so Rogan explained to him what they needed to do.

The colonel shook his head. "I sure hope they have some fuel to help out because it takes fuel to run the snowcat too."

Rogan didn't say anything, knowing that the colonel was grousing about all the problems of late, not just this one.

"Fine, get him up there, one last trip. Get the rest of the stuff that he needs to shut everything down, and that will be your focus this time. I want no more trips up there. If you think anything else is needed or can be utilized, such as if they have a lot of fuel left," the colonel explained, "let me know."

"Will do."

By the time Rogan got Myles up to the scientists' camp, Myles was almost on the edge of the seat with worry.

"I'm sorry, was there something else we were supposed to do?" Rogan asked him.

"No, just call me obsessed, but ..." Myles shook his head. "It's just that all of our work is here."

"And you couldn't back it up?"

"Sure, it's backed up, but I don't know how anything handles these kinds of temperatures for this length of time."

"And I understand that," Rogan replied, "but let's get up there, and we can figure this out."

Once they parked outside the front door, with Myles leading the charge into the camp, Rogan had a little more time to walk around and to check out things.

Myles quickly packed up boxes and boxes full of books and equipment. By the time he was done, a good stack sat in front of him.

"You really want to haul all this out?" Rogan asked him.

Myles winced. "No, not under normal circumstances," he said in exasperation. "However, if we won't come back for quite a while, it won't be easy to get anybody to support us for funding, especially if we lost this data, and then they must come back here after this mess," he explained. "So, we'll take as much as we can."

Rogan frowned and looked at him curiously. "How will you get it out of our training center?"

"I don't know," he admitted. "At least if we have it there, we can work on backing some of it up, or maybe secure it somehow." Myles shrugged. "Some of this is research material we could have left, if need be, but I'll need it for the next little while. I'm hoping we can come back and do a couple more visits here over the next week." He looked over at Rogan anxiously. "Is that possible?"

Rogan shrugged. "Theoretically it's possible, though, at this moment, the colonel wouldn't be in favor of it. But, considering that some of your team still isn't back yet …"

"I know, and I'm starting to get worried."

"Starting to get worried?" Rogan asked, looking at him intently. "Honestly the rest of us were trying to figure out why you weren't worried before."

"Because I didn't want to panic. Amelia has been doing this for the last five years, and she's got a good team member with her. They've both got good heads on their shoulders, but we lost communication with them somewhere around the same time that everything at our camp blew up," he added. "So, at this point, I don't really know what to say."

"And yet at no point in time did you request any search and rescue for them. Why is that?"

"Let me tell you this. I did once with Amelia in the past, and, as it turned out, she was completely fine and quite royally pissed that a search team showed up. So honestly I don't really know when I'm supposed to do that."

"Has she exceeded her check-in date?"

"I was unconscious," he reminded Rogan, staring at him with a hard look. "Remember that? That's when they would have supposedly checked in. So, I don't know whether they attempted that or not."

"Well, Christ." Rogan stared at him. "So, at this point, you don't know if they're overdue or not."

"Exactly, and I don't know if they know that we're here, or if they checked in and assumed we couldn't answer because of generator problems."

"But they would also be smart enough presumably to understand—in the face of serious generator problems—how you would be at the training base with us."

"Yes, that would be my assumption," he agreed.

With that, Myles took another walk around the scientists' camp. "I'll shut down everything as much as I can, but, if we could come back one more time to save some further materials that I don't want to haul out during this trip, that would be very helpful. I need everything here to continue the work that I'm doing right now, and, when I'm done, some of these core materials can come back."

"Right," Rogan noted, knowing that the colonel would not be terribly impressed. "The cost of the fuel for the snow Cat is an issue, and it's made a lot of trips up here," he shared, with a shrug. "So, you might get some blowback."

"Right, hopefully it can go under the heading of community assistance."

Rogan laughed at that. "You can try that, but don't be surprised if the colonel contacts your sponsors and gets them to pitch in."

"That would not be good," Myles replied, with a groan, "because nobody has money in our world. This is all grant money, remember?"

"And maybe the government will suck it up. I don't know," Rogan admitted cheerfully. "The more we can limit all this, the better. Let's get these back to the center, and, if it can be discarded, surely it doesn't matter where."

"None of it is to be discarded. It's meant to be reference materials for the next team," he noted.

"Right. We'll do our best, but I can't make any promises, let me put it that way."

"Good enough. I don't think I'll be capable of staying here."

Even then he started to cough, and Rogan shook his head. "No, nobody's staying here," Rogan stated, "not until we can get this generator fixed."

"And that is not the easiest thing to sort out either," he noted, a bit angry. "It's an old piece of equipment, and we're dealing with parts and pieces at this point. It's a real mess."

"It is, and this facility was what? One of the original hunting lodges up here?"

He nodded. "Yes, and then they brought in materials, a little bit at a time to slowly insulate and secure it," he added. "I know that they're fairly protective of it, partly because of its historical value, but also because it's done the job for many, many years."

"And it can still do the job for many years, but you'll have to ensure that some money is put into upkeep."

"Yeah, and that goes right along with that whole grant BS," Myles complained, with a groan.

Rogan took twenty-five minutes to load up all the boxes, and, even then, he looked at the cart attached to the snowcat and winced. "Hope you don't mind scrunching in with the boxes."

"I'll ride on the roof to save all these," Myles declared determinedly. When Rogan looked at him, he nodded. "Hey, I'm a scientist, and coming up here is a big deal. The information we get, the data we collect," he explained, "that's a big deal too."

"Hopefully we can do better than have you riding on the roof." It was a tight squeeze, but, by stacking boxes both on and around Myles, Rogan managed to get everything in, including the two of them. Getting back to the base was another story though because visibility was now at a really crappy level.

As they trundled forward, Myles mentioned, "You guys seem to handle these conditions really well."

"I don't know about that," Rogan replied. "Some of us certainly do, while some of us don't, but we're all up here specifically to learn to adapt." He shrugged and added, "Mother Nature can be a bit of a bitch, especially when it comes to her more unhospitable areas on planet Earth."

"And yet I've always found it so beautiful out here," Myles replied, his voice almost dreamy. as he stared off into the sheer whiteness around them.

"I get that too," Rogan agreed. "I still prefer to be safe though."

After that, neither had anything more to say on the whole trip back. By the time they pulled into the training center, it looked as if Myles had dozed off. Rogan nudged him awake, and Myles blinked at him several times, then jerked up and looked around. "Good God, did I sleep?"

"You did," Rogan confirmed, "which is a good reason to get your ass back inside again and maybe hook up to that oxygen for a little while."

Myles winced. "Sounds awful when you put it that way."

Rogan laughed. "I don't mean to put it in any particular way, but the fact that you could sleep on a trip like we just made means you're obviously still not up to snuff. The weather is no good either."

"And cold," Myles confirmed, as he started to shiver.

With that, Rogan immediately sent Myles inside, while Rogan started to unload the boxes. The storm had picked up, and it was getting pretty crappy outside. Bringing the first load in, he called out for help and got two other men to give him a hand, getting the rest inside.

They moved everything to the room Myles was in, as he'd been given a room to himself. And now, with boxes stacked all around him, Myles sat wrapped up in a warm blanket, hugging a cup of coffee, grinning like a fool. He looked up when the last load came in and cried out, "Thank you, thank you so much."

Rogan laughed. "Don't know if you realize this, but most people aren't usually this happy to see paperwork," he muttered.

"Yeah, most people aren't," Myles agreed, "but I am, and I'm very grateful. You've saved our mission, not to mention our lives."

"Let's make sure we've saved the people," Rogan repeated. "No point in saving the data if we lose the team."

DAY 7, MORNING

THE NEXT MORNING, Lisa stopped by the medical clinic and asked Sydney, "Do you need me here in the clinic today?"

Sydney looked over and smiled at her. "No, we're just keeping an eye on Myles and Anna."

"How is she doing?"

"Not as well as Myles," she admitted. "She was doing better but has slid slightly. She's staying pretty close to the oxygen, but she's slowly recovering."

"Do we have an update on the rest of their team?"

"Yes, three of them are doing better, but one, ... not so much," she replied.

Lisa winced at that. "It's bad when the brain is starved of oxygen."

"Let's not go there," Sydney muttered. "That's the last thing we need to even think about."

"And yet how do we not?" Lisa asked in frustration.

"It's hard. I know. There will be an investigation, and that won't be easy either. I don't know whether it would be run by us, their own team, or by another party," she stated, "but obviously somebody has to figure out exactly what happened."

"I thought the generator malfunction at the scientists' camp was just a bad accident, wasn't it?" Lisa stared at

Sydney in sudden horror. "Please tell me nothing suggests otherwise."

"We don't know anything yet," Sydney noted immediately. "I'm not quite so quick to accept things."

"No, of course not," Lisa agreed, "but I think in this case it was just stupid human error, plus failed equipment."

"We've seen plenty of both of those. Anyway, if you want to go do some training, off you go."

"The teams have already been set up. I'm a floating member these days," she admitted. "I can go out with them, if they have room for me." She sighed. "I almost feel …" She stopped, faced Sydney, and shrugged. "I don't belong at either place, it seems. I don't quite fit here because you don't really need me, although they assigned me here." She looked around the empty clinic office. "And yet I don't fit with the teams now because I don't have an assigned group." Lisa raised her hands, palms up.

"Do you want me to step in and make sure that you are assigned to a particular group?"

"No, because, when you need me, I do want to be here for you."

"Got it." Sydney nodded. "We do have some inventory to do, which I know is never anybody's favorite, and it's a whole ten-minute job," she added, with a chuckle. "And I have some reports to write, but I need to handle those. Plus I'll be checking in on our two outpatients. Still, I can handle it all myself."

"Which I'm glad for," Lisa replied. "However, I feel out of it."

"I don't know what I can do about that, and I am sorry. I didn't intend to ruin your training session."

"Not your fault," Lisa said. "I just want to get out and

do something."

"Go talk to Magnus and see if he's got something you can do out there. Or Mountain or the colonel or the staff sergeant or somebody. Be proactive. And even if the teams have already been sorted out, that doesn't mean everybody showing up is feeling good. Maybe you can step in for one of them."

And, with that, Lisa nodded. "I'll go check." Then she quickly raced to talk to the staff sergeant, who was doing the schedule.

Chester looked up and stared at her intently. "I suppose you want to go out today too, don't you?" he asked in a grumpy voice.

She winced. "I want to go out as often as I can to get the training that I came for," she replied. "I understand that's a complication for you, and I'm sorry."

"No, it's all right because, when we need you in the medical clinic, we need you, but I can see that the rest of the time you're probably bored out of your mind."

"I am, and boredom doesn't sit well with me," she murmured. "I'd much rather be doing something."

"You and me both." He snorted. "Fine then, why don't you go help with the dog care today."

"Oh, now that would be fun. Thanks!" she cried out in delight.

"Maybe, but you know Joe is a bit of a stickler," Chester added, "so you do it his way or no way."

"That's fine with me." And, with that, she headed into the dining room for a quick breakfast, quite content with her assignment for the day. She would request more dog interactions.

Indeed, after she'd been working with the dogs for several hours, she looked over at Joe out of respect. "You really do have the best job in the place, don't you?"

He turned to her, smiled, and nodded. "Absolutely, and don't you forget it," he muttered. "These dogs are everything to me."

"And what about Benji and Toby? How are they doing now?" Lisa asked, looking over at the two sled dogs that had been shot. They were playing together—less energetic than usual, however.

"They're doing much better." Joe grinned at the two dogs. "However, I need to get their muscles strengthened, and that's a different story. When we're in a training session, the dogs are also in training. So it's hard when you have some that need special attention," he explained. "I'll be working on that today too."

"I could give you a hand," Lisa offered.

He looked at her, assessed her carefully, and then nodded. "Maybe, you seem to handle the dogs pretty well."

"I love dogs," she replied, "and I've done quite a bit of work with them. Mushing too, but more for fun than missions."

He nodded. "It's obvious, but you still need to do the training that they set out."

"Right, and that's the thing about here." She sighed. "I know I shouldn't complain, but it's frustrating to come into this session with some experience, but they don't care. They start everyone out as beginners."

"They don't care because that prior experience isn't the experience *they*'ve given you. It isn't the training *they*'ve given you," he reminded her. "The military—be it the army, navy, air force, marines—it doesn't matter what branch you're serving in, they have their own system, their own methodologies, their own rules, and their own very particular way of doing things. So, you can come in with all the experience you want, but, if it isn't their own, it doesn't make the cut. They'll look at your experience and give you a job because, at least, you'll have a passing familiarity, but they won't give you a free pass."

"No free passes in the military," she agreed, with another sigh.

"How are you doing on the winter training?"

"Unfortunately I get freezing cold every time I go out now," she admitted, with a wince, "so I seem to be a dead weight out there."

"You are to a certain extent, but that dead weight also has medical skills, and you never know when we'll need them. We've had way more medical emergencies this trip than I am at all happy with."

"I know, right? I was wondering if I'm paranoid."

"You're not. And now the latest at the scientists' camp? What a mess that is," he noted, with a headshake. "How are they doing now?" he asked, straightening up and looking at her curiously.

"Of the four who got airlifted out, three of them are apparently on the road to recovery, but one is not so good," she shared. "I don't know whether that'll be a permanent situation due to the lack of oxygen or …" Lisa let her words trail off.

Joe nodded.

Lisa continued. "And we still have two here, Myles and Anna. Myles is doing better. In fact he made a trip back to their camp with Rogan. Apparently he needed to get their research materials."

"Yeah, I heard the snowcat head out."

"Right. However, the rest of the team appears to be an issue."

He looked at her curiously. "What do you mean, the rest of the team?" She realized he hadn't heard about the other team members, so she filled him in on Dr. Amelia's situation, and her coworker, Dr. Robinson.

Joe stared at her, wide-eyed. "And they haven't checked in?"

"The problem is, their scheduled check-in time was when all this blew up over their generator, so nobody was able to receive the message, and now nobody is there at all. So the other two scientists may have returned, then left again."

"And Myles doesn't have any way to get a hold of them?"

"He says not, or maybe he's tried but hasn't had any luck, I guess." She stopped then, confused at that too. Then she shrugged. "I'm not sure on that. I know that Rogan is on it now at least."

"Isn't that all a little on the suspicious side?" Joe asked, with an odd expression. "If that was part of my team, I would be out there, making sure that they checked in on time every day."

"You and me both," she confirmed. "But apparently the last time he sent out a team looking for Amelia, she got quite pissy because she and her team had to come in, and that's not what she wanted."

He snorted. "Then she should have done more check-ins."

"Apparently in that previous case, she was checking in, but somebody else was of the opinion that she didn't know what she was doing." Lisa hesitated and then added, "Quite possibly because she's female."

Joe laughed at that. "Some of the best team members are females," he stated. "They have good instincts. And, as long as they haven't been too messed up with too much training, they're fine."

"What do you mean, when you say, *messed up with too much training?*" She stared at him in astonishment.

"Sometimes training overrides instincts," he stated, with a nod. "Training should increase instincts. Training should augment your instincts, honing them, not replacing them. All too often, people think that because they have training, they're good to go," he shared, "and it's not that way at all."

As it was, when Lisa went into the main building on base to get lunch later on, she saw Rogan off to the side, talking to the colonel and some others. She had questions for Rogan but decided it was probably not her place, particularly when he was in the middle of a discussion with the higher-ups. She sat down with a group and quickly ate her lunch.

When she stood to put away her plate and to head back out to the dogs, Rogan stopped her.

"Hey," he greeted her in a pleasant tone. "You're at Joe's today, aren't you?"

She smiled and nodded. "And believe me. I'm happy to be there. I absolutely love those dogs."

He nodded. "He's got a hell of a team out there."

She asked curiously, "Any word on Amelia and her coworker?"

He shook his head. "No, but we do have the coordinates for where she was heading. She is now two days overdue, so we're setting up a search party to go look for her."

"Oh, good." Then she stopped. "Dogs?"

"Joe has been given the word and, yes, dogs. We are setting up four parties, and we'll have the snowcat at the ready, in case."

"In case?"

"It still takes gas to run it, and we're low on supplies. If we go retrieve them, and the dogs can't handle pulling two people on the sleds, then it's a different story," Rogan explained in a hushed tone. "We'll take out the Cat then."

"Right," she murmured. "So, do you expect this to be a search and rescue operation, or is this a recovery op?"

"Search and rescue," he declared immediately. "It's way too early to assume it's a recovery. Apparently these two scientists are very experienced."

"That's good to hear," Lisa replied in relief. "We've had quite enough trouble around here, haven't we?"

"We have, but, at the same time, there will be a full investigation into what happened at the scientists' camp and here with our own generator," he shared in a low voice, "so be aware."

"Like right now?"

"Like right now," he confirmed. "The rest of the team members have given their side of the story, and some of it's not jiving." And, with that, Rogan was gone, leaving her staring behind him, open-mouthed.

THE SEARCH AND rescue teams set out a large grid map, with Rogan heading into the northern quadrant of that grid, with one other team member and six dogs.

As he headed out, Joe gave him a hard look.

Rogan understood and nodded. "I promise, Joe. I'll look after the dogs. You look after Toby and Benji." He flashed a grin. "Especially Benji."

"Yeah, you *will* take good care of my dogs," Joe declared, "and we all know the reason why. And don't you worry about Benji. He's fine here."

Rogan smiled at that. Even when injured, Benji was always willing to get out in the tundra but not yet recovered enough for this trip. Injured or not, Benji had quickly become Rogan's favorite. "If we run into trouble," Rogan admitted to Joe, "that will have everybody in trouble."

Joe nodded at that. "Get the two lost scientists back tonight. Time is running out for them."

"I know," Rogan agreed, "and we've got a bad storm coming in again."

Now Rogan was two hours into his route, and, so far, nothing had jumped out at him. He thought Magnus or Mountain may have gone back to the village to talk to the locals, but Rogan had no confirmation of that. With so many teams out, everybody was using it as a training run as well, which made sense. He wasn't against that, but, at the same time, they needed to find out what the hell was going on with this other team of scientists, still deemed missing— as were some of their own team members from the military base.

While the Shadow Recon team were here in a covert investigatory role, Ted was designated by the base CO and other higher-ups as the face of the investigation, the lead investigator handling this craziness at the training center and surrounding areas.

Yet Ted wouldn't speak to Rogan. Then Rogan didn't have the clearance that Mountain and maybe even Magnus had. Rogan wasn't sure. Up here no one ever really knew who was doing what. Rogan didn't appreciate being shut out, but, hey, welcome to being in the service. Things were frequently on a need-to-know basis, and, in this case, Ted obviously decided that Rogan didn't need to know.

As frustrating as that was, he also understood it. They didn't want any half-cocked suppositions or suspicions flying around, yet they needed something happening on the ground to publicly confirm an investigation was underway, plus some general announcements occasionally to all in the base to attempt to quell the rumor mill.

Besides, Rogan reported to Mason—and Mason only—when it came to what was going on here. Rogan had sent several updates, but clarity was thin on the ground, so answers were nonexistent. He was mostly concerned about Lisa and Sydney and anything around the clinic, but nothing weird had happened lately, except for Lisa's nighttime stalker.

When Rogan got back hours later—tired, frustrated, and cold—he saw Lisa in the dining room, having dinner. He walked over with a hot cup of coffee and sat down. When she winced, he groaned. "Don't tell me that I look *that* bad."

She nodded. "Rough day?"

"Rough trip, no answers, no nothing," he muttered. "It's as if the two missing scientists were never there. Never went out. Ghosts." She grimaced at that, and he nodded. "I know, sorry. I didn't mean to make it sound quite that bad."

"And yet it probably is that bad."

"I don't know." He lowered his voice and added, "Have you had any other trouble?"

She shook her head. "No, I sure haven't. Why?"

"I'm trying to figure out what's going on," he replied. "I don't want to lose sight of the fact that, regardless of the problems at the scientists' camp, we also have problems here that can't be ignored."

"I know," she agreed. "I'm not sleeping as well as I would otherwise, mostly out of exhaustion, but also from worry about what's happening here at the base and now at the scientists' camp, with their missing team. My heart's a little on the soft side for this job," she admitted, with half a smile.

"Absolutely. Anyway I may stop by later tonight and take a look."

"Take a look at what?" she asked.

He didn't say any more and got up and walked out, leaving her staring after him.

DAY 7, EARLY EVENING

LISA TRIED NOT to wait for Rogan to stop by, but, when he didn't, she decided to get up and take a look to make sure he was okay. She didn't have any reason for her worry, except that he'd looked so tired earlier that it tore at her heartstrings to see him that exhausted, that down. Maybe it was that sense of defeat, knowing that he hadn't found anybody out there and worried that, because of his failure, that team of scientists might die.

She couldn't even imagine what the missing team was going through. Experienced or not, they were trying to beat Mother Nature when she was at her most inhospitable. *Even some of our own survivalists didn't stand up to the test*, she thought.

When she got to Rogan's room, she turned to see if anybody was watching, then knocked on the door. When no answer came, she frowned, opened it, and stepped inside, but he wasn't here. She stepped out and looked around again, but she saw no sign of him. Quickly walking to the dining area, she popped into the kitchen, finding only Chef there, doing prep for the next day's meals. "Have you seen Rogan?" she asked.

He turned to her and nodded. "He's in a meeting with the colonel."

She winced. "Okay, that's probably not good."

"Can't be all bad though. Nothing around here is happening as it should be anyway."

Not sure what to make of that, she nodded and headed back to her quarters. She'd barely gotten settled in her room when a knock came at her door. She opened it to see Rogan standing there. "I was at your place, then in the dining area," she said. "Chef told me that you were in a meeting."

He nodded, his face grim. "Yeah, I was in a meeting all right." She looked at him, opened her mouth and he shook his head. "Don't ask. I can't tell."

Her jaw snapped shut, and she nodded. "That's the difficult part of being here."

"Very true," he agreed. "Anyway, I need to crash. We're heading back out early in the morning."

"Did you get more intel?"

"Nope, more questions." With that, he pulled her into a rough hug and held her. She wasn't sure if the hug was for him or for her, but she welcomed it regardless and held him in her arms. When he stepped back, he smiled. "Thank you for that." And then he was gone.

What the hell should she make of that?

She would have brought him inside and spent some quality time with him, but he obviously was in a very different space. Worried, she tossed and turned throughout the night, but it was hard to get any decent sleep.

DAY 8, MIDMORNING

WHEN LISA GOT up the next morning, it was already later than her usual time to rise. Knowing she was staying inside—and grateful for it today—she headed to the dining area, while she noticed Chef staring at her. "I know. I'm late," she muttered.

He shrugged. "Late doesn't matter so much, but the place has been agog with news, and you look as if you're completely complacent about it," Chef noted. "And you're the only unnerved one who I've seen so far."

"What news?" She stared at him, wondering what she'd missed. "This place is a shit show already. What else has happened now?"

Chef laughed. "It has been a shit show, but now it's about Myles."

"What about Myles?"

"It seems he's gone missing."

"Missing?" she cried out. "How did he go missing?"

"I don't know, but apparently a full-scale search is underway. I'm surprised you aren't a part of it."

"Part of it? I didn't even know about it." She swore under her breath. "I had a restless night, woke up late and came for coffee. This is horrible."

"Anything in particular keep you up during the night?"

She winced and nodded. "Yeah, footsteps walking up

and down the hall and stopping outside my door. Not the first time either. It's had me on edge for a while." Chef stared at her in shock; she nodded. "It's happened several times since I've been here, so, yeah, it's unnerving. Now I realize it really is an issue."

"Ya think?" Chef took a cautious look around. "Did you tell anybody?"

"I did. I told Rogan, and Sydney knows, and by extension that includes Magnus. So the colonel has also been informed."

Chef lowered his voice. "Do we need to be worried about this?"

"I don't know," she muttered. "I hope not, but I can't see what anybody standing outside my room does for anyone."

"No, but you need to be careful. Way too much shit is going on around here."

"I know," she agreed, "but still, it's nothing serious. It's not as if they're knocking. Or trying to get in. Still, it's … unnerving."

"Right. Sounds as if they're stalking."

She paled, feeling all that fear from the night crowding back inside her again. She wrapped her arms around her chest. "You're right about that and also how I wasn't contacted to help with the search. Do you know anything about it so far?"

"No, I sure don't. They've already been through my kitchen area. As if I've got people hidden in there." He snorted.

"Yeah, maybe in your freezers."

"The freezer is in the great white north outside," he stated, "so, if they're hiding there, they could be anywhere."

And, with that, Chef went back to his food prep.

She took her coffee and headed over to a table and huddled there, while she sipped the hot brew. However, her mind was still caught up in Chef's words about her stalker from the previous nights.

She hadn't considered it as stalking before. She thought maybe somebody was... what? She didn't know. Maybe pacing the hallway to get a text message through? Maybe better reception was there? She just didn't know. But it was the first time someone had put a word to it, and it wasn't a word she appreciated. She got up and headed to the medical clinic with her second cup of coffee. As she stepped in, Sydney sat there, a worried look on her face. Lisa walked over and sat down in front of the doc. "What the hell is going on?"

"I don't know," Sydney admitted. "I didn't see Myles this morning at all, and apparently some equipment is missing."

"And dogs?"

"No, not that we know of."

"The snowcat?"

She looked over at her nurse and frowned. "Maybe. I don't know."

"Oh, Jesus. Why would he take it? It's not as if he could hide his tracks."

"I know, right? Nobody is quite sure what's going on here, but one suggestion made was that he might have been responsible for the accident at the center."

"Responsible or to blame, as in, did he do something deliberately?"

Sydney shrugged. "I won't make any judgments because I really don't understand what's going on. All I can say is that Myles is now part of that main investigation into the scientists' camp."

"Jesus. Can you imagine someone trying to kill off your entire team?"

"And yet he didn't, did he?" she asked. "He didn't kill anybody."

"Sure, but one of the team members may very well be better off dead," Lisa replied, "and I know that sounds harsh."

"I know what you mean though." Sydney gave a wave of her hand. "I doubt the family feels that way, but, at the same time, he may not recover."

Lisa let out her breath. "That's awful," she murmured. "Now they're looking for somebody to blame, I presume."

At that, Sydney gave her a crooked smile. "People always feel better when they have somebody to blame," she declared. "It doesn't matter if it's the right person or not, ... as long as they have a target."

"That sucks," Lisa stated. "Do you think Myles took off because of that? Afraid of repercussions?"

"I don't know. I don't understand any of this." Sydney leaned forward and asked, "Are you okay? You look a little off."

"I had a rough night," Lisa shared. "And then, when I was talking to Chef, he put a word to it that I hadn't really thought about before."

Sydney shook her head in confusion. "Wait. You want to back up and this time add a few more details?"

Lisa explained what had happened several times now with footsteps outside her door, stopping there and waiting.

Doc's eyebrows shot up at that. "So, you mentioned it the one time, but, after that, I assumed it had stopped. You never told me anything more."

"I just reported it that one time. I didn't say anything about the other times."

"How many times has it happened?"

She winced. "Pretty much every night."

"Jesus, Lisa," Sydney exclaimed. "With all the problems we've got going on, you didn't let anybody know?"

"*Because* of all the problems going on, it's hardly a priority."

"Until we find your dead body one day," Sydney snapped, her voice harsh. She turned and looked around, snatched a pad of paper and tossed it at her. "Write down everything that's happened and don't you dare leave out a single detail."

"But it's footsteps," Lisa protested, surprised at Sydney's reaction.

"Good, I'm glad it's *just* footsteps up to now." The doc motioning at the pad of paper and the pen. "Let's make sure it stays that way. I don't want to hear any argument. Do it."

Lisa stared at Sydney for a long moment, then asked, "You really think it's a problem?"

"Yes, I *really* think it's a problem. We can't afford to mistake it for something benign." Sydney shook her head. "I don't know what you were thinking, trying to keep this hidden."

"I wasn't trying to hide anything," Lisa said. "I was focused on all the other problems going on around here. It's all been a hell of a distraction."

At that, Sydney turned and stared. "I wonder how much of it is exactly that."

"What do you mean?"

"What if all this *is* a distraction, trying to keep us from seeing the real reason everything is under fire."

Shocked, Lisa studied Sydney and shrugged. "But what possible reason could there be for footsteps at my door too many nights in a row?"

"I don't know, but we damn well better find out."

ROGAN CLOSED HIS eyes briefly against the biting snow and wind, as he raced across the tundra. There had been a weather warning about the snow moving in and an ugly front coming in after that. The trouble was, he didn't even know how many people he was looking for. When things got wild, they really got wild, as far as everyone was concerned. Myles was now credited as responsible for the carbon monoxide poisoning at the scientists' camp and potentially for the other team not making it back.

Yet Rogan hadn't seen any proof of these matters. It was hard to reconcile that theory with the man he'd met. However, knowing that he'd disappeared, Myles looked guilty now, and everybody was questioning everything.

Rogan called out to his dog team as they raced behind the tracks of the snowcat left in the snow. Rogan had shown Myles how to run the damn machine. It wouldn't have been a hard thing for him to figure it out on his own, so Rogan shouldn't feel guilty about that.

At the same time, something really fishy was going on, and Rogan didn't want any part of it landing on his plate. He followed the tracks to the scientists' camp, only to find the tracks carried on to the north.

First priority was to find Myles and to get back that damn snowcat. That one piece of equipment was worth millions, but, for the people here, it was directly related to safety, and that pissed off Rogan more than anything.

When he caught sight of the snowcat up ahead of him, he sighed with relief. Even the dogs, seeing their quarry ahead, seemed to pick up their pace, as if understanding what the problem was. When they got to the machine, they milled around. Rogan checked out the equipment, and, of course, it was out of fuel. Fuel was a priceless commodity here. Even as he checked out the tracks, he located a single set of footprints heading off, so Myles was on this trek alone and on foot.

With that, Rogan returned to the dogs and the sled and tracked Myles's prints. Rogan followed Myles's tracks right until they met up with other tracks. He frowned at that, wondering what was happening, and realized that Myles had met up with another dog team. Now this was getting even more suspicious.

Moving carefully and trying to read the signs as he went, Rogan followed the unknown team out into the wilderness, farther and farther away from this camp and the military base. Where the hell were they going? Rogan came over a rise to see a local hunting party. Up ahead, smoke rose from small dwellings—half were tents, and half were holes dug into the snow, with a few people milling around.

Rogan slowed and approached. As soon as he arrived, several of the local hunters came out and stared at him. He asked about the tracks and the man who had come in with them. It took a bit to understand what had happened, but apparently one of their hunting teams had gone out and had found Myles walking. They had brought him back to this campsite, and even now Myles was in one of the enclaves, recovering, but he wasn't doing very well.

The hunters invited Rogan in.

Inside he found Myles curled up in a ball, wrapped up in furs, near a small smoking fire. Rogan bent beside him and checked for a pulse. When Myles opened his eyes, Rogan glared at him. "What the hell was that for, some kind of a stunt?"

Startled, Myles cried out, then calmed down as he recognized Rogan. "Had to get away."

"Had to get away? But why?" Rogan asked, relieved to find him—and alive—but frustrated over the chase. "Why did you really think you had to get away? And why on earth did you take the snowcat?"

He blinked at him. "Only way to get out, had to get out." He kept repeating that over and over again, to the point that Rogan wasn't even sure what was going on. He looked around at the others, but nobody seemed to have any idea what the problem was, or, if they did, they lacked the ability to communicate it.

Groaning, Rogan checked his watch and realized he, Myles, and Rogan's dogsled team would be damn late getting back. If he could even get them back before the major storm hit. He assessed his options and then realized he pretty-well needed to stay and deal with the circumstances here right now and try to get Myles back in the morning.

He sent out several text messages, saying Myles had been found, but it was late, and Rogan wouldn't get him back anytime soon. Plus they would need to send fuel in this direction to drive the snowcat back to base. When confirmation of that had been received, Rogan turned to his host and asked, with as guttural a language as he could, if he could stay for the night.

He was immediately acknowledged with a bright yes,

and, if anything, they all seemed to be excited to have company. Rogan could understand that, yet the circumstances sucked. But, with bright smiles and cheerful goodwill, the local hunters quickly gave him several fur robes, food, and then they all proceeded to curl up and crash. Rogan unleashed the dogs, checked that they were okay, brought them inside, but all preferred to stay outside.

As he checked his watch again, he realized how late it was. Rogan needed sleep tonight because tomorrow would be even longer. But it was hard to sleep because he kept fearing that Myles would run off. Even though he wasn't in great shape, he still seemed to be struggling to get up and leave.

As it was, Rogan caught Myles getting up several times in the night, but each time he was disoriented and incoherent, muttering how he had to leave. Worried now that something other than what Rogan expected was going on, he sent several more text messages. By the crack of dawn, he heard the sound of the snowcat coming toward him.

He stumbled out of the hunters' dwelling and turned in the direction of the sound and used a flare to help them locate his position. They came over the crest and saw him, and he waved. The dogs barked happily, milling around him. Something about seeing that snowcat—powerful, strong, with a bright light—moving its way toward him, made Rogan breathe a sigh of relief.

Rogan immediately ducked back in to check on Myles, who was muttering feverishly in the tent. When the Cat arrived, he was happy to see Magnus at the helm, with two dogsled teams behind him, bringing up the rear.

Several of his hunting group came out to greet the new arrivals. When Magnus hopped out, Rogan explained, "They found Myles walking alone, after he ran out of gas."

Magnus nodded grimly. "What shape is he in?"

"Not very good. He's incoherent, babbling, and running a fever."

He nodded. "Okay, let's get him back to the doc."

With many thanks to Rogan's new friends, Magnus left the hunters something which Rogan didn't see. He then hopped up into the snowcat with Myles and Magnus, his dogs and sled redistributed to the other two teams. "What did you leave them?" Rogan asked Magnus.

Magnus laughed. "The little bit I had with me and the promise of future gifts, as my thanks for treating our friends as well as they had. They are simple folks, and they live a simple life. I've met many like them, and they live a truly comfortable life out here."

"How can it be comfortable?"

"Because they live a peaceable existence. They don't try to change their environment. They live with it," he stated. "And there is a certain lifestyle to this that they all embrace."

Rogan wondered at that, having never had that exposure, but he could imagine spending some time out here under different circumstances, and he could definitely appreciate the beauty. "They were extremely welcoming," he acknowledged. "I admit I was damn happy to see Myles."

"Of course. They know all too well that being in trouble out here is a death sentence. It's not their way to turn their backs on someone needing help," Magnus stated.

DAY 9, MORNING

LISA AND SYDNEY waited in the clinic for the men's return. When they finally got Myles onto a hospital bed, Sydney went to work, while Lisa asked Rogan, "Any idea why he left?"

"Something about being in danger." She stared at him in shock. He nodded. "More to this crazy mystery," he muttered. "I'll go grab a change of clothes and get some hot coffee."

"And food," Sydney called out. "Get something to eat." Then she looked over at Lisa. "Do you want to go with him?"

"No, I'm fine. I'll stay here and give you a hand."

Lisa studied Myles, as they quickly worked on him. Once he was settled, warm, hooked up to oxygen again, the two ladies stepped away for a private conversation about their patient.

"What would make somebody take off like that?" Lisa asked the doc.

"What if he thought he would get shanghaied into being blamed for something he didn't do? He's not in the military, so maybe he doesn't understand how it works. What if one of the guys had a little fun at his expense, telling him what would happen to him or something? Maybe that was all he needed to get spooked."

Lisa stared at her boss and shook her head. "I understand fun and games, but then there's straight-up suicidal talk," she muttered, "and, for somebody like Myles, that would have been deadly."

"Not only deadly, he wouldn't have understood any of it. Everybody wants to think there's justice, until people tell you that you'll never get it."

"Right," Lisa murmured.

They stayed there for the rest of the day and far into the night, watching over Myles, who alternated between delirium, then a few minutes of coherence, then out again. When at last he fell into a deep sleep, Sydney sat back with a frown. "His vitals are too low, and, although he keeps waking up, it's almost as if …" She shrugged. "It seems he's been drugged."

At that, Lisa's heart clenched, and she stared at her boss. "Please don't say that."

Sydney turned toward her. "Why?"

"I was thinking that it was still some side effects from the carbon monoxide poisoning and that we should have gotten him out at the same time as the others."

"Maybe." Sydney looked him over. "But he was the better of the group, and he seemed fine. He'd been back to their camp on his own, with no ill effects."

"Which is why I don't understand what's going on, unless something at the scientists' camp continues to poison everybody?"

"And yet Rogan is fine."

Sydney stared at her nurse and asked, "Is he?"

Lisa frowned, and then something clicked. "On that note"—she pivoted, already racing to the kitchen—"I'll go talk to him."

ROGAN DEBRIEFED THE colonel, while huddled over a cup of coffee in a secluded corner of the kitchen.

"Do you have any concerns that anything at that scientists' camp is still dangerous?" the colonel asked him.

Rogan shook his head. "I don't, but it's possible. I don't have any way to explain Myles's behavior, unless it's delirium or paranoia and who knows what else. We didn't check his belongings, so maybe he brought recreational drugs with him."

At that, the colonel's face thinned, and he nodded slowly. "That's a consideration too, isn't it? You can search his room when we're done here."

Rogan nodded. "I also know that some of the guys were insinuating that Myles had something to do with the poisoning. People were bugging him for sport, about how he would pay the price and be dealt with here instead of in a court of law."

"Of course." The colonel shook his head. "They've got nothing better to do than to hassle somebody, right?"

"In this situation, it certainly appears to be that way."

When Lisa walked into the dining room, the colonel frowned and nodded toward her. "Your girlfriend is here, probably checking up on you."

He turned and saw Lisa standing there. "Am I done, sir?"

"For the moment, yes. I still want it all in writing."

"Of course."

He got up and walked closer to Lisa. As soon as she saw him moving in her direction, her face lit up, flushing in response. "Hey. We're a little worried that you may have some ongoing symptoms from exposure to something in the scientists' camp."

Rogan shrugged. "I feel fine. That's what the colonel was asking me about as well."

"I'm glad to hear that, but it's not quite the same as getting checked over."

He smiled. "Are you telling me that you want to play doctor?"

She flushed again and rolled her eyes. "As if I haven't heard that a million times."

"I'm sure you have." He chuckled. "Sorry, I couldn't resist."

"Whatever," she muttered. "I know that Sydney wants to confirm you're okay, and, to do that, we need you to come to the clinic for some tests."

He winced at that. "Really not my favorite thing."

"No, I'm sure it isn't," she agreed. "It's nobody's favorite. On the other hand, we don't want to take any chances that we've missed something."

"She can only do so much though, right?"

"Yes, but more help is available by phone, if she needs it."

He nodded. "*Great*, let's go do your tests, but honestly I feel fine."

"And that's good. Yet I don't understand what's going on with Myles," she muttered, as they walked out to the hallway. "And neither does Sydney."

"I'll search his room."

"Why?" she asked, looking at him wide-eyed.

"What are the chances he has some recreational drugs with him?"

"Oh." Lisa frowned. "I'm not sure Sydney thought

about that, considering this is a 100-percent drug-free camp." Rogan laughed at that, and she nodded. "Right, nothing is 100 percent, not when you have people involved."

"No, it sure isn't." He smiled. "You do what you can and hope that you don't get caught. And if you do get caught, it could get you busted out of here pretty-damn fast, but we all know that it happens." After he walked into the clinic, he told Sydney the same thing.

She nodded, then gave him a one-arm shrug. "I wondered that myself, but I don't have any visible proof that Myles has had any drugs. I've pulled his blood, but it'll deteriorate if I can't get it tested fast enough. And, before you ask, no I didn't come equipped with testing for drugs." She then checked Rogan's eyes, his mouth, took his temperature, his blood pressure reading, and his pulse rate. "All seems fine with you, Rogan. However, if you get any delayed symptoms, be sure to come see me ASAP."

Rogan nodded. "You would think that drug testing would be mandated here."

"Sure, live drug testing, urine testing," she replied, "but, in Myles's case, too many hours have gone by."

"Right," Rogan noted. "Sorry, I should have thought of that sooner."

She shrugged. "Only so much I can do in this facility."

"You've mentioned that a couple times, as if you're frustrated that you don't have more available to you."

She laughed. "Show me any medical professional who doesn't want to have more available," she stated, with a head shake. "With this, it can be fatal. What we also considered is if somebody else gave him the drugs."

In a low voice, Rogan whispered, "What about the drugs that went missing from here? That wasn't something he could have been given, was it?"

"*Hmm.* We never did recover those drugs, but, unless Myles had some bad reaction to it, I wouldn't have thought so." Rogan turned and looked over at the unconscious man. She frowned, as she pondered it. "Sorry," Rogan said. "I'm really not trying to cause trouble."

She snorted. "Rogan, I think some of you guys live for trouble."

He grinned. "I'll go do a full search of his room."

"Good, let me know what you find," she said absentmindedly. "Anything right now, any tidbit of information, could be helpful."

And, with that, he walked out of the clinic and headed to the room that Myles had been given. The doc was right; anything would be helpful. One little bit of information could make a massive difference as to whether Myles lived or died, and right now he looked damn close to dying.

As Rogan opened the door, he stopped because it was still completely full of all the research boxes they'd moved in from the scientists' camp. Boxes that Myles had been almost giddy to have. For the first time, Rogan wondered if Myles had legal rights to these boxes. Yet, if everything at the camp could be destroyed by weather, vandals, animals, whatever, before somebody arrived to properly safeguard these documents, it did make sense to preserve them.

Rogan hoped Myles would wake up enough that he could be questioned because nothing made a whole lot of sense at this point.

Whatever Myles had brought with him for his escape would most likely be in his personal gear, but his bag was gone. Maybe Myles had taken it with him, and yet Rogan hadn't found any sign of it at the hunters' campsite. But then again, Rogan hadn't asked. He frowned at that because, if something dangerous was in Myles's bag, Rogan didn't want anybody in the local hunting party to be harmed by trying it. He finished searching Myles's room, then went to find Magnus. When he quickly explained the problem, Magnus nodded.

"I've got his bag."

"You do?"

"Yeah, I picked it up. Let me go grab it." He headed back out to the snowcat, and there it was.

Relieved, Rogan sighed. "I was afraid something might be in here that somebody from the hunters' camp might have gotten into. We don't know exactly what Myles has been up to and why he's so sick."

"Good call," Magnus noted. "While you were loading him, the locals gave me the bag."

"I'm grateful for that." Together, the two of them opened it up and went through everything, item by item. Rogan found a USB key, which he palmed. "I wonder how much of this is his research? It also occurred to me how much of that research he's entitled to," Rogan mentioned, looking up at Magnus.

Magnus caught his drift immediately, and he frowned. "That is a little disconcerting."

"Yeah, my thoughts too, though I hate to even think of that, particularly when the man can't defend himself."

"No, but his actions are extremely suspicious," Magnus noted.

Looking at the USB key and realizing nothing else was suspicious in Myles's bag, Rogan asked, "Will we get in trouble if we open this thumb drive?"

"Doesn't matter whether we do or not," Magnus stated.

Then above them, a shadow loomed. "Fine, but you share." Mountain gave them half a smile. "Anything that's wrong up here," he declared, "I will be very involved with." His tone was incredibly gentle, but nobody had any doubt of the meaning behind his words.

Together they walked to a private room, where Mountain worked alone. He came and went like a ghost.

"Anybody comment on your presence here?" Rogan asked lightly. "Or your lack of presence?"

"Not more than once. I go out and do training, and I keep to myself. I think they consider me the secret brass."

"That's pretty funny," Rogan noted, with a chuckle.

Mountain shrugged. "They can think whatever the hell they want. I really don't give a shit." And that, of course, was pure Mountain.

Mountain inserted the USB key into his laptop. They brought up the disk drive, opened it up, and confirmed that it was definitely research. As the names scrolled by, on all the papers and all the data, Mountain tapped a portion and stated, "Look at this. It's not his data."

"And yet we can't really hold that against him, considering that he's the only one here to save everything. This is a backup, and there should be a cloud storage backup as well," Rogan reminded them.

"Yes, but it also depends on whether he's left it available for anybody else to access."

Pondering that, Mountain looked off in the distance. "Time to have a conversation with some of the other survivors, who were airlifted out."

"Good idea," Magnus agreed.

The three walked to the communication center. Rogan asked, "What is it you're thinking?"

"I'm thinking about good old greed. I'm thinking somebody had done the research, and maybe Myles wanted it published under his name."

"Or the flip side of that," Rogan suggested immediately. "Myles may have found something that he doesn't want published, and he's trying to destroy it."

Mountain looked at him and nodded slowly. "And it could be that as well. But we need to talk to the other scientists to find out whose research this is. Not to mention the fact that we still haven't found the other two-man team of scientists."

"No, we haven't," Magnus agreed grimly. "And I really want to know more about that scenario."

"Nothing seemed suspicious anytime I was there at their camp," Rogan noted.

"Nor while I was there," Magnus piped up. "So, I'm not sure what the hell is going on."

"No, and because we don't know, it's important that we find out. I'll get back to you guys." And, with that, Mountain disappeared.

Rogan looked over at Magnus. "He comes and goes, doesn't he?"

"Yeah, that's Mountain for you. He's big, but that guy can move. He can also stay quiet and live in the shadows, like nobody I've ever seen."

"Do you know anything about why he's here and what it's all about?"

Magnus stared at Rogan for a moment. "I guess you're on a need-to-know basis, aren't you?"

Rogan nodded. "Yes, but sometimes there's a need to know a little more than you've been given, so you can stay alive."

Magnus pondered that and nodded. "Let's say that one of the missing men is somebody very close to him."

"Ah, shit." Rogan shook his head. "He's here trying to figure out what happened to him?"

"Yeah, he sure is. Let's hope he figures it out before anybody else dies."

"And are we taking on the missing team of scientists as part of our nightmare too? That would double our work almost overnight."

"Not if we find the missing team soon," Magnus noted. "I still have faith."

"I'm glad you do," Rogan replied. "At this point in time I'm running a little low."

"Don't give up," Magnus ordered. "We've seen all kinds of feats of people who have survived, and Amelia's got a lot of experience. I've talked to several people about her, and, according to them, … if anybody can pull this off, it's her. Don't forget. We don't even know that they're really missing. Just because she didn't check in or her check-in didn't get logged doesn't mean she is in trouble."

"I hope not," Rogan said. "I really hate to think somebody else is out there lost because of this mess."

"You and me both. Now why don't you go back and keep an eye on Myles and Lisa. Whoever is stopping outside Lisa's room at night is a concern."

"What's a bigger concern is that it's happened several times, and it makes my stomach clench to think of it," Rogan shared, his voice low. "I can't believe she didn't say anything more to anybody."

Magnus eyed Rogan. "I'm really not a fan of short-term relationships at bases like this, but being close to Sydney has helped me watch out for her better. So you might want to consider moving forward with your relationship with Lisa."

"I keep thinking about it," he muttered. "I had hoped we could have some time under normal circumstances to take it to the next level, where I can approach her."

"Don't wait," Magnus stated. "I've got to tell you. When things go to shit, … they go to shit fast. So don't wait for that to happen. Get your relationship started now, and then, whatever comes, you'll be in a position to save her."

"Or"—Rogan gave a laugh—"she'll be in a position to save me."

At that, Magnus gave him a wide grin and nodded. "Exactly."

DAY 9, LATE EVENING

LISA WAS READY for bed and tucked under the covers, feeling the chill in a way she hadn't expected. Yet she knew it had absolutely nothing to do with the temperature but everything to do with the strange happenings here. When a knock came at her door, she was startled. She hopped out of bed and leaned closer, then heard footsteps walking away. Waiting a little bit, she opened the door, trying to see who had been here. If it had been Sydney, Magnus, or Rogan, they would have identified themselves. At least she hoped so.

She couldn't see any sign of anybody. They had escaped, abruptly but smoothly, though it could have been that they went in another bedroom door down this same hallway. She'd been making so much noise herself that she wouldn't have heard. Frowning at that, she turned to go back into her room, only to see Rogan walking down from the other end.

He frowned at her. "Problems?"

She shrugged. "Somebody knocked on my door, but, when I opened it, nobody was here."

"I was coming to talk to you about that."

She motioned him inside. "Come on in." Once they were inside, and the door was closed, she asked, "So, what is it you wanted to talk about?"

"Combining our rooms." She stared at him and flushed,

which made him grin. "As much as that would be fun," he acknowledged, with a smirk, "I'm thinking of it more in terms of your safety."

She winced. "*Great.* You sure know how to make a girl feel sexy." He stared at her with raised eyebrows, as she shrugged, feeling embarrassed. "Don't mind me. That slipped out."

"Maybe so, but, honest to God, I'm looking at the sexiest woman in this place."

At that, she burst out laughing. "Nice try."

He shook his head. "No, I mean it—at least for me."

"Ah, well, that's a qualifier."

"Yeah, but that's the one that counts," he argued in a smooth tone. "Regardless, the purpose of this visit was because of your constant nighttime visitor. Have you turned anybody down since you've been here? Rejected any advances?"

"No. I haven't even been asked." She gave a mock shudder. "Really appreciate your making me realize that."

"Does that bother you?"

"No, God no," she stated. "It's exactly the way it should be."

"What do you think a knock on your door at nighttime is about?" he asked.

She winced. "I guess in your book, it's probably not an ask, is it?"

"It would certainly make me curious," Rogan replied. "I'm not sure of the who, what, and why of it all, but I would feel better if somebody wasn't coming to your door all night long."

"Me too, particularly the ones who don't say anything."

"Do you think it's the same person?"

"I don't know who was here," she admitted, "and, if I would have opened the door faster, I would have found out. However, I deliberately didn't because I honestly didn't really want to talk to anybody. It could even have been Sydney. I don't know."

"Do you want to go find out?"

She hesitated, then nodded. "I'd feel better, yes." She got up, threw on a sweatshirt, and, with him at her side, padded down to the medical clinic.

Sydney was still in there, and she looked up. "You two together at this time of evening? Is there a problem?"

"You didn't happen to come to my door a few minutes ago, did you?" Lisa asked the doc.

Sydney shook her head. "No, I sure didn't. I've been here, finishing off these reports and keeping an eye on our friend here."

At that, Rogan walked over. "How is he doing?"

"Not the best," Sydney noted. "I feel as if I'm losing him. Whatever he took or was given seems to be taking over his system."

"I guess we can't get any more help for him, can we?" Rogan asked.

"It would be nice, but, with the storm outside, flights can't get in or out. Plus the naval ship that was here earlier has moved away with our other injured personnel," she pointed out.

"Right," Rogan said. "Damn."

Sydney nodded. "You guys should go get some sleep." She looked at Rogan with a curious gaze. "Are you staying with her tonight?"

He nodded. "That's the plan."

"Good," Sydney stated, her tone sharp. "I don't want

any more trouble here when I wake up in the morning."

"Yeah, you and me both," Rogan confirmed. And, with that, they turned and left Sydney in her office.

As they walked away, Lisa asked in a low voice, "Do you think she's safe in there?"

He nodded. "I do. Magnus will be along soon."

"Right," Lisa murmured. "A pretty pair, those two." Then she thought about it. "What about any other women here?"

"There are two others, and, last I knew, they have Anna bunking in there too, so they are all together," Rogan shared, "and they've been warned."

"Right, not exactly what we thought we had to watch out for or worry about."

"No, but it's a given in any situation, isn't it?"

"Yes," she admitted, "to some degree, it absolutely is. Unfortunately, with all this going on, extra caution is definitely called for." And, with that, they headed into her room. She looked at the bed and frowned.

"I can sleep on the floor if you want," Rogan offered in a jiff.

"God no, Rogan. You'll be frozen in the morning, and I'll have a hell of a time waking you up."

"Not at all. There are ways to wake people up."

She rolled her eyes at the sexual innuendo and added, "If you came here for that—"

"Nope, I sure didn't." He raised his hands. "Not that I'm against it, so you know, but that's not why I'm here. Something rotten is going on here, and you've got a stalker."

"I wish I knew what that was all about." She stared at her door. "It's creepy and weird. Yet, at the same time, it doesn't really make any sense."

"There must be a reason for it," Rogan said, "and it could be as simple as somebody hoping to get lucky."

"He's not getting lucky in my bed," she snapped, as she again looked it over. "It's awfully small."

He nodded. "It is, and that's why I suggested that I sleep on the floor."

"Yet that won't be very warm, so we'll make the best of it. You get the edge though."

He burst out laughing and asked, "Why is that?"

"If you end up being a gentleman, you'll stay close to the edge and give me space."

"I'll try," he promised.

And, with that, she gave him a quick hug. "In that case, let's grab some shut-eye. I don't know what tomorrow will bring, but, chances are, it won't be anything good."

At her comment, he frowned, then nodded. "Let's hope that we find some answers and damn fast."

"We're finding bits and pieces but not any real answers."

"I know, and the moment we get a little more in the way of intel, we get more questions."

"Right. It's not just me thinking that, *huh*?"

"No." He smiled. "Not just you."

"I wish to God that this would all go away, but it's not likely to anytime soon"—she sighed—"at least not while we're here."

"It'll go away," he declared calmly, "after we get out of this nightmare and find out what the hell is going on with the scientists' camp and our base."

"Yeah, that camp event," Lisa noted, "I was talking to Sydney about it earlier. We wondered if it was a diversion."

He looked at her with a surprised expression, considering it thoughtfully. "That's an interesting take on it."

"Since everything else around here has been completely sidelined because of that scenario, then somebody succeeded in getting our focus elsewhere."

He nodded. "Not a bad theory."

"You can look at it however you want, but I'm not looking at anything until morning." With that, she yawned.

And he tucked her up close. "Go to sleep."

She laughed. "I really didn't expect this."

"What?" he asked in a sleepy voice.

"You being here tonight."

"You should have," he said, with a smirk, as he pulled her closer. "It's not the first time I've made the offer."

"I know, but even allowing you here says something."

"Yeah? But so does asking," he murmured. "So don't worry about it. Get some rest and relax."

She fell asleep fairly quickly, yet woke several times in the night, startled to find arms wrapped around her. Once she realized who it was, she smiled, and went back to sleep again.

DAY 10, MORNING

LISA WOKE THE next morning feeling rested, even if her bed was completely empty. And maybe it was better that way, since she'd always had a preference for early morning lovemaking. And he made her want things, permanent things she'd never considered before. But that was not necessarily something they should indulge in while they were here. Yet it would be hard. Feeling way better than expected, she got up, dressed warmly, and headed to the medical clinic.

As she got there, she heard voices on the inside. She rapped on the door and then pushed it open, not giving anybody a chance to answer. As she stepped inside, somber expressions worn by all. "Oh no."

Sydney nodded. "Yes, Myles didn't make it through the night."

"Jesus," Lisa murmured, as she sagged back. "Do we know why?"

"No, we don't. I'm putting his body in the cooler right now, until we can get him airlifted out. In the meantime, nobody has any idea what happened or why, and now there will be an even bigger investigation," she added, "which is not on us."

"So, his death is not our responsibility?" Lisa asked.

"No," Sydney stated, with a pointed look at the others. "Though it did happen on our base and under our watch."

"So, of course, you feel responsible," Magnus noted.

Sydney shrugged. "How can I not? I don't have a clue what he may have been taking or was given, but I can tell you that his behavior wasn't normal. I don't know that he was fully responsible for any of his actions, including leaving our base. All I know for sure is that, as a result of his escape, he has now passed away."

"Will you put that down as cause of death?"

She shrugged. "That will be for the Medical Examiner to determine cause of death. It could very well all have stemmed from the same thing." She shrugged and turned. "He wasn't responding as well as I would have liked to the oxygen, and he kept refusing to take it, which is also a symptom of lack of oxygen."

"I've seen that happen, but this was over a longer time period," Magnus noted.

"And that's why I'm stumped," Sydney admitted. "It shouldn't be something that happened the way it did, but I don't have any way to test for drugs. They'll do a complete analysis later."

"That's good," Magnus noted, "and what about Anna?"

"I haven't told her yet. She's been huddled in her bed and not feeling great. She's probably wishing she'd gotten moved out with the others, but she was one of the healthier ones at the time." Then came a knock on the clinic door, and Anna stepped in.

"I had a horrible vision that Myles died overnight," she cried out, visibly shivering. "Please tell me that I'm wrong." Then she saw Sydney's face and spun to look around the room, noting others were here. She turned back to face them all. "What happened?"

"Myles did pass away during the night." Sydney got up

and walked over. Lisa was immediately at her side, seeing the tears on Anna's face. "I'm so sorry," Sydney said, taking Anna's hand.

The other woman sniffled. "I don't know what happened to him. I feel as if it's all related to what happened to us at our research camp."

"And that's quite possible," Sydney replied. "Lack of oxygen can affect us in a lot of different ways."

Anna nodded, starting to sob.

Lisa looked over at Sydney and offered, "I'll take her back and get her settled." And, with that, she led Anna back to her room. Once there, Lisa got Anna quieted down and back to bed. "Can I bring you a coffee or something?"

Anna sobbed harder. "I want the others, the rest of my team."

Lisa nodded. "When Rogan took Myles back to your camp to collect the data, is anything there yours that you needed? Because we only got one thumb drive."

"Everything should have been backed up to the cloud," Anna replied, bewildered. "Why? What difference does it make?"

"Maybe nothing. We don't know if, on that second journey back to the camp, Myles might have picked up another dose of something."

Anna winced. "God, that doesn't even bear thinking about. He has two adult kids. His wife passed away quite a few years ago, but he was always the one with the most common sense," she noted.

"And was there any dissent in the group?"

That question wasn't Lisa's. She turned to see Rogan standing here, his voice gentle, as he questioned Anna.

"No, there wasn't. A few were upset about the generators, the crappy equipment, and all that stuff, but it goes along with grant work." Anna snorted. "Unless you happen to have a ton of support, there's never enough money to go around. But, no, we all got along well. You have to in these scenarios," she stated earnestly, looking up at them. "I don't know what happened, but I sure hope they do an overhaul on that equipment before anybody else comes back up here."

"I'm sure they'll have to," Rogan noted. "We wondered if the research might have had anything to do with the problem."

She shook her head. "No, though I want to take a look at that later, if I could," she murmured. "However, I was backing up everything of mine to the cloud storage—although our reception wasn't always very good. So we were all keeping backup keys." Then she stopped, frowned, and asked in an undertone, "Did you say he only brought one key?"

He nodded. "Yes, one key."

"Interesting." Anna then shrugged. "Until I see it, I won't have a clue."

"Maybe after breakfast, we can do that."

She sniffled several times and then asked, "How about doing it now? If I stay here, I'll bawl my eyes out, and that won't help anybody. Let's see if I can do something useful for a change." Enough bitterness filled her voice that Lisa and Rogan frowned at her.

Anna shrugged. "It feels terrible. I came here to do a job, and I got mostly finished, but I couldn't quite get it all done. It seems as if we never ever get everything all done," she admitted, with a sad smile. "And now look. I'll probably never come back up here." She looked around, winced, and added, "Although, honest to God, I'm okay with that too."

Rogan nodded. "I'm sure you are. Once you have a bad scenario like this, it's hard to imagine ever wanting to do it again."

"Exactly. Anyway, if you can point me in the direction of the computers, if our stuff is there, I want to see that research." Instead Rogan brought her a laptop. "And the key?" Anna asked.

He handed it over, and she immediately plugged it in and checked out the information. "It's the main server backup," she stated, "which makes sense too. He's been making sure that everything we did up here is secured." She smiled. "That's so like him."

"So, nothing is suspicious at all about this?"

She looked at him and then shook her head. "No, of course not."

"What about the team we have yet to hear from?"

She winced immediately. "God, that's Amelia. This may sound rude, but checking in has not been her strong suit. Not that she doesn't, but sometimes when she does, it's much less often than we want."

"So, any theory on why that is?"

"She has some military background, and she's always been hyper-suspicious."

At that, Rogan stiffened and then studied Anna closely. "You want to give me an example of that?"

She shook her head. "God no. I couldn't even begin to, and I'm pretty sure it was all in her head. She saw everything peculiarly," she muttered.

"Who is she suspicious of?"

She hesitated and then whispered, "Myles." Anna took a moment and added, "Mostly Myles."

A PALL FELL around the base for the rest of the day. Everybody was upset over Myles's death, and there was still confusion over what had happened. When the search party came back after a second day with no sign of Amelia and her companion, the depressing atmosphere deepened. People were talking about it, and then, all of a sudden, not talking about it. Lots of murmured conversations took place in secluded corners, and, when anybody else joined, the conversations would immediately switch. Lisa joined several and found the same thing happening, wondering if it was because of her presence that everybody was shutting down the talk but found it occurred with others as well.

People were insecure, suspicious, and not sure who could be trusted. Lisa understood the sentiment.

Later that evening she was sound asleep but woke with the sudden strange feeling of *wrongness*. Almost immediately she felt Rogan gently put a finger to her lips, and he whispered in her ear, telling her to stay quiet. All she heard was loud breathing outside her door.

Rogan slipped out of bed in his boxers and tiptoed to the door. She knew he would open the door to see who was out there. By the time he got the door unlocked, she heard footsteps racing down the hall and around the corner. Rogan ran in pursuit, but she knew it was already too late. This guy already had an exit plan, and, whatever that was, enough doorways were up and down the hallway that Rogan wouldn't know who had just been here.

She sat up and wrapped the blankets around her shoulders, and, when Rogan returned, his expression was grim.

"I presume you didn't get him," she noted gently.

He shook his head, but, as he stared at her, his hands on his hips, his frustration was evident. "What the hell is he after?" Rogan asked.

"I don't know, but one thing is for sure. Now he knows I'm not sleeping alone."

He eyed her and then slowly nodded. "And that's something he didn't likely know beforehand or was testing to find out, isn't it?"

She gave him a nod back. "The question is, will it change anything?" she asked.

He frowned, as they both contemplated what that could mean. "I'm here now, and you can bet I'm not leaving. But this guy's still here, still coming to your door at nighttime." Rogan stared off in the distance.

"And I always expected that my stalker would be somebody trying to get to me in the night," she replied, "and maybe he didn't have the guts to do it at first. Maybe he was working up to it."

"It's possible," Rogan said. "And I don't know if my presence here will stop that now or anger him."

"I was hoping you wouldn't go out there."

He gave her a half smile. "Hiding your head in the sand won't help."

"Sand sounds good right about now." She laughed.

He flashed her a bright grin. "A holiday in the South Pacific when this is over?"

She appreciated the change of subject, absolutely loving the idea. "The two of us?"

"I sure don't want to bring the entire contingent with us," he added, with a suggestive smile.

"No, I wouldn't either," she muttered and nodded slowly. "That would be a hell of a nice thing to look forward to."

"Okay then." He settled on the bed beside her and gently dropped his forehead against hers. "You'll have some time to figure out exactly where."

"I've never been, but I always wanted to go."

"That's easy enough. I have time coming. Do you?"

"I do, and it seems to be the perfect way to take it, ... particularly after being up here." She shivered, as another wave caught her.

He wrapped her up in the blankets again. "Stay here?"

"What are you doing?"

"I'm going to get coffee." Her eyebrows shot up. He nodded. "I want to make sure that nobody else is up and walking around."

"So, what makes you think there'll be coffee?"

"Maybe there won't be, but I can always put on the teakettle. Hey, I'm awake now." He shrugged it off and grabbed his pants.

At that point, she realized he stood here, basically nude. "I don't understand how come you are not shivering too. I mean, you are standing in your boxers in these temperatures."

"I'm used to it. I've always been the hot-bodied type."

"I've always been the cold-bodied type," she shared, "but I've spent a lot of time in winter conditions. However, I've never felt like this."

"There are all different kinds of cold. Particularly once you caught that chill." And, with that, he leaned over and gave her a firm kiss. "Do not open that door unless you hear my voice on the other side." And, with that, he was gone.

Lisa didn't know whether that meant Rogan would come right back or that he wasn't planning on coming back for a while. Yet he was back within minutes, offering her some hot tea.

"It may help you get back to sleep," he suggested.

Either way, she drank the hot tea, and it stopped her involuntary shivering. "Did you see anybody roaming the halls or in the dining room?"

Rogan shook his head. "Let's try to get some sleep." He crawled into bed with her, as she snuggled up against him.

She would love to fall back asleep, but how could she, knowing her stalker might have seen Rogan leave her room earlier and may wait for him to do it again? Yet she was cold enough and tired enough that she fell asleep pondering it all.

DAY 11, ALMOST MIDMORNING

THE NEXT TIME she woke, Rogan's voice was in her ear. He came in bearing coffee this time, and she grinned. "A lot to enjoy about this living arrangement."

He chuckled. "I'm glad to hear that, and hopefully there's more to it than coffee delivery."

She curled back up in bed, pulling the covers tightly around her, as she sat up, hugging the coffee. "What time is it?"

"It's a quarter to nine." She stared at him in shock, horrified that she had slept so late.

He nodded. "I told Sydney that we had another midnight visitor and that you're not feeling all that great."

She wanted to protest, then realized he was right. She started to shiver again. "Damn, I'm cold."

"Once you catch that chill, it's pretty hard to get rid of your susceptibility to getting cold. Plus you went back out and got cold again."

"But I didn't really," she countered. "It's not as if I caught a chill every time I went out."

He nodded. "But your body obviously still wasn't ready to deal with that temperature." As he stood, he looked around. "The good news is that there are no more dead bodies this morning, at least not that we know of."

She snorted at that. "That we know of," she repeated,

rolling her eyes. "Not exactly reassuring, if you say that."

"Right, and, of course, everybody isn't up yet."

"*Great*," she said in an even louder sarcastic tone, as he stood there, his hands on his hips, frowning at her. She shrugged. "So what's the plan for today?"

"You'll stay here, whether you like it or not."

She nodded. "I'm not arguing that today. I'm definitely feeling the cold more than I want to."

He nodded. "I don't know that anybody else is going out on search and rescue anyway. It may have been called off, since our resources are also getting thin, and that delayed storm looks set to hit and hit hard."

She winced. "What about Anna? She didn't look too good yesterday."

"We definitely need to have some more conversations with her. She's going over the research data and told me that, when it comes to Amelia, she would most likely be fine living off the land for a long time, out of all of them. However, she only had supplies for four or five days."

Lisa winced at that. "And that four or five days is several days past, isn't it?"

"It is," he murmured. "And, if there's one thing that's unforgiving, it's the northern tundra."

She didn't have anything to say to that, and, when he was long gone, she took her time getting dressed. When she finally made it to breakfast, Chef looked at her intently.

"I hear you're not doing so well."

She shrugged. "I had a good night, so, in theory, I should be doing fine."

He snorted at that. "Theory doesn't work so well up here, so, in the end, it doesn't mean much."

"Got it. Anyway I'm doing fine—as long as I stay inside," she muttered. "I know Rogan's really worried about me, but it's that stupid chill I got. I still get cold easily."

"Yeah, that's not hard to do out here," Chef noted. "Grab some hot food. That should help."

With a hot breakfast, she sat down at an empty table. When she looked up, Anna stood nearby with a tray, looking lost. Lisa immediately motioned to her. "Please sit."

The other woman smiled gratefully. "Still feels weird to be here."

"I'm sorry. I know it's hard when you're out of your own space."

"I am, indeed." She lowered her voice and shared, "I don't think they're looking for Amelia anymore."

"If so, it may be a matter of low resources and Mother Nature amping up again," Lisa responded kindly.

At that, Anna winced. "I hadn't really considered that. I've sent out an email, asking for assistance from our universities, anything that would help move this along."

"Move what along?" Lisa asked.

Anna shook her head. "Amelia. I hate to think that she's lost out there forever."

"I can't imagine that happening, but I don't know if anybody has contacted the locals to see whether they've found her or not." Then came a loud shout from somewhere in the kitchen, and several people took off running.

"Something's happening." Anna stood, yet remained in place.

"Absolutely, I don't know what though," Lisa noted. Anna looked around nervously, and her nervousness got to Lisa. "You don't have to be afraid here, Anna."

She jerked, spilling coffee on the table, and immediately apologized. "Oh, I'm so silly," she whispered, as she grabbed napkins and tried to mop it up, while Lisa watched her curiously.

Lisa repeated, "I know it's not your space and all, but nobody here is out to hurt you."

At that, Anna stopped her frantic motions and flushed, embarrassed. "Thank you for that, and I wish I could believe you." In a low voice she added, "However, I'm pretty sure Myles was murdered."

"Good God." Lisa stared at her. "Why would you ... How did you even begin to think that?"

She shrugged. "Some of the data that he'd collected ... wasn't his data."

"So? You've got the other team members heading back home again." Lisa eyed her curiously. "Isn't he supposed to safeguard that data? You said it was all backed up, and you're a group working together."

"Yes, but some of that data I don't recognize."

At that, Lisa sat back. "That's an interesting twist."

"And I don't have any way to talk to the others to know if it's something they were working on."

"So, it's not necessarily that this is a problem. It's mostly that you don't recognize the data."

"Exactly," Anna agreed, with relief. "And I know it sounds foolish to even bring it up."

"No, I think everything needs to be brought up at this point in time," Lisa stated, equally honest. "We've got enough going on without having to worry about more people trying to hide stuff."

"I'm not trying to hide anything," Anna stated, "and I've certainly backed up as much of that work as I can. Yet, with Myles gone, it feels very much as if I'm the last one and alone."

"And you are, at least here, depending on what the outcome of Amelia's trip is."

Anna nodded and didn't say anything more but finally sat down again and quickly worked away on her food. She didn't seem to be short in terms of her appetite, even if she was nervous.

When she looked around again, she lowered her voice and asked Lisa, "Has everybody here been vetted?"

"Yes, of course," Lisa confirmed. "The same as everybody in your place is vetted."

She winced at that. "Sure, but we're scientists. I'm sure somebody does a criminal background check and all that good stuff somewhere along the line, but I don't know how much vetting is done to come up here."

"Yet why would they be worried about it?" Lisa asked. "Unless there happens to be some deeper issues that you're not sharing. Were there arguments over whose names were on each research paper? Maybe over whose materials we're talking about?"

Anna stared at her. "Not that I know of."

"So, what possible reason could there be for anybody causing trouble up here in your group?" she asked, sincerely trying to understand.

"That's like asking what possible reason anybody in your group could be causing trouble. Who the hell knows?" Immediately Anna slapped her hand over her mouth, embarrassed at her own raised tone. She sighed. "I can't even sleep. I'm so worried."

"Worried about what? If you know something, something that you suspect, something that you have some idea about, then please speak up, so we can put some of this to rest. And now you've got a room to yourself, as I understand."

"Yes, I'm all on my own, thank God. I couldn't sleep at all well when sharing that other room with two women."

Again, not sure what to say to that, Lisa nodded. "I don't know what you'll be doing all day, but, if you want to find me, I spend my time here in the dining room or in the medical clinic. I have reports to write, other things to do, like training and such. And sometimes I'm assigned to spend some time with the dogs." Lisa shrugged. "Everything is very strange this trip. Normally there's a lot of training, then we get some downtime, but, at the moment, things are messed up."

"I know, right?" Anna agreed, with a nod. "Messed up in so many ways."

"Is this your first trip up?"

Anna snorted in response. "I wouldn't even be allowed to come this time," she admitted, with a resigned nod, "except Amelia okayed my application."

"That's interesting," Lisa murmured. "Why wouldn't you be allowed here?"

She shrugged. "Too many applicants for too few positions, but one pulled out suddenly, so I got the call," she explained, with a half smile. "Now I wish to God I hadn't."

"But if you weren't here," Lisa noted, "you'd still be wondering how it was to research in the Arctic and wishing that you could be a part of it. And now that you did, you got a chance to experience it."

"And now all I want to do is go home," she muttered.

"And that's coming too," Lisa added, trying to calm Anna down.

"How fast is the real question, and is it fast enough that I'll survive?" And with that cryptic tone, Anna got up. "I'm heading to my room. I'm really tired."

When Lisa got to the medical clinic, she told Sydney about what Anna had shared. Sydney frowned, then slowly nodded. "That makes sense. I did speak with her yesterday a little bit, and she's quite paranoid that something deliberate happened to Myles."

"And yet what could it be?" she asked.

"Other than drugs, I have no idea."

"Maybe somebody else could check on Anna, as she doesn't seem to be very happy."

"Of course she's not very happy," Sydney confirmed. "Her entire team has been moved out, is dead or is missing, and she's the only one left behind."

"Right, and she did go over the research material on the thumb drive, and some of it she didn't recognize."

"Which doesn't mean anything," Sydney pointed out. "I've been on lots of research missions, and believe me. It's not that nobody is willing to share. It's that not everybody has time. You're there writing reports, collecting information. There isn't always time for a whole lot of group discussions. If we had any idea what was happening to Amelia and her partner, I know the colonel would be more than happy to get them picked up and shipped out and put a stop to all this. But we don't."

"I hear you, but it sucks." Lisa groaned, leaned forward, and asked, "Anything I can do here today?"

Sydney chuckled. "Nope, go find something else to do. Maybe go visit with the dogs. Do something you enjoy."

"Now that I can get behind," Lisa said.

"Although, if we run into any more trouble, I might call you back."

"And that's fine too," she said, even with an eye roll. "If

I can help you and still get a little bit of training in, I'm good. And, if I'm needed anywhere else, I'm fine with that too."

She headed to the dog barn, dressed warmly. Joe welcomed her, as did the dogs. Especially Benji. She cuddled him for several minutes, before the others interrupted, looking for their quota of love. It was so wonderful to have all this canine energy. It was heartwarming and so damn innocent. It helped to handle the darkness in the main building. She spent a few minutes visiting with them and loving them.

"How are things over in the base?" Joe asked her.

That reminded her how little time Joe spent there. She frowned at him and asked, "Do you go over there at all?"

"Sure, I go and get food, then return." He smirked, then chuckled. "It's not that I'm antisocial or anything, but my dogs are my responsibility."

She winced. "Are you expecting trouble?"

"I wasn't expecting trouble to begin with," he stated, "but believe me. I haven't forgotten that somebody shot two of my dogs."

"I understand," she murmured. "At the same time, we've still got missing people out there."

"Any chance that they're a part of all this?" Joe asked in a hushed tone, looking around to confirm they were alone. "Nice and convenient that somebody turns up missing right when a lot of other people get hurt."

"I don't know that it's very convenient for Amelia. There's a good chance that she and her dogs are suffering, wherever they are."

At that, his face thinned, and he nodded, staring off into the distance. "Someone here went to the village and checked, and nobody's seen her. They do have several hunting parties out, so, when they come back, there's a chance that they could have news."

She nodded. "And they're all quite used to this weather, I presume."

"They are. They live it, but they don't take chances with it either. They know when to get in out of it."

"Amelia's also very experienced, I'm told."

"That's good," he replied. "I hope *very experienced* means the same for Amelia as it does for the local hunters. I have every faith in their ability to get home again, but I don't know so much about her training. But then I don't know her. I don't know her abilities, and it's not right to judge her for it."

At that, Lisa nodded. As she turned to leave, she asked, "Has Anna, the scientist, our newest arrival, come in to see the dogs at all?"

He shook his head. "No, and a lot of people don't even know that me and my dogs are out here or that they're allowed to visit. A few of you insist on coming over and being social, even though nobody's invited you."

She burst out laughing, and he grinned. "I guess that's the way you like it, *huh*, Joe?"

"Damn right," he muttered. "Don't know what's going on over in that corner, but I'm okay to stay here by myself. That way nobody else gets a second chance at my dogs."

With the sentiment, she wholeheartedly had to agree. After a prolonged goodbye she headed back to the main quarters. As she did, she thought she saw somebody else walking toward the generator. Thinking it was Rogan, she headed around to take a look, though in the back of her mind she thought he'd already left with the snowcat.

Although why she didn't know.

When the person snuck around the power plant area and acted suspicious, looking around behind him, she froze, wondering what was going on. She sent Rogan a quick text, asking where he was. When she didn't get a response, she sent a message to Mountain. **Somebody is at the generator shed, acting suspicious.** Lisa immediately got a warning in response.

Stay put. Don't approach.

She winced at that because, if she didn't approach, how the hell would she know if they were doing something stupid and/or sabotaging the generator, putting the rest of the base in trouble again?

As Lisa watched, the figure once again looked behind and crept into the generator shed. Lisa immediately sent off a message to both men. **Someone in the power plant now.**

What was going on here was beyond her, and, definitely not liking the turn of events, she immediately crept closer, trying to stay in the shadows as much as possible. She was dressed fully in white, as so many of them were. When she approached, she noted that the door was open. Pushing the door a hair bit wider, trying to be ever-so-quiet, she took another step, searching the darkness.

Suddenly the door slammed shut behind her, and, before she had a chance to react, something came out of nowhere and slammed against her head.

Lisa collapsed into blackness.

ROGAN RACED TO the medical clinic, only to be stopped at the door by Magnus, who grabbed him and gave him a hard shake.

"She's fine," he said, his voice calm, as he tried to get Rogan to hear him. "She'll be fine."

Rogan took several deep breaths, glaring at the man who stood between him and Lisa, yet knowing there was no way Magnus would let Rogan in there until he calmed down. When he finally managed several long breaths, he calmed down a bit. "Do we know what happened?" he asked in an almost calm voice.

"Not yet." Magnus shook his head. "Mountain found her at the generator. She'd texted him how she saw somebody going inside, acting suspicious. He told her to stay where she was, but she didn't follow instructions."

He winced at that. "No, of course not. She would have gone right in there to find out what was going on."

"Exactly, but we don't know who it was or what they were doing because, by the time Mountain got there, they were gone. And it was a really quick escape because Mountain was already on the way. That's one of the reasons she's doing fine right now because Mountain picked her right up and brought her back into the warmth. The generator was untouched."

"So, all is well there?"

"It appears to be. Mountain's back in the generator shed right now, and I'd be with him, except that I knew you were coming in all hot and bothered, and we don't need that right now."

Rogan took several slow deep breaths again, glaring at Magnus, who smiled.

"I know exactly how you feel. Remember that."

Rogan winced, remembering Magnus had already been through something similar with Sydney. Rogan nodded.

"Still sucks."

"Yes, it does, and even more so when it's people we care about. But, if you're calm, and it's safe to leave you, I'll head on out." Magnus stopped, his gaze narrowed, as he waited for the appropriate response from Rogan, who immediately nodded.

"Yes, I promise. I won't terrorize them."

He snorted at that. "Don't worry, I trust Sydney to slap you down, if need be," he related, with a smirk. "Still, I don't want you going in there and upsetting Lisa either. We need her as calm as possible when we question her."

Rogan ran his hand through his hair, pushing it off his face. "I'm fine. Let me go see her." And, with that, Magnus stepped back.

"You get five minutes, and then I want you out at the generator with me." And, with that, Magnus was gone.

Pushing open the clinic door, he stepped inside to find Sydney and Lisa talking softly. She was stretched out on the bed, but her eyes were open. It was all he could do to not rush over, pick her up, and hold her close.

Her face broke into a soft smile when she saw him. "Hello. And here I figured you'd be racing in, yelling at me."

"Racing in maybe, but Magnus caught me outside and made sure I didn't come in here *terrorizing anybody*." Rogan sent a quick look over at Sydney.

She tossed him a laughing glance. "Yeah, that would be appreciated. It's still my medical clinic, and everybody needs to follow my rules."

Rogan nodded, then looked down at the hand he tightly clenched in his, then released it a bit to be sure he wasn't hurting Lisa. He bent down and kissed her hard and asked, "What the hell happened?"

She opened up her arms instead, and he collected her into a warm hug. When she could, she sat back and whispered, "I was being stupid."

"*Uh-huh.*" He nodded, without saying anything else.

She glared at him. "I suppose you've already heard."

"I've heard some things, but I sure as hell haven't heard enough. Explain why Mountain ordered you not to go in there, but you went anyway."

"Because I wasn't sure what they were doing, but it was definitely suspicious. I knew Mountain would be on the way, and I figured that maybe we could finally get to the bottom of some of this nightmare. We had a real opportunity, and I didn't dare let it go by." She squeezed his hand a long moment, then continued. "I saw them go inside, and they were checking the equipment. I hid, and then I snuck up behind him, hoping I could see who was in the room, or even what he was doing. But, of course, with all our gear on, it's damn hard to see anything," she muttered.

"Anyway, I stepped inside, but I didn't even get a chance to see anything before the door shut behind me. I gather they were behind the door and knocked me out with something." She reached up a tentative hand to her head. "And, for that, I'm really sorry. I really didn't need that."

"No, you didn't." Rogan inspected the wound himself. "Thankfully it's not too bad." He looked over at Sydney for confirmation.

The doc nodded. "Hey, I got knocked out myself here, so welcome to the club. I'll keep her here for observation, confirming everything is okay. I'll also do a full checkup and blood work."

At the term *blood work,* he stared at the doc. When she gave him a flat stare back, he realized that, because Lisa had been unconscious, anything could have happened.

Obviously Lisa herself hadn't put two and two together earlier because she turned and stared at Sydney in horror. "Seriously?"

Sydney nodded. "I'm not taking any chances."

At that, Rogan smiled down at her, then leaned over and kissed her gently. "I have orders to get up to the generator shed and see if we can find out what the hell is going on. You have absolutely no idea who it was, correct?"

She nodded. "Right. Not a clue. I saw a large figure wrapped up in winter gear, suspiciously looking all around, then heading into the generator room. That's it."

He nodded and stood up. "In that case, I'll leave you in Sydney's capable hands, and I'll join the guys." He stood outside the closed clinic door for a long moment, staring down at his clenched fists, as he tried to get his temper back under control. It was a hell of a thing to come home to, a hell of a thing to hear while he had been out. Thankfully the message that she'd been knocked unconscious had come from Mountain himself, so Rogan knew he could trust it. Plus there was some chance of keeping things relatively contained emotionally.

But now that he'd seen her and had been assured that she really would be okay, he could breathe again. However, along with that breath came the fury that somebody was out here playing this game in these temperatures, knowing exactly what a broken-down generator would do to them all. Obviously the base had backup options, but it brought to mind the ongoing and suspicious generator problems at the scientists' camp.

Rogan raced out to the generator shed. Magnus stood there, his hands on his hips, glaring at it. "Problems?" Rogan asked immediately because he didn't like Magnus's current body language.

He shook his head. "No, that's the problem. I don't see any tampering. I can't see anything."

"Any chance that Lisa stopped him before he got that far?"

"Sure," he replied, staring at him. "And believe me. That's really not an answer I'm particularly happy about. We'll post a guard here twenty-four/seven from now on, not only at nighttime."

"Who's got the time and inclination for that?" he asked, staring around at the equipment.

"No one, but it's mandatory. ... The colonel has ordered it regardless. Everybody already knows how dangerous it is to have anybody messing around with our generator. That was one of the problems with always going up to deal with the scientists' camp, but having to do it here, all the damn time? That's not okay. We would be sitting ducks in this cold."

"What are the chances it's the same person?"

"It's a long way to travel and not an easy path either, just to come here to mess with a generator—but it would explain our daytime saboteur."

"Right, but so was the scientists' camp, depending on where their saboteur was coming from. Although that puts the attacker as one in our circle." Rogan shook his head and added, "And nobody keeps track of everybody all the time."

"Except now," Magnus stated. "The place was put on lockdown after Lisa was attacked, in case you hadn't heard."

"No, I hadn't heard, but I'm all for it." Rogan let out another slow breath. "Can't say I'm terribly impressed."

"No, of course not," Magnus agreed, looking past him, "but maybe it'll make the colonel move a little faster."

Rogan winced. "Or maybe not."

"I'm pretty sure he wants to put in his time and get the hell out of here," Magnus stated.

"Maybe, but it won't be that easy, will it?"

"No, and it certainly hasn't been easy up until now, and that's a problem in itself," Magnus noted. "We need to make sure that everything here is copacetic."

"Preferably better than just okay," Rogan added, with a glance in Magnus's direction. "Nobody here can leave, and nobody else can come in, … not until this is all straightened out."

"Yet we still have the same missing people."

"We do, and believe me. There will be a lot of questions about that too. We could bring in new people to help us, if we already had this current issue dealt with, but, because of the scientists' camp and their missing team members, the brass has decided to leave it to us for the moment."

Rogan shook his head at that. "And that makes sense?"

"Nothing makes sense right now," Magnus snapped, with a hard tone. "That's the biggest problem we have. Somebody is messing with us, and that is pissing me off."

"Have you talked to Mountain?"

"No, not since I came out here to deal with this." Magnus pointed to the massive generator system they had. "He came, found her, and then came back here to ensure everything in the generator shed was okay. Afterward he's been with the colonel—for a while now."

"*Great*," Rogan groaned. "Better him than me."

"Yeah, you're not kidding," Magnus muttered. "Better him than all of us right now."

"Mountain seems to have some pull."

"I don't know about pull *per se*, but he's certainly managed to get more done than any of us, especially when we're up against the colonel. So, yeah, maybe *pull* is the right word." He turned around and said, "Listen. I want you to go do a full maintenance inspection on this first system. I'll work on the second one and ensure nobody's had a chance to do anything. The guards out here will be on alert for twenty-four/seven now, until we figure this out. And even still, it may not be enough," he warned him.

Rogan looked over at him and nodded. "That could mean one of our guards gets taken out. Also one of the guards may be the perpetrator."

"That could happen either way. We know that it could. So, what are you suggesting?" Magnus asked curiously.

Rogan hesitated, then shrugged. "I know we don't really have the manpower for two at a time."

"No, we sure don't, but, on the other hand, if it's that important, we'll find it, won't we?"

"Two would be better and safer. Besides that, we do have another issue. It's not terribly warm in here, yet it's not that cold either. Plus there is all the exhaust from the actual generator itself." At that, he stopped and winced. "Right?"

"That's another reason for two men at a time," Magnus agreed, "because that's exactly what happened up at the scientists' camp. All that exhaust …"

"Exactly. Let's see what Mountain says about the whole scenario."

Right then Mountain joined them. "I heard my name," he said, his voice harsh.

Magnus looked at him and nodded. "We were talking about posting full-time around-the-clock guards on the generator systems."

MOUNTAIN NODDED. "WE'RE doing two at a time. The guys want training? Well, they'll get training. It may not be the kind they had in mind." And, with that, Mountain turned and walked away again. "And, no, I'm not playing. I have another quadrant to check." Then Mountain turned to look at Rogan and Magnus. He noted the looks on his friends' faces. "I know the odds are slim, but it's Teegan. He's my kid brother. If our positions were reversed, he'd find me. I can do no less."

"I get it," Magnus murmured. "Don't kill yourself trying to recover his body. That's not what Teegan would want."

"Good thing that's not happening." With that parting shot, Mountain headed to gear up.

DAY 12, MIDMORNING

LISA HAD MISSED the warmth of having Rogan in her bed last night, as she slept in a hospital bed in the clinic. She shifted uneasily most of the night, hating that she was constantly listening for footsteps at the door, yet there was no reason for it. Whoever had been hanging out around her door surely knew now that she was no longer sleeping solo. That alone should put an end to whatever pursuit they had going on in their mind.

At least that was the thought, but now that she was stuck in the clinic, if anybody knew about this event, it meant that they knew where she was. Not exactly something she wanted to contemplate.

When Sydney walked in this morning, she looked at Lisa in exasperation. "You don't look as if you got much sleep."

"No, I didn't."

"I thought telling you about the guards at the door would calm your fears."

Lisa shrugged apologetically.

"When I checked on you in the middle of the night, you were sound asleep." Sydney studied her and immediately checked her vitals.

"Did you come in and check on me?" she asked.

Sydney smiled and nodded. "Sure did, and I know that Rogan was in here twice."

"You let Rogan in?" she asked.

"It's more a case of managing him, versus telling him no, which gets him angry."

Lisa laughed at that. "That's a good point. I hadn't really expected people to keep a watch on me overnight."

"You were attacked. We don't know why. We don't know who did it, and we don't know if they are coming back to silence the witness."

Lisa shook her head. "No need for that. I didn't recognize him."

"But they don't know that," Sydney replied.

"Oh God," Lisa muttered, staring at her friend. "I would rather not consider that."

"Maybe, but that doesn't change the fact that it's now on the docket, as far as a lot of people are concerned. You must take better care of yourself."

"You mean, not go off and try to solve problems on my own?"

"That's one thing." Sydney smiled. "But, hey, I'm not saying that's what you did. That's not my department. I'm saying we don't want a repeat of another blow to your head and a return of that headache. Now, how about some food?"

"That sounds great. I'd love to go down to the dining room and get a little something," Lisa said, trying to get up.

"That's not happening."

The word of warning was too loud and very clear, and Lisa glared at the doc. "I am fine."

"Glad to hear it," Sydney said gently, "but, no, you aren't getting up and walking around. We'll do some walking around, once I can get your blood pressure down again," she explained, holding up the meter.

"Oh, come on. Surely that's just stress."

"Maybe, but that doesn't matter to me. That's the reading, and we've got to get it down, so you're not going anywhere."

"It's not even an issue really."

"Stop now, and let me work. I do have some blood pressure medication, which I may need to consider for you, but I'd rather not if we don't have to. However, I'm concerned about the fact that this is not a normal state for you, is it?"

"No, I don't think so," she admitted. "Yet I have been under a tremendous amount of stress."

"Yeah, all of us have," Sydney noted, "but not everybody is showing these high blood pressure readings."

A little bit later Lisa was allowed to get up, and, with Sydney at her side, they made their way to the washroom, where Lisa used the facilities and scrubbed her face, Sydney stood on watch the whole time.

When they got back to the clinic, Lisa collapsed on the bed and winced. "That was very discouraging."

"Yet it's very encouraging from my perspective," Sydney stated, with a bright smile, as she walked over with a hot cup of coffee for Lisa.

"How do you figure that?" Lisa muttered.

"You didn't collapse, and you made it there and back, mostly on your own. I'll take that as a good sign for now."

"Yeah, but I was so weak," she grumbled in frustration.

"What did you expect? You got hit over the head. You're lucky you had contacted Mountain, so he was on the way. … Otherwise, it would be a whole different story."

"How long do you think it would take to die out there, if you're not prepared?"

"Under most temperatures here? Ten minutes," the doc stated immediately. "You were injured in the generator room, which kept you out of the full force of Mother Nature and went a long way to saving you. However, more than that was the fact that Mountain got you in here so quickly, and at least you were decently bundled up."

"I was because I'd been over visiting with the dogs," she added.

Sydney smiled. "I go over there on a regular basis too. Something is very healing about being around them. I do love Toby. I know Magnus is quite taken with him too, to the point where I think he's wondering about asking Joe if he would sell Toby to him. Particularly now that Toby's injured and might not be up to working standards any longer."

"I adore the dogs," Lisa replied, with an agreeable nod. "Joe tends to ignore everybody here because he doesn't like anything that's going on." She looked over at Sydney, who stared at her with a wry look on her face.

"Why do you think *I* go over there?" Sydney asked, with a half laugh.

"Right, I guess that's a good point, isn't it?"

"When shit goes down here, it's usually the people kind of shit," Sydney noted. "I'm here to try to pick up the pieces, but, this time around, this base had way more issues than I would have expected. That's very depressing because almost all of these problems are man-made."

"And you're staying here, yet you're probably needed elsewhere," she pointed out.

"If I am, I'm pretty sure they know where to find me," Sydney added. "So lie back on that bed and rest and stay there."

Groaning, Lisa did as she was told, which was a good thing because, when Rogan and Magnus showed up a little later, they both nodded at seeing Lisa still in bed.

She glared at them. "I'm perfectly fine."

"If you're perfectly fine, the doc would have you up and running around." Rogan glared at her.

"And, if you were perfectly fine, you wouldn't have ignored your orders." Magnus chipped in from his side, and she snorted.

"I wasn't taking it as an order," she argued, with a roll of her eyes. "Maybe I should have."

"Yeah, well, I don't see Mountain in here talking to you, so that probably means he's still pissed."

"Oh, crap." Lisa stared at Magnus. "Now I'll have to apologize, won't I?"

A snort came from the door, and she turned to see Mountain staring at her.

"Right," she said, with a nod. "I apologize for not listening." He waited. She glared and tried again. "You told me not to go any farther and to stay where I was, and I ignored you."

"Want to explain why you did that?"

"Because, ... well, so much shit is going on around here," she explained in a resigned tone. "I was in a position, whether a good position or not, to find out what somebody was up to. I'm only sorry that the moron took me by surprise."

He nodded. "Not something you were expecting, I presume?"

"No, I wasn't at all. It's not what any of us expect, right?"

"Yet you thought he was acting suspicious, so it's not as if you were *not* prepared for that." Mountain raised one eyebrow at her, his mouth grim.

She realized she'd basically walked into a trap. She glared at him, and he smiled.

"Next time anything like this happens, you follow orders. Do you hear me?" Mountain stated. She stared at him, nonplused, as he looked her full in the face.

Mountain continued. "If the generator had gone down, it would have gone down. We would have been able to fix it."

"But would we though? After all the problems with the generator at the scientists' camp?"

"We've done full servicing on all the systems, and everything is running nicely. So whoever was here didn't get a chance to do anything," Mountain told her in an agreeable tone. "So, thank you for that." She gave him a half smile. "Don't do it again, *huh*? Machine parts and equipment we can replace, but lives? … We can't. So hear me when I say this. Don't ignore my orders again." He turned to face Sydney. "We're running guards, two at a time, twenty-four hours a day now," he shared calmly.

She nodded, the relief evident in her voice, as she replied, "I won't argue with that."

"I didn't think you would. Keep in mind that we could have a few more cold-related injuries because of the guards."

"Presumably they will be prepared."

"Which is why we're doing them two at a time. In normal conditions, one is enough, but right here, right now? No way." And, with that, Mountain was gone again.

Sydney looked around the room and asked, "Does anybody know what Mountain does around here?"

They all laughed in unison, and the responses came all at once as well.

"Nope."

"Nada."

"Zilch."

AFTER DINNER AND a visit with Lisa, Rogan headed back to the dining room area, trying to mingle with the others and see what the talk was, getting a measure of how things were going. As he poured a coffee, he saw Anna sitting by herself. Wondering about that, he walked over and smiled at her. "May I sit here?"

"Sure." She gave him an odd look. "You're the only one who wants to."

He winced. "Everybody's had a bit of a shock. They are also on the distrustful side right now."

"Yeah, you and me both," she muttered. "It's not where I expected to be, and honestly I would very much prefer not to be here." She looked around nervously. "I keep asking for a way to get out, and they keep telling me that I must wait, that it's not time yet. I admit that, when they say, *it's not time*, I get more paranoid that it won't ever be time and that I'm a prisoner here," she explained, with a half laugh.

He nodded and smiled. "Sometimes it can seem to be a life sentence, when you are where you don't want to be."

She shuddered. "Not now, not with everything that's happened." She looked around and asked, "Did anybody consider that maybe Amelia is behind all this?"

He frowned. "You mean, Amelia, the missing scientist?"

She nodded.

"Is that something she is likely to do?" he asked, studying her intently. That was the first time anybody had mentioned that theory to him. Yet it should be considered.

"She's the one who's missing," Anna stated in a hard tone. "I was trying to figure out who would be involved in this attack, but how could anybody be when you're all here under watch all the time? It doesn't make any sense, so I wondered about Amelia, considering she's the one who's not here."

"Now that you've brought it up, we can look into it."

She nodded. "And before you say it, no, I'm not trying to throw a team member under the bus. I've had absolutely no problems with Amelia at all. I just..." And then she shrugged.

"No, I hear you." Rogan stared off in the distance. "What can you tell me about her?"

"Not a whole lot. She's friendly but distant. She's got a hell of a reputation at the university and has been doing these trips for a long time." Anna waved her hand in a dismissive manner. "She was always friendly enough, but I never really got to know her. She kept to herself."

"Which I imagine is something that a lot of people do at the scientists' camp."

"And yet so few of us were there," Anna added. "So it's not as if you can really stay isolated."

"That's not healthy either," he pointed out.

"Exactly," Anna replied, "but any attempt I made to get friendlier with her was always rebuffed. Gently, of course, but rebuffed nonetheless."

"Maybe she was there to get the work done, and that was it."

"Maybe. I don't know. It was just something that occurred to me."

"I'll look into it," he repeated.

"I figured that you had some pull around here," she

shared, looking around at the rest of the people here in the dining room. "They all seem to be followers."

"It's not that they're followers," Rogan corrected, stiffening ever-so-slightly. "They're under orders."

"Right, that whole soldier thing."

"In this case it's a mixture of soldiers, including army, navy, marines, and air force, with international partners as well."

"If the air force is here," Anna asked, "why the hell can't we get out?"

"Because we don't have planes here at the moment," Rogan explained, trying hard to keep his voice calm, but Anna was definitely frustrating him. "They can only fly in certain weather conditions. We may have a supply plane coming in tomorrow, if this storm quits."

She looked at him hopefully. "Maybe I can go out on that one."

"Maybe, particularly if it's a problem."

"It's a problem," she stated, with an eye roll. "I really, really, really want to leave."

"I can talk to the colonel about it."

She looked at him hopefully. "Would you? I don't seem to have a voice here."

"I don't think that's it at all," Rogan replied. "I think it's just that, every time the planes fly in and out, the payload is already reached."

"And yet surely they can handle one more person," she argued. "When was the last time they came in?"

"It's been a while. The last one was the rescue for the rest of your team."

"And they didn't bring supplies?"

"Of course not."

"So, supplies should be coming then, right?"

"I believe tomorrow, if the weather cooperates. We also need fuel."

She winced. "God, I want to get out of here before you guys run out of fuel." Anna shook her head. "That doesn't even bear thinking about." She shuddered. "No fuel equates to no heat, and I went through that up at our camp. I want to go home and never leave again."

"I'm sorry it's been such a traumatic experience for you."

She shrugged. "It's nobody's fault, and I get that, but I don't belong here, and I'm definitely a fish out of water."

"Let me talk to the colonel," he repeated.

She looked at him gratefully. "If you could, that would be awesome, particularly when you guys are short on people. Getting me out of here would mean you'd have one less to look after."

He laughed. "I don't think one person will make much difference to our workload or our supplies."

"Every person counts," she pointed out. "Particularly if you're running low."

"We're not that low."

She didn't say anything, just looking at him like a dog lost in the city. "I would appreciate it if you could talk to the colonel." Then she got up and left.

Rogan wasn't sure what he'd let himself in for because talking to the colonel was not exactly something on his wish list. When Magnus joined Rogan later, he confessed what he'd done. Magnus stared at him and shook his head. "It's not as easy as that. You can't just go in and tell him this lady wants to leave and he should let her."

"I know. I know," Rogan admitted. "I shouldn't have even told her that I would talk to him."

"And now that you did, what will you do about it?"

He winced at the thought of the colonel yelling at him. "I have no clue. ... I probably should go talk to him, but that doesn't mean anything I say will be well received."

"Probably not," Magnus agreed cheerfully.

"There are so many puzzles right now. I'd love to see the autopsy reports on all the dead men we shipped out," he muttered. "Could drugs have been in their systems? I haven't seen any autopsy reports, and chances are we won't get access to them. But considering drugs have been an issue already ..."

"So, the colonel can say whatever the hell he wants then, in order to keep the peace."

"That's not how the brass works though."

"Come on. That's exactly how the brass works," Magnus countered, with a head shake. "You and I both know that. Anything to keep things quiet."

"They can't keep it quiet. Not here at least."

"Not much we can do about any of that from here."

"That's what I mean. So it's not as if we have a whole lot of choice. We're sitting ducks here."

"Really wish you wouldn't use that term." Magnus winced. "What you need to find out is who the hell attacked Lisa," he declared.

"That's a completely different story." Then Rogan groaned. "Okay, it's all tied up together. I also have some concerns about Anna's mental health."

"I noted that too. It would be best if she left here."

"It makes sense to send her out on the next flight."

But when he heard that the trip was delayed for another two days due to the latest weather forecast, he nodded, because it's what always happened up here. Best laid plans and all, but Mother Nature still prevailed.

When he explained that to Anna later, she had tears in her eyes, but she didn't do anything more than thank him. He added, "You'll get out of here. Just not tomorrow or the next day."

She looked up at him with a haunted expression and nodded. "I'm glad you think so."

He winced. "Is there any reason in particular you think you won't?"

She shook her head. "No, of course not. I just get the feeling that this is a life sentence."

That was something she had relayed before. "But, in this case, the life sentence will be commuted." She burst out laughing at his choice of words, and he grinned.

"Thanks for that." She got up and headed to her room.

He didn't even know what she did all day. She still had one of the laptops, so he presumed she was working, but he hadn't seen any of the work that she did and probably wouldn't recognize it anyway.

That was the thing about this base. Everybody had their jobs; everybody had a reason for being here, and generally people went about their business and took care of their own responsibilities. Anna had had too many shocks to her system lately. Rogan hoped that the colonel would see the wisdom in sending her back out on the next supply run.

And, with that, Rogan headed off to visit with Lisa.

DAY 12, LATE AFTERNOON

FROM HER HOSPITAL bed in the medical clinic on base, Lisa heard Rogan and Sydney talking in whispers off to the side. Lisa groaned and announced, "I'm right here. Feel free to include me in your discussion."

"It won't do any good though," Rogan commented, as he walked closer to Lisa. "You were already told to look after yourself, and you didn't." She glared at him, but he smiled and added, "Come on. Time to go to your room."

"Really?" She looked up at Sydney, with a delighted expression.

Sydney nodded. "Yes, but only because Rogan is staying with you," she stated in a cautionary voice.

"Right, so a babysitter."

Sydney shrugged. "Hey, take it or leave it."

"I'll take it. I'll take it." Lisa laughed. And, with Rogan's help, she walked carefully to her room. As soon as she got inside, she sat down on the bed with a big smile. "What is it about having your own personal space that makes everything so much better?"

"I don't know," Rogan replied, with a smile, "but I'm sure everybody on the planet would agree with that statement. And you're lucky that you do have a personal space."

"I know. I know. Ever since I got here, I've been the lucky one with my own room," she noted happily. "It's hard to argue when the gods smile on you."

He nodded. "I'll head to the washroom before we call it a day."

She nodded. "Okay." He frowned at the doorway, and she groaned. "Look. You can at least leave me alone to go to the bathroom. I'll be fine. You won't be gone that long."

"I'm not planning on it," he agreed. "Otherwise I'd be taking you right back to the medical clinic."

"I'm fine," she declared, glaring at him, and he laughed as he finally stepped away. Not long afterward, a knock came at her door. Knowing it wasn't him and not at all sure that she should open her door, Lisa then heard Anna's voice. Lisa opened the door and looked at the nervous woman, noticing how very pale she appeared. "Hey, Anna. Are you okay?"

"I was checking to see if you were okay," she said, giving Lisa a half smile. "I heard that you were still in rough shape from your attack."

"I don't know how you heard that. I certainly haven't talked about it to anybody." Lisa frowned, as she studied Anna, watching the expressions on her face.

"But, with the rumor mill and the gossipers here, you don't have to in this place." Anna gave a wave of her hand. "People love to talk."

Lisa nodded. "True. People will be people. It's not so much that they seem to talk, as they need to know that everything is okay."

"Maybe," Anna conceded, with a shrug. "I haven't had much exposure to this stuff."

"Hopefully you can get out of here pretty soon, and you won't be worried about it again."

"That's what I keep hoping, but, so far, it hasn't happened."

"Ah, but the supply run will be in tomorrow or the next day," she shared. "However, with the harsh weather conditions here, it's always late."

"Is it?" Anna asked.

"Sure, flight times are always subject to the weather. That's one of the reasons why the base has to sometimes tighten our collective belts, based on what we get for food. At that point, Chef will stretch what he has as far as he can."

At that, Anna laughed. "I'm checking in to make sure all is well with you. That's all." She glanced behind Lisa, checking out her accommodations. "You have the room to yourself too, *huh?*"

"I do." Lisa smiled. "I ended up being one of the lucky ones."

"Nothing wrong with being lucky," Anna noted. "Enjoy it while you have it." And, with that, she gave her a smile and headed down the hallway—oddly enough, passing Rogan on his way back.

As he reached Lisa's doorway, where Lisa still stood, she looked down the hallway to confirm that Anna was gone.

"Was Anna just here?" Rogan asked Lisa, motioning at her open door.

She nodded. "Anna knocked and announced herself, so I opened the door to talk." He frowned at her, and she sighed. "I know. I know. I shouldn't have opened the door, but, as you can see, … everything's fine."

"*Sure*, everything's just *peachy*," he growled, as both of them stepped inside her room. He closed the door carefully behind them, as if trying not to set off an explosion.

She showed both her palms and explained, "Even if I am injured, I highly doubt that Anna would do anything to hurt me. She was checking that I'm okay."

"And that's fine, *in theory*," he stated. "First, we don't know if a man or a woman attacked you. Second, I'm not all that sure of Anna's mental health at the moment."

"It can't be very good," Lisa agreed. "She's pretty much lost all her team members in one way or another, plus her work may be useless, since their research was cut short, and some may even be lost. I'm sure she's got to be devastated."

"I know, and that's why I took time to visit with her earlier today. I wanted to let her know that I had requested she get out on the next supply run, but I didn't get confirmation from the colonel on that yet. Hopefully he'll decide before the supply plane makes it through here."

"No need to keep Anna here," Lisa noted, "particularly when she's as distraught and as upset as she is."

"I'm pretty sure she's not terribly impressed at not making it out with the others."

"I would have been too," Lisa pointed out. "Considering that her coworkers were airlifted out, but she wasn't, then dealing with Myles's death, all that had to be hard for her."

"Yet, the rationale was valid to airlift those in greater danger after their carbon monoxide poisoning to a full-service hospital. And, at the time, Anna was okay with it."

"Maybe that's because Myles was still here, and, as long as she had one of the other scientists with her, and a very steadying one at that, then Anna was okay. But then he died ... and under odd circumstances. We still haven't heard more on Myles, have we?"

"No," Rogan replied. "And don't forget that his body is still here."

"Oh God. So whenever Anna does leave, she'll likely end up going out with his body, won't she?"

"Yes, and that won't be easy on her either."

"I can't imagine," Lisa replied, as she shook her head. "Anyway, maybe we can park that conversation and get some sleep tonight." She yawned.

"I would have been totally okay not having that conversation, but somebody opened the door when she wasn't supposed to."

She gave him a wry look. "We've moved past that, haven't we?"

"Yeah, we have—as long as the next time, you remember to let her sit outside. You knew I was coming back, so you could have waited until I came back."

"Maybe, but it's not an issue now. So we can afford to be nicer to her and to help her get through the next few days."

"That's what I like about you," he admitted. "You're all heart, but I still reserve my right to keep you safe."

"Hey, we've all been in tough circumstances. It won't hurt us to be nice to Anna for the few days she's here," Lisa explained. "Honestly everybody would benefit from a little more niceness."

He smiled and motioned toward her bed. "Get in. I'm already much more concerned about keeping an eye on you. So chances are, I won't get any sleep tonight."

She frowned at him. "That's not very good."

He laughed. "Let's get to bed and hopefully get some sleep."

And, with that, she curled up in his arms and closed her eyes.

When she woke a little later, she heard him snoring gently at her side. Yet something had woken her, and, not sure what it was, she looked at him, but she didn't want to disturb him. As she shifted upright in the bed, his arms tightened around her.

Even in sleep he was trying to protect her. She leaned over, kissed him gently on the forehead, and whispered, "I have to go to the bathroom."

His blurry eyes looked at her and frowned.

"I know," she admitted. "It really sucks."

He shifted around and got up. "I'm coming with you."

"I'm fine," she said, looking at him. "I'll be back in a minute." She took advantage of the fact that he was still throwing the sleep off, when she slipped out of the door and walked to the bathroom. As she got inside, she heard somebody sobbing, muttering.

She winced, recognizing the voice. She softly called out, "Anna, are you okay?"

The sobbing stopped. "No, I'm sorry. I got a little overwhelmed." And, with that, she added, "Please, please leave it alone." Then she quickly escaped the bathroom, leaving Lisa staring after her, wondering what was wrong. When Lisa got back to Rogan, she explained what had happened.

"Is that unusual?" Rogan asked.

"I don't know, maybe not. She is obviously upset, but it sounded as if her heart was breaking."

At that, he stopped, then turned and asked her, "Do we know if there was a relationship between her and Myles?"

"I don't know," Lisa replied. "We don't know anything about these scientists."

"Only that they ran into trouble, and now everything about them will be exposed," Rogan added.

"That's never much fun for anybody," she murmured. "But I can tell you that, the way she was bawling, she seemed absolutely devastated."

"Maybe it's a delayed reaction because she is still here,

and Myles is gone—maybe even that Amelia is lost. I don't know. Your guess is as good as mine."

"Not really because, when it comes to women and emotions, I understand a lot of it, but sometimes? … Sometimes it all seems beyond me too." She laughed at her own insight. "It's beyond all of us sometimes, including ourselves. We get overwhelmed, and tears are a release. We get to a point where we don't know anything else to do, and the tears come out because pressure has to be released somehow."

"I'm glad to hear that it works." As they settled back in bed and got curled up, he asked, "How's your head?"

"It's good." She gave him a smile. "How's yours?"

"Mine is fine," he replied, frowning at her.

She chuckled. "See? You don't enjoy being asked about it either."

He winced. "None of us do, do we?"

"No, particularly not when we're in the field that we're in," she noted. "It's all about being a tough guy."

"It is, and it isn't," he stated. "It's also about not being stupid."

She snorted at that, wrapped her arms around him, and added, "So, does that mean the idea of taking this relationship to the next level is being stupid?"

"God, I hope not, but …"

"But what?"

"Your head," he confessed.

She groaned. "My head's fine."

"Is it though?" he asked. "The last thing I want is to get reamed out by Sydney."

Lisa burst out laughing. "So, let me get this straight. You're scared of Sydney?"

"Anybody in their right mind would be scared of Sydney," he admitted, chuckling. "She's very good at what she does, and she can see through everybody."

Lisa smiled. "Which means that I really should be talking to her about Anna's state of mind, to see if she has something to recommend."

"Probably talking and being friendly with the woman would help," he suggested.

"Which is what I was doing today, but I'm not sure she was all that receptive."

"Again, she doesn't know you that well, so how receptive will anybody be? She may believe you were prying."

"Got it," Lisa concurred, and she snuggled up closer to Rogan. "My head is fine."

"How fine?" he asked.

She grinned and nudged her hips toward him several times.

He groaned, and she was gratified with an instant hardening of his body.

She chuckled. "See? I knew my condition wouldn't be a problem."

"Only if you are sure," he muttered, his voice thick, raspy, as he nuzzled against her neck.

"Oh, I think I'll be fine," she murmured. "Besides, we don't want to be too loud anyway. These walls are very thin."

"Way too thin." He smiled down at her as he moved in and kissed her gently.

She wrapped her arms around him. "The first time you kissed me was quite a surprise, but it was so natural," she shared passionately. "It made me realize where our relationship was going."

"Hell, we've been going in this direction for a very long

time."

She stiffened at that, looked up at him, and her gaze searched his, before she asked in a whisper, "Did it bother you when I was married to Barry?"

He nodded. "Yes, because I'd already heard some rumors that he was rough with other women, and I was worried about you." He shrugged, still studying her. "Yet you appeared to be okay. Then, all of a sudden, I didn't see you two anymore. And the next thing I knew, you were split up and divorced. I never knew what to say to you about those rumors. Should I warn you or not warn you? It was super awkward, and I didn't have any proof. The rumors were all from disgruntled girlfriends."

"Right, so you didn't know if you could trust them to tell the truth. He wasn't violent with me," she repeated. "And, for that, I'm very grateful because I don't think I would have handled that very well."

"No, I don't think any woman should either," Rogan stated, with a smile, as he kissed her again. "But I'm grateful that he didn't hurt you. I was feeling pretty guilty there for a while, and then, when he was in prison, I didn't know what to do. I stared at the announcement in shock, but then, in many ways, it made sense."

"It may have made sense to you, but I'm really glad I missed it all," she shared. "I can't imagine the guilt."

"That was the thing for me. It was all guilt," Rogan admitted. "When you are friends with somebody like Barry—and you don't know what they're truly like, you don't realize what they're going through, what they're doing—so it's pretty rough to hear about."

"In that case," Lisa said, "I highly suggest we park all of that and realize that Barry had one life to live, and he chose to waste it. However, that is not our pathway, and we won't ruin it. This is about you and me—and hopefully for a whole lot longer than our time up here."

"Yeah, remember that whole thing about taking a holiday after this?" He kissed her neck and nuzzled her throat.

"Yeah, I do, and, man, I can't wait. Sandy beaches, here we come."

He chuckled. "Me too." And, with that, he lifted his head and took her lips in a searing hot kiss that left her breathless.

"Good God," she murmured, "where have you been hiding that?"

"Waiting for you."

"Really?"

"No, not really," he corrected, "but it was always in the back of my mind."

When another kiss scrambled her brain, she had to catch her breath before speaking again. "I'm really glad that the opportunity arose to bring it to the forefront." She gasped against him. "Jesus, I don't know whether it's me, the injury, or what, but, holy crap, I don't want to wait."

"You don't have to wait at all," he noted, "but I do think you need a little more attention." And, with that, he slowly worked his way down to her chest, taking one nipple at a time into his mouth and sucking deep, making her shudder in response, as her body twisted beneath him.

"Good God," she whispered, unable to keep herself from saying the same thing over and over again. When he finally slipped inside her, she was panting and more than ready. She wrapped her thighs around him tightly and held on.

He groaned, as she clenched her inner muscles tightly around him. "You do much more of that, and it's over."

"It'll be over in seconds anyway," she declared, as she pushed up against him.

He moved gently at first, but then she tightened around him again, and he lost it, moving at a rapid pace until she exploded beneath him. He followed in a moment, gasping for breath when he finally collapsed beside her. Holding her close and trying to regain his breath, he whispered, "I think you killed me."

"No, I definitely don't want to do that. No encores with dead men."

He burst out laughing again, trying to muffle it so they didn't disturb other people.

She nodded. "It's very strange to be in this place where everybody can hear everything."

"And yet they can't," he reminded her. "We do have privacy."

"Some privacy," she corrected, "not necessarily a whole lot."

He nodded. "Now, how about getting some sleep?"

"I might manage that." She yawned, as she curled up in his arms. "Especially now."

"Good. So glad to have helped."

She chuckled. "I can take that sleep aid any old time."

He smiled, pulled her against him in a spooning position, and whispered, "Now sleep."

And she closed her eyes and drifted off.

DAY 13, EARLY MORNING

ROGAN HELD LISA gently in his arms throughout most of the night, not wanting the time to disappear. He knew it would, and, in the morning, everything would revert back to normal because it always happened that way. But, for the moment, he wanted to hold her close. He hadn't really expected this, but the minute he'd seen her, it was certainly something he wanted. And now that their relationship had bloomed into true intimacy, he would do a whole lot to make sure that nothing destroyed it.

She was very special, and she'd already been attacked once. And so had he, for that matter. He wanted very much to leave this base behind, but he wouldn't bail on his friends and leave them here to deal with whatever the hell was happening at the training center and beyond. They needed to solve this, and they needed to solve it now. But, with everything that had happened with the scientists' camp, it had all gotten more confusing, making it even more difficult to solve the many mysteries, as these latest events just muddied the waters.

As he thought about what Lisa had suggested earlier—about Anna nursing a broken heart—Rogan had to wonder if there had been a relationship between Myles and Anna, or between Anna and one of the other scientists at their camp. Hell, with the proximity between this training base and the scientists' camp, maybe one of the military guys had had relations with Anna. Rogan pulled out his phone and quickly sent off several texts to Mason, hoping that there would be some internet capability.

With a sigh, Rogan then drifted off to sleep.

WHEN THE PHONE rang not too much later, Rogan groaned into it, "Hello?"

"Hey," Mason replied, flint in his tone. "It is six in the morning here. Sorry if I woke you."

"That's fine. If it's six o'clock there, it's high time to be awake here anyway."

"That's what I thought," he agreed, with a note of humor. "You guys have got yourself a hell of a mess up there."

"Yeah, and, when we think maybe we're getting on top of it, something else goes wrong." He sat up in bed and got up, looking to see if Lisa was awake. "With these latest events, I really think they are diversions, not related to our issues at the base. But, with so little intel, I can't rule out anything yet."

"That text you sent proved to be interesting."

"Oh? In what way?"

"Anna did have a relationship with a scientist previously, a couple years or so ago. He also passed away at the same scientists' camp. She apparently took it really hard, and, as I understand it, he went out to read his instruments one day, and they found his body several days later. He'd ended up getting completely disoriented and didn't have enough experience to get himself out of trouble and died of hypothermia."

"God, and she wasn't here at the time, I presume?"

"I need to double-check who else was up there back then, but seems Anna supposedly wasn't at the base some two years earlier, and that was one of the reasons she fought so hard to come on this trip. So, yeah, maybe she wanted to say goodbye to him or something."

"Ah, well, she's definitely depressed and despondent, so maybe that's what this is all about."

"Maybe," Mason noted, "but there was also a suggestion that Myles had a habit of having relationships with young women at these camps as well. Not just the camps either. I won't say it's inappropriate because I don't know the circumstances, but generally when you have a relationship with a student under your tutelage, it's considered inappropriate by college and university standards."

"Yes, I would think so," Rogan agreed. "So, we don't know if maybe she hooked on to him as a way to heal from her other relationship."

"Possibly. The other scientist was Dr. John Willowbee, and he died two years ago."

"So, long enough to grieve and hopefully to move on."

"Exactly, not that I'm sure if it has anything to do with what you've got going on there though."

"No, and what we really need is to get Anna out of here, so that she can be evaluated and get some mental health support. She's not in a position to get it long-term here."

"What about trying Sydney in the interim?"

"Anna hasn't opened up to Sydney that I know of, but I will verify that this morning. I'm getting dressed now, and I'll go talk to her in a little bit. I'll send you a message afterward."

"Good enough," Mason said, then he hesitated. "Any

news on any of the missing people?"

"No, not yet."

"Do you want out of there?"

"No, no at all. Why?"

"I understand Lisa's been hurt."

"You too, *huh*?" he asked, with a groan. "She's fine." He tossed a glance at the woman still sleeping in her bed. "I'm not sure she wants out either. Last time it came up, she was pretty adamant about staying."

"Not surprising," Mason replied. "Almost everybody we've talked to has been willing to go the distance."

"We also know that, if we don't bring anybody else in, you're dealing with the pack of cards that you've got. Once we start adding new elements, such as the scientists," he offered, "everything falls apart, and you don't know who can be trusted."

"Good point," Mason agreed.

"And," Rogan added, "Anna did suggest that it could have been Amelia, going in to tamper with our generator."

A shocked silence came from the other end. Then Mason asked, "The other scientist? The one who's missing?"

"Yes, and I don't know why the hell Anna would say that."

"No, I don't know either," Mason muttered.

Rogan cleared his throat. "I'll just throw this thought out there too. Maybe Anna is a black widow of sorts?"

Mason snorted. "I'm off to do some more research. I'll get back to you." And, with that, he was gone.

Rogan looked down at his phone, glanced down at the sleeping woman, then leaned over and gave her a gentle kiss. "I really hate to leave you." And, with that, he slipped out the door and headed to the kitchen.

He grabbed two coffees and, stopping to check on Lisa first—who was still sleeping—he continued to the clinic and stepped inside to talk to Sydney, who sat there, huddling over a coffee. He nodded. "I feel the same way."

She gave him a bleary smile. "I didn't sleep all that well," she muttered.

"I was hoping to ask you about Anna's mental health."

She nodded. "It's a concern, and, from what I see, she's definitely not adjusting. I've asked the colonel to get her out."

"Good," Rogan said. "Maybe if enough of us ask, he'll do it."

She rolled her eyes at that. "It's not that, and you know it."

"I know." He smiled. "But, when we get the next supply run, Anna should be going home, wherever that is." He shared what Mason had discovered about Anna's history, and Sydney winced at that.

"If Anna came up here to get closure, this is a pretty rough version of it," the doc muttered.

Rogan nodded. "I was wondering that myself, but maybe this is also her grieving mode."

"That in itself would make sense." Sydney shrugged. "Thanks for that information. I'll talk to her a little later."

"Good. I've got to get some work done today."

"I know. You're not just on nursemaid duty."

"It's my turn guarding the generator," he noted.

"Right." Sydney winced. "That's where everybody has to do a shift currently."

"Well, yeah, a lot of us are here still, but it's my turn. Plus I wanted to ensure that we all got a shift, so we share the burden and the exposure, you know? Anyway, I left Lisa sleeping, and I'm pretty uncomfortable with that."

"I'll go sit with her," Sydney offered.

"Okay. Thanks, Doc."

And, with that, Rogan turned and headed out to guard the generator at the base.

DAY 13, LATER THAT MORNING

LISA YAWNED, OPENED her eyes, then gave a start. A woman sat in her room. Startled, Lisa reared back, then relaxed. "Anna?"

Anna smiled and nodded. "Yes, it's me."

Lisa looked around and frowned. "Gosh, you startled me. What are you doing here?"

"Visiting."

She stared at her in shock. "Visiting while I'm asleep?" She was quickly trying to make sense of it, and nothing came to mind. "Why would you do that? Why come in while I'm asleep?"

She shrugged. "You told me that you had a room to yourself, but you lied. So I wanted to see what he saw in you."

Lisa stared at her in shock. "Excuse me?" She rubbed her eyes, not sure exactly what this conversation was all about. She shuffled back onto the bed, only to have Anna point a small handgun at her. "I wouldn't do that if I were you."

She stared at the handgun in shock, then looked back at her. "What on earth?"

"Yeah," Anna replied, with a sad but venomous tone. "Nobody ever really understands, do they?"

"Pretty hard to understand what *this* is," Lisa declared in a biting voice. "Seriously, you're here because we saved you guys from some serious trouble in your own camp, and now you're holding a gun on me? What the hell is that all about?"

Anna shrugged. "It seemed to be a much better thing to do."

Lisa snorted. "Look, Anna. You need to talk with somebody, get some professional counseling."

"What kind of counseling?" She studied Lisa with interest.

"Anything to help you deal with your life. I understand that you lost somebody out here."

She nodded. "He was the love of my life, ... but I wasn't his."

She blinked at that switch. "What do you mean?"

"I wasn't his. The great white north was his first love."

"Ah, well, lots of people are in love with their work," she stated cautiously, as she looked around the room, trying to figure out what she was supposed to do right now. Unfortunately, after making love last night, she hadn't put any clothes back on, so she was literally wrapped up in her blankets, without a stitch underneath. Not that that would matter. She would heal from the cold, but a bullet she wasn't so sure about.

"That's the thing, you see? When you love somebody, but they don't love you back, it hurts," she said.

"So, you had problems with your relationship with him? Or with Myles?" She kept asking questions, trying to keep her voice calm and steady.

Anna nodded and stared off in a dreamy state. "I knew he loved me, but that love wasn't enough."

"It wasn't enough for you?"

Anna turned her gaze and narrowed it at Lisa. "It wasn't enough to keep the relationship going."

"And so?"

"And so I killed him."

At that, Lisa almost choked. "What? How could you do that to somebody you love? You killed him?"

"Because he didn't love me back," she said with emphasis, giving Lisa a surprised glance in her direction. "I just explained that to you, didn't I?" She shook her head, frowning. "I don't understand why people have so much trouble with that."

"Maybe because that isn't what love is all about," Lisa replied, gritting her teeth.

"No, but that is what rejection is all about." Anna again turned the gun on Lisa.

"And did he reject you?" Lisa asked.

Anna shrugged. "He certainly didn't choose me, … not over the great white north."

"How did you kill him?"

She smiled. "I exchanged his pills, which I knew he took on a regular basis for arthritis, with sleeping pills. So, when he took them while out on one of his many data collection trips, he would freeze to death. I didn't know when he'd die, I just knew he would." Her smile deepened as if she'd enjoyed the anticipation.

"Oh God." Lisa tried to make sense of it, tried to see a way out of this mess. She needed a route, some way to escape.

"But think about it—it's really the best way to go. You can't argue that point."

"Falling asleep is a nice way to die, but he certainly didn't need to die early."

"Absolutely he did," Anna declared, "and so did Myles."

And there it was. Lisa stared at the woman in front of

her, too confused to really hear it. She'd initially thought Anna was talking about Myles but had described killing someone else previously. So did she kill Myles too? What is happening here? "So, you weren't talking about Myles before? I thought maybe you were getting some details mixed up or something."

"Oh, please, as if I would. That would be John."

"John." And that was that. She knew that Anna was the viper here and that Lisa needed to know more. "Please tell me that you didn't kill Myles."

Anna shrugged. "I switched up his medications too. I wasn't even sure exactly what would happen to him, but he started to get pretty paranoid."

"So you gave him some of your own medications?" It was a shot in the dark.

Anna nodded. "Yes, but whatever. I take several drugs for a bipolar disorder. And I knew that Myles had his own prescriptions, but not for the same condition of course. Still, it's pretty easy to open the capsules and switch them up." She shrugged. "Besides, I helped him pack up all that stuff."

"*Great*," Lisa muttered. "You killed Myles. But why?"

She raised her eyebrows at Lisa. "For the same reason."

"Rejection?" she asked after a moment, and then Anna nodded.

"Yes, we were an item, until we weren't," she stated bitterly. "And it seemed so unfair that, once again, the great white north would win over me. I mean, the Arctic's so beautiful, and she's so cold, and she's such a bitch, and yet everybody chooses her over me," she wailed, talking about the great white north as if it were a human, with feelings and emotions and actions.

"Dear God," Lisa whispered.

"I know," she agreed, turning to face Lisa. "It's really sad, isn't it?"

"It is sad," Lisa said, for completely different reasons, while contemplating the broken woman in front of her. "It's sad that rejection hits you so hard."

Anna frowned at her. "How else does rejection hit you?"

"If you care, you care," Lisa replied carefully because the woman was clearly unhinged.

"It's not as if you can hide your feelings," she muttered. "Emotions are emotions. They're not exactly something you can just stop." And there was a certain amount of truth to that, and Lisa understood that part. "I'm sorry that you feel as if you must kill everybody in order to make this better."

"Oh, not everybody," she corrected, with a sweet smile. "At least I wasn't really planning on it being *everybody*. However, when we had such continuing generator problems, and then we made the switches in the lines to try to run the exhaust at a safe level to help heat us, well …" She laughed. "That wonderful opportunity presented itself."

"Oh God," Lisa muttered. "So you switched everything out so that the exhaust would run inside, didn't you?"

"Oh, it was running inside. I had to drop the pipes, though Myles had made it very clear about how dangerous it would be and had made sure everybody knew what they needed to follow through on and what needed to happen to make it safe. When everybody fell asleep, I got up and switched it," she admitted. "I figured it would be an easy answer for all of us, you know?"

And again, there was that dreamy tone to her voice. Lisa asked her, "Including yourself?"

"Yes, of course. I don't care about living anymore. Why should I?"

"You were hoping to get out of here though," Lisa mentioned in confusion. "That means you do want to live."

"I want to live, away from here, and I sure as hell don't want to die here." She snorted. "And, if the opportunity presents itself for life over death, I guess I would take it, especially if it means getting out of here. … I didn't want to be punished for what I did because I only did what I needed to do."

"You needed to do it for whom?"

"For myself," Anna declared, looking at Lisa. "That's pretty obvious, isn't it?"

"But you hurt a lot of people."

"But they'll be fine," she stated. "I really only wanted to hurt Myles, but tempers were growing short, and everybody else seemed to have some sort of a beef, and that made it easier for me to decide everybody at the scientists' camp should go."

Lisa frowned, trying to figure out how to distract this deranged woman so Lisa could kick away the gun, but she was tangled up in the sheets. "And how does that possibly involve me?" She still couldn't quite understand Anna's motive here. "Why the devil would you come in here after me with a gun?"

"I figured you knew," Anna stared at Lisa, nonplused.

"Knew what?" Lisa asked.

"Knew that I loved Myles."

"Ah, you mean because you were crying so much in the bathroom?"

Anna stared at Lisa, and Anna's anger glinted through. "You know I had every right to cry," she snapped, "and you sure as hell shouldn't have been there."

"I woke up in the middle of the night, and I needed to

go to the bathroom," Lisa stated, both legitimate everyday happenings. "What else was I supposed to do?"

"I don't know what you were supposed to do," Anna replied. "That's not my problem. I thought I was alone."

"I didn't know you were in the ladies' room. However, we do share that bathroom with other women. So our privacy is limited to access the same bathroom by the other women here," Lisa explained, as if to a child.

"You intruded on my privacy," Anna snapped again.

Lisa frowned. "I didn't plan to, and I didn't mean to." Yet per Anna's twisted point of view, Lisa had intruded.

"But you did, and, having guessed that I was heartbroken, I'm sure you decided to tell everybody."

She winced. "No. However, I know others suggested to the doctor that she might need to talk to you, but that's about it."

"Talk to me about what?" She spoke with a snarl. "About being depressed? I am on an antidepressant, but I'm on a lot of things." Anna shrugged. "So, it doesn't really matter anyway. Doctors just give you prescriptions. They don't really care about whether it's working or not."

"I think you've been seeing the wrong doctors," Lisa suggested gently.

Anna snorted. "It really doesn't matter. You'll end up taking some antidepressant yourself because you're upset over still being here and especially after the attack …"

"You mean, your attack on me?"

She looked at her. "Figured it out, did you?"

"Only just now," Lisa admitted, staring at Anna in complete understanding, with a true grasp of the situation. "Were you trying to mess with our generators?"

"I was trying to figure out if I could do something similar to what I did at my camp, but honestly yours is a far more complicated system, and I couldn't see how to reroute it right away."

"God, so you really would have tried to kill everybody here? Thirty-something people are here."

She shrugged. "I don't think any of them really want to be here anymore, so it would have been a nice release for them. They would have appreciated it."

"Oh my God." Lisa stared at Anna in horror. "You don't get to decide that for all the people here."

"Why not? And don't look at me as if I'm crazy," she snapped. "I know exactly what I'm doing."

"Yeah, that's what worries me. So, what next? Would you force me to take some sleeping pills and then, … then what?"

"And then I would get up and walk away from all these people here. However, you told me that you were sleeping alone, had a room to yourself, and yet you weren't alone at all. Don't you dare play me for a fool. You were sleeping with somebody," she stated bitterly, with menace in her tone. "You know that'll go badly in the end, and you'll get a broken heart."

She lined up her gun with Lisa and pulled the trigger back ever-so-slightly. "We never really learn, do we? So, understand this. If I kill you now, it's to save you," she explained, with a beaming smile.

The woman was clearly past the point of making sense or even hearing sense when spoken to. Lisa shook her head. "I would just as soon go through that rejection on my own, thank you. I'm not afraid of emotions. Sometimes the most beautiful events come from a relationship that is no longer."

The other woman stared at her in confusion. Anna was

too far gone to understand.

"I see that you don't understand, and I'm sorry for that."

"You don't need to be sorry for me," Anna snapped again. Then she bellowed, "Nothing is wrong with me!"

"Nope, *nothing*," Lisa quipped. "Except that you're totally okay to set up a mass killing of people who don't deserve it."

"Everybody deserves it," Anna argued. "Everybody's done something wrong in their lives."

"But this isn't about justice. This isn't even about vengeance. This is because you enjoy killing too much, Anna."

"Do I?" She replied in a singsong voice, as she turned and looked around the room. "I don't know if it's that or not."

"It would be nice if you would put down the gun and let's go get a cup of coffee at least, and we can talk about it. We have a lot to talk about."

Anna laughed. "Yeah, that's not happening." She pulled out a bottle of sleeping pills and chucked them at her. "You can have coffee after you take all these."

She stared at the full bottle and shook her head. "God no," she declared, though she couldn't readily see a way out of it.

"Oh yes, absolutely yes," said Anna, cocking the gun. "It's not as if you'll get out of here. You don't even have a stitch on." Anna sneered at Lisa's predicament.

That made Lisa shake with anger. What was Anna thinking?

"And you're still dealing with all the cold issues, I hear. You best not get a chill." Anna laughed. "So, you won't be going anywhere, will you?"

"I can assure you that I'm not taking these pills. I'll take a bullet first. So, believe me when I say, you'll get caught right after that."

She shrugged. "And I'll turn the gun on myself, not that you'll care," she replied, with a smile, "because you'll already be dead."

Anna spoke with such a calm voice that Lisa had no doubt about it.

"So, what'll it be? Ticktock. ... Time is wasting. A bullet for sure or sleeping pills? Of course, if you're lucky, somebody might get here in time and pump your stomach."

"Sleeping pills, it is then," Lisa stated, as she snatched the pill bottle. But, as she opened it, she tossed the pills all over the floor and threw the blankets off her and onto Anna. The gun fired, reverberating through the room, as Lisa tussled with Anna to get control of her gun from under the covers. It fired several more times, and then suddenly the door burst open, and two people rushed in.

At least Lisa thought it was two. Rogan picked her up and pulled her off of Anna, then quickly wrapped her up in another blanket and stuffed her on the corner of the bed. She turned in time to see Sydney pulling the blankets off the shrieking, bellowing woman, who turned, struggling to get away. Finally she stopped, and buried her head in her hands, sobbing.

Sydney checked over Anna, then whispered, "She was hit at least once." Turning to Rogan, she said, "Help me get her to the clinic."

He quickly picked up Anna and raced to the clinic.

The doc looked back at Lisa. "Are you okay?"

"I'm okay," she replied, shivering, "but, dear God, that woman is nuts."

"Yeah," Sydney agreed. "That's apparent. As soon as

you're dressed, come on down, and I'll check you over." And, with that, Sydney was gone.

ROGAN HAD STOPPED to see whether Sydney had gone to be with Lisa or not, when he realized that other people had stepped in to talk to her, so she hadn't had a chance to leave yet.

She looked up at him with a smile. "I'm coming. I'm coming."

But he turned and left and was just steps away from Lisa's room when he heard the first shot.

Even now, with his heart in his throat, he wanted to be with Lisa, but he was helping a seriously injured woman. Personally he was okay to take Anna out in the snow and leave her there, but he would do better than that. He would be a better person than Anna was.

Once he reached the clinic, he laid her on one of the two hospital beds, and Sydney shooed him away. "Go check on Lisa and bring her back here." He didn't need to be told twice, and he raced down to find Lisa struggling to put on another layer of clothing.

As soon as he sat her down, Rogan quickly helped Lisa pull on heavy Arctic-weather socks, and, with her bundled up, he picked her up in his arms and carried her to the clinic.

"I can walk. I'm fine, really," she muttered, her arms looped around his neck.

"I know you are," he said. "If you weren't, I'd have taken you to the clinic first."

She tightened her hold around his neck and kissed him gently. "I'm sorry. I woke up, and she was already there in my room."

He nodded. "Sydney was supposed to check up on you, but she got waylaid at the clinic."

"Don't get mad at her for that. She's our only doc and is supposed to be there, after all."

"I know," he admitted, with a groan. "I was supposed to do my shift at the generator, but apparently there was a schedule mix-up, and I wasn't needed after all."

"Anna was also my attacker in the generator room," Lisa added. When he frowned at her, she nodded. "So, you can stop the security rounds on the generator and get those guys out of the cold." She explained what had happened and why.

"Good God," Rogan exclaimed. "Obviously she lost her way and has been troubled for a long time."

"I think the second breakup was the final straw, and, when eliminating the offender worked so well with the first one, she did something similar with Myles. And then, with the scientists' generator being such a problem, in her twisted mind, it seemed that would be an easy answer for *saving* everybody. Especially figuring that all relationships were destined to end badly, per Anna."

"They don't," he replied, squeezing her gently. He stepped into the clinic to see a hell of a mess. Sydney turned to look up at them and shook her head. She was covered in blood. "I'm sorry, but she bled out. I don't have anywhere near enough blood to do the transfusion she would have needed."

Sure enough, the deranged woman lay dead but still warm on the bed.

"Give me a moment," Sydney said, as she tried to clean up some of the mess, including herself. Rogan put Lisa on a chair and joined Sydney to give her a hand. Soon they had the bulk of the blood contained, if not completely mopped up.

"Jesus, you don't realize how much blood is in the human body, until you see this," Rogan noted.

Sydney nodded.

Lisa added, "Five, six liters ..." She stared at Anna, now harmless and sad in death. What a waste.

"Grab some of those bags, will you?" Sydney barked at Rogan. And, with that, they soon got most of it cleaned up. Then she explained, "I need to get her wrapped up and moved quickly, before everybody else is here." However, it was almost too late for that.

Thankfully Mountain was the one who strolled in, took one look at the residual mess, and stared. "This would be a great story to tell," he suggested, but he quickly helped Rogan bundle up Anna's body under Sydney's direction. "There was no hope?" Mountain asked Sydney.

"None, the bullet went through and ripped multiple arteries," the doc replied. "I don't have any means to do anything with that here. The damage was too severe."

"I trust you in that, Doc. Too bad I didn't get to interrogate her first." And Mountain was gone with the body in seconds.

From the sound of it, he went out one of the exterior doors to avoid going through the main part of the base. Lisa pitched in to do another round of cleanup and to make the clinic presentable. Rogan quickly cleaned the bloody trail in the hallway and in Lisa's room.

"Rogan says you're okay, but are you sure you weren't hurt?" Sydney asked Lisa.

"No, I'm fine. I am still a little shocked."

"We can deal with that now," the doc said. And for the

next twenty minutes, she checked over Lisa from head to toe.

"Did you ever expect to be dealing with these nightmares up here?" Lisa asked her boss.

Sydney shook her head. "No, I sure didn't," she muttered. "But that's the thing about being on the spot in this place. When shit happens, you can only do so much. No point in trying to save Anna from her injuries because I couldn't possibly give her enough blood or surgically stitch up all the holes in her various organs. Always a tough decision to make to allow someone to die moments later. I really couldn't do anything for her."

"I'm just grateful the bullet took her out and not me."

Sydney gave her a big smile. "Yeah, me too." She patted her nurse on her shoulder. "It's a little hard to find nurses up here."

"Hey, we should get hazard pay," Lisa teased, with a laugh, yet a serious note filled her voice.

Sydney nodded and smiled brightly. "You're not kidding, especially right now."

About twenty minutes later Mountain returned and, with Rogan now at Lisa's side, she gave a clear accounting of everything that had happened with Anna in Lisa's room.

Mountain stared at her. "So, she's the one who rerouted the exhaust system at the scientists' camp, and she's the one who attacked you in the generator room."

Lisa nodded. "Yes." She hesitated and then added tersely, "Anna also admitted to switching up the medications on her lover who died up here before, but I don't know how long ago."

"Two years ago," Rogan replied from behind Mountain, and they all turned to look at him.

"And you know this too? How?"

"Mason told me. I asked him to check Anna's history, and he got back to me this morning, before I left Lisa in her room." They were all looking at him curiously, and he added, "Lisa heard Anna crying in the bathroom last night, so I had Mason check her out."

Mountain glared but this obviously wasn't the time, so he turned to Lisa. "Continue."

"After killing her previous partner, she ended up doing essentially the same thing here with Myles."

Rogan shook his head at that. "Jesus Christ, so she was killing off everybody?"

"I think she felt as if life would be better for everybody if they all died," Lisa offered. "As I've noted before, she had a lot of mental health problems."

"Ya think?" Rogan gave a hard snort. "Oh, it'll be some fun explaining it all to the colonel."

And, with that, Mountain quickly turned to leave, but, before he stepped out of the room, he added, "Get all of that in your report. Now are you looking to get out of here?" he asked, looking at Lisa.

"No, not at all. Why?"

"Because, if you want to go, I can arrange to have you airlifted back out again."

"I'm fine," Lisa said, with a smile. "Besides, I've got Rogan here to keep an eye on me, if I get any more homicidal visitors."

Mountain rolled his eyes. "Let's not forget that the homicidal visitor was only one issue," he emphasized, with a bitter tone. "We still have another homicidal maniac on our base, but, if you're sure that you're okay to stay behind, we can use you." Mountain eyed Sydney. "Are you okay with that decision?"

The doc nodded. "Yeah, we'll keep an eye on her."

"Good enough." Mountain turned to Rogan. "Good job." And, with that, he was gone.

Lisa looked up at Rogan. "What did he mean by *Good job?*"

Rogan smiled. "You're not dead."

"*Great*," she muttered, "but that holiday is looking better all the time."

"You can leave, but I can't, not until it's time, not until I'm done here," Rogan stated. "A part of me wants you safe and a long way away from here."

"Nope." She shook her head forcefully. "We're together. I'm staying. Besides, it's not just me who's been attacked. You were too. So were Magnus and Sydney."

Rogan reached out an arm and pulled Lisa to him. "I promise to look after you better."

She laughed. "I don't know that you could have done much in this case," she noted, "but the good news is that it's over with—at least the part with a deranged woman with a gun coming after me."

Rogan raised his pointer finger. "At least it seems Anna's activities were not distractions but unrelated events to our own problems here at the base, for which we still need answers. However, all Lisa-related matters are not solved with the removal of Anna. We still don't know who has been stalking your doorway at night."

Lisa grimaced. "Thanks for the reminder. However, I have you in my life, so I choose to focus on the good things right now, how we have our whole future together." She looked back at Sydney and smiled. "And I see why you stay."

"Of course," Sydney confirmed. "At least if you're both here, you can look after each other."

Rogan tilted up Lisa's chin, lowered his head, and, before his lips touched hers, he stated, "I'm all for taking on that job." Then he lowered his head and kissed her.

EPILOGUE

MASON STARED DOWN at the phone. "Jesus Christ."

Mountain responded, "I know. I know," his voice booming through the phone. "The trouble is, we're still not getting to the core issues," he said, with a brewing anger deep inside. "Plus we're still missing the other scientist team. At this point, although we don't have any answers, I have a suspicion that Anna may have done something to that team, taking them out as well."

"Christ," Mason muttered, running his hands through his hair. "This is not what we expected."

"No way we could have known there would be these problems," Mountain noted. "I understand that the university is planning on sending somebody to clean up the scientists' camp. They'll stay with us, unless we can get their camp up and running soon. However, they really don't want to engage with any of us, as they have suspicions of their own about the entire base. Regardless they want a few days, four, five, maybe six days up there. I think they're also looking at sending out their own search-and-rescue team. They have different coordinates and are potentially looking at finding Dr. Amelia. She's an important member of that community but has ties up here and is a bit of a wild card. I did try to get them to share those coordinates with me—maybe they will but later—and to promise that they would alert me if Amelia and her coworker were found."

"So, either she's got powerful friends or somebody else is financing this?"

"Her brother is some dot com wizard, and he doesn't believe she's dead. And I gotta admit that, if there's a chance she's alive, I'm encouraged to believe there's a chance that Teegan's alive too. I know there isn't another soul up here who believes that, but, in some way, this missing Dr. Amelia is giving me hope."

"Good," Mason said. "It's not that late for her yet. Teegan has been longer though," he added gently.

"No, it isn't too late for Amelia. Again that's not our main problem. And I'm not shifting on Teegan," Mountain growled stubbornly.

"Fine. And, no, Dr. Amelia sure as hell isn't our main problem, yet it's not that easy." Mason groaned. "Anyway, thanks for the update. Have you had any luck with the new arrival?"

"Hardly a new arrival." Mountain laughed. "But Egan has been pretty busy being friends with everybody. He enjoys socializing with everyone."

"Sometimes that's a good thing too."

"Sometimes, and, as long as he can get information from people, … I am good with it."

"That's Egan's specialty," Mason noted, "and exactly why he was assigned to be there. Give him a chance."

"Yeah, believe me. He's got all the chances he needs up here. People are more than interested in something to take their minds off the hell that's been going on all around them," he shared, "and everybody is more than happy they're not the ones involved."

"Of course," Mason agreed, "but we've still got several

dead people and too many who have gone missing. So, short of something else going wrong, how about the next time you call me, it's with a positive update?"

"Yeah, I'll try that next time." Mountain gave a hearty laugh. "So, besides Magnus, Rogan, and now Egan, do you have anybody else up here?"

"I do …" Mason hesitated. "Yet I won't tell you who that is right now."

"*Great*," Mountain muttered. "You really think I don't need to know?"

"I think that this person is not the person you would expect, but they're very good at what they do." And, with that, Mason hung up.

MASON EYED HIS wife, a small smile playing at his lips.

"What is that look for?" Tesla asked.

"Rogan's one thing, and Egan is the newest addition to our SR team," he began. "However, Mountain also has a covert female operative up there, which Mountain won't like. It will supercharge his instincts to protect, maybe even to overprotect and to distract him. So better to keep that secret from Mountain for now."

This concludes Book 2 of Shadow Recon: Rogan.
Read about Egan: Shadow Recon, Book 3

Shadow Recon: Egan (Book #3)

Shit happens but at the arctic camp, it's happening too much and too often. The mess from the scientist camp has left a pall over the training camp. And still there is no sign of Teegan, Mountain's brother. The surrounding tundra has been gridded and searched but so far, nothing… except another body…

Berry's sister convinced her to try a new experience and apply for this training camp with her. Except none of her training prepared her for what lay ahead. Being in close quarters and cooped up due to the ugly weather, several people struggle to stay calm and in control. When her sister shows a side of her personality she'd never seen before, she's wondering what she can do to fix this, but was it even fixable?

And if she'd been taken in, how many other team members had been as well? And did it have anything to do with the nightmare happening right under their noses. Egan and Berry need to find out, before they become the next victims…

Find Book 3 here!
To find out more visit Dale Mayer's website.
https://geni.us/DMSSREgan

Author's Note

Thank you for reading Rogan: Shadow Recon, Book 2! If you enjoyed the book, please take a moment and leave a short review.

Dear reader,

I love to hear from readers, and you can contact me at my website: www.dalemayer.com or at my Facebook author page. To be informed of new releases and special offers, sign up for my newsletter or follow me on BookBub. And if you are interested in joining Dale Mayer's Reader Group, here is the Facebook sign up page. http://geni.us/DaleMayerFBGroup

Cheers,
Dale Mayer

About the Author

Dale Mayer is a *USA Today* best-selling author, best known for her SEALs military romances, her Psychic Visions series, and her Lovely Lethal Garden cozy series. Her contemporary romances are raw and full of passion and emotion (Broken But … Mending, Hathaway House series). Her thrillers will keep you guessing (Kate Morgan, By Death series), and her romantic comedies will keep you giggling (*It's a Dog's Life*, a stand-alone novella; and the Broken Protocols series, starring Charming Marvin, the cat).

Dale honors the stories that come to her—and some of them are crazy, break all the rules and cross multiple genres!

To go with her fiction, she also writes nonfiction in many different fields, with books available on résumé writing, companion gardening, and the US mortgage system. All her books are available in print and ebook format.

Connect with Dale Mayer Online

Dale's Website – www.dalemayer.com
Twitter – @DaleMayer
Facebook Page – geni.us/DaleMayerFBFanPage
Facebook Group – geni.us/DaleMayerFBGroup
BookBub – geni.us/DaleMayerBookbub
Instagram – geni.us/DaleMayerInstagram
Goodreads – geni.us/DaleMayerGoodreads
Newsletter – geni.us/DaleNews

Also by Dale Mayer

Published Adult Books:

Shadow Recon
Magnus, Book 1
Rogan, Book 2
Egan, Book 3

Bullard's Battle
Ryland's Reach, Book 1
Cain's Cross, Book 2
Eton's Escape, Book 3
Garret's Gambit, Book 4
Kano's Keep, Book 5
Fallon's Flaw, Book 6
Quinn's Quest, Book 7
Bullard's Beauty, Book 8
Bullard's Best, Book 9
Bullard's Battle, Books 1–2
Bullard's Battle, Books 3–4
Bullard's Battle, Books 5–6
Bullard's Battle, Books 7–8

Terkel's Team
Damon's Deal, Book 1
Wade's War, Book 2
Gage's Goal, Book 3

Calum's Contact, Book 4
Rick's Road, Book 5
Scott's Summit, Book 6
Brody's Beast, Book 7
Terkel's Twist, Book 8
Terkel's Triumph, Book 9

Terkel's Guardian
Radar, Book 1

Kate Morgan
Simon Says... Hide, Book 1
Simon Says... Jump, Book 2
Simon Says... Ride, Book 3
Simon Says... Scream, Book 4
Simon Says... Run, Book 5
Simon Says... Walk, Book 6

Hathaway House
Aaron, Book 1
Brock, Book 2
Cole, Book 3
Denton, Book 4
Elliot, Book 5
Finn, Book 6
Gregory, Book 7
Heath, Book 8
Iain, Book 9
Jaden, Book 10
Keith, Book 11
Lance, Book 12
Melissa, Book 13

Nash, Book 14
Owen, Book 15
Percy, Book 16
Quinton, Book 17
Ryatt, Book 18
Spencer, Book 19
Timothy, Book 20
Hathaway House, Books 1–3
Hathaway House, Books 4–6
Hathaway House, Books 7–9

The K9 Files
Ethan, Book 1
Pierce, Book 2
Zane, Book 3
Blaze, Book 4
Lucas, Book 5
Parker, Book 6
Carter, Book 7
Weston, Book 8
Greyson, Book 9
Rowan, Book 10
Caleb, Book 11
Kurt, Book 12
Tucker, Book 13
Harley, Book 14
Kyron, Book 15
Jenner, Book 16
Rhys, Book 17
Landon, Book 18
Harper, Book 19
Kascius, Book 20

The K9 Files, Books 1–2
The K9 Files, Books 3–4
The K9 Files, Books 5–6
The K9 Files, Books 7–8
The K9 Files, Books 9–10
The K9 Files, Books 11–12

Lovely Lethal Gardens
Arsenic in the Azaleas, Book 1
Bones in the Begonias, Book 2
Corpse in the Carnations, Book 3
Daggers in the Dahlias, Book 4
Evidence in the Echinacea, Book 5
Footprints in the Ferns, Book 6
Gun in the Gardenias, Book 7
Handcuffs in the Heather, Book 8
Ice Pick in the Ivy, Book 9
Jewels in the Juniper, Book 10
Killer in the Kiwis, Book 11
Lifeless in the Lilies, Book 12
Murder in the Marigolds, Book 13
Nabbed in the Nasturtiums, Book 14
Offed in the Orchids, Book 15
Poison in the Pansies, Book 16
Quarry in the Quince, Book 17
Revenge in the Roses, Book 18
Silenced in the Sunflowers, Book 19
Toes up in the Tulips, Book 20
Uzi in the Urn, Book 21
Lovely Lethal Gardens, Books 1–2
Lovely Lethal Gardens, Books 3–4
Lovely Lethal Gardens, Books 5–6

Lovely Lethal Gardens, Books 7–8
Lovely Lethal Gardens, Books 9–10

Psychic Visions Series
Tuesday's Child
Hide 'n Go Seek
Maddy's Floor
Garden of Sorrow
Knock Knock…
Rare Find
Eyes to the Soul
Now You See Her
Shattered
Into the Abyss
Seeds of Malice
Eye of the Falcon
Itsy-Bitsy Spider
Unmasked
Deep Beneath
From the Ashes
Stroke of Death
Ice Maiden
Snap, Crackle…
What If…
Talking Bones
String of Tears
Inked Forever
Psychic Visions Books 1–3
Psychic Visions Books 4–6
Psychic Visions Books 7–9

By Death Series
Touched by Death
Haunted by Death
Chilled by Death
By Death Books 1–3

Broken Protocols – Romantic Comedy Series
Cat's Meow
Cat's Pajamas
Cat's Cradle
Cat's Claus
Broken Protocols 1-4

Broken and... Mending
Skin
Scars
Scales (of Justice)
Broken but… Mending 1-3

Glory
Genesis
Tori
Celeste
Glory Trilogy

Biker Blues
Morgan: Biker Blues, Volume 1
Cash: Biker Blues, Volume 2

SEALs of Honor
Mason: SEALs of Honor, Book 1
Hawk: SEALs of Honor, Book 2

Dane: SEALs of Honor, Book 3
Swede: SEALs of Honor, Book 4
Shadow: SEALs of Honor, Book 5
Cooper: SEALs of Honor, Book 6
Markus: SEALs of Honor, Book 7
Evan: SEALs of Honor, Book 8
Mason's Wish: SEALs of Honor, Book 9
Chase: SEALs of Honor, Book 10
Brett: SEALs of Honor, Book 11
Devlin: SEALs of Honor, Book 12
Easton: SEALs of Honor, Book 13
Ryder: SEALs of Honor, Book 14
Macklin: SEALs of Honor, Book 15
Corey: SEALs of Honor, Book 16
Warrick: SEALs of Honor, Book 17
Tanner: SEALs of Honor, Book 18
Jackson: SEALs of Honor, Book 19
Kanen: SEALs of Honor, Book 20
Nelson: SEALs of Honor, Book 21
Taylor: SEALs of Honor, Book 22
Colton: SEALs of Honor, Book 23
Troy: SEALs of Honor, Book 24
Axel: SEALs of Honor, Book 25
Baylor: SEALs of Honor, Book 26
Hudson: SEALs of Honor, Book 27
Lachlan: SEALs of Honor, Book 28
Paxton: SEALs of Honor, Book 29
Bronson: SEALs of Honor, Book 30
Hale: SEALs of Honor, Book 31
SEALs of Honor, Books 1–3
SEALs of Honor, Books 4–6
SEALs of Honor, Books 7–10

SEALs of Honor, Books 11–13
SEALs of Honor, Books 14–16
SEALs of Honor, Books 17–19
SEALs of Honor, Books 20–22
SEALs of Honor, Books 23–25

Heroes for Hire
Levi's Legend: Heroes for Hire, Book 1
Stone's Surrender: Heroes for Hire, Book 2
Merk's Mistake: Heroes for Hire, Book 3
Rhodes's Reward: Heroes for Hire, Book 4
Flynn's Firecracker: Heroes for Hire, Book 5
Logan's Light: Heroes for Hire, Book 6
Harrison's Heart: Heroes for Hire, Book 7
Saul's Sweetheart: Heroes for Hire, Book 8
Dakota's Delight: Heroes for Hire, Book 9
Tyson's Treasure: Heroes for Hire, Book 10
Jace's Jewel: Heroes for Hire, Book 11
Rory's Rose: Heroes for Hire, Book 12
Brandon's Bliss: Heroes for Hire, Book 13
Liam's Lily: Heroes for Hire, Book 14
North's Nikki: Heroes for Hire, Book 15
Anders's Angel: Heroes for Hire, Book 16
Reyes's Raina: Heroes for Hire, Book 17
Dezi's Diamond: Heroes for Hire, Book 18
Vince's Vixen: Heroes for Hire, Book 19
Ice's Icing: Heroes for Hire, Book 20
Johan's Joy: Heroes for Hire, Book 21
Galen's Gemma: Heroes for Hire, Book 22
Zack's Zest: Heroes for Hire, Book 23
Bonaparte's Belle: Heroes for Hire, Book 24
Noah's Nemesis: Heroes for Hire, Book 25

Tomas's Trials: Heroes for Hire, Book 26
Carson's Choice: Heroes for Hire, Book 27
Dante's Decision: Heroes for Hire, Book 28
Steve's Solace: Heroes for Hire, Book 29
Heroes for Hire, Books 1–3
Heroes for Hire, Books 4–6
Heroes for Hire, Books 7–9
Heroes for Hire, Books 10–12
Heroes for Hire, Books 13–15
Heroes for Hire, Books 16–18
Heroes for Hire, Books 19–21
Heroes for Hire, Books 22–24

SEALs of Steel
Badger: SEALs of Steel, Book 1
Erick: SEALs of Steel, Book 2
Cade: SEALs of Steel, Book 3
Talon: SEALs of Steel, Book 4
Laszlo: SEALs of Steel, Book 5
Geir: SEALs of Steel, Book 6
Jager: SEALs of Steel, Book 7
The Final Reveal: SEALs of Steel, Book 8
SEALs of Steel, Books 1–4
SEALs of Steel, Books 5–8
SEALs of Steel, Books 1–8

The Mavericks
Kerrick, Book 1
Griffin, Book 2
Jax, Book 3
Beau, Book 4
Asher, Book 5

Ryker, Book 6
Miles, Book 7
Nico, Book 8
Keane, Book 9
Lennox, Book 10
Gavin, Book 11
Shane, Book 12
Diesel, Book 13
Jerricho, Book 14
Killian, Book 15
Hatch, Book 16
Corbin, Book 17
Aiden, Book 18
The Mavericks, Books 1–2
The Mavericks, Books 3–4
The Mavericks, Books 5–6
The Mavericks, Books 7–8
The Mavericks, Books 9–10
The Mavericks, Books 11–12

Standalone Novellas
It's a Dog's Life
Riana's Revenge
Second Chances

Published Young Adult Books:

Family Blood Ties Series
Vampire in Denial
Vampire in Distress
Vampire in Design
Vampire in Deceit

Vampire in Defiance
Vampire in Conflict
Vampire in Chaos
Vampire in Crisis
Vampire in Control
Vampire in Charge
Family Blood Ties Set 1–3
Family Blood Ties Set 1–5
Family Blood Ties Set 4–6
Family Blood Ties Set 7–9
Sian's Solution, A Family Blood Ties Series Prequel Novelette

Design series
Dangerous Designs
Deadly Designs
Darkest Designs
Design Series Trilogy

Standalone
In Cassie's Corner
Gem Stone (a Gemma Stone Mystery)
Time Thieves

Published Non-Fiction Books:

Career Essentials
Career Essentials: The Résumé
Career Essentials: The Cover Letter
Career Essentials: The Interview
Career Essentials: 3 in 1

www.ingramcontent.com/pod-product-compliance
Lightning Source LLC
LaVergne TN
LVHW021654060526
838200LV00050B/2346